Elizabeth Stuart Phelps, Herbert Dickinson Ward

The Master of the Magicians

Elizabeth Stuart Phelps, Herbert Dickinson Ward

The Master of the Magicians

ISBN/EAN: 9783337395803

Printed in Europe, USA, Canada, Australia, Japan

Cover: Foto ©Andreas Hilbeck / pixelio.de

More available books at **www.hansebooks.com**

THE
MASTER OF THE MAGICIANS

BY

ELIZABETH STUART PHELPS

AND

HERBERT D. WARD

. . . " The man the son of his god,
Like heaven may he be pure !
Like the midst of heaven may he shine ! "
BABYLONIAN INCANTATION

BOSTON AND NEW YORK
HOUGHTON, MIFFLIN AND COMPANY
The Riverside Press, Cambridge
1890

NOTE.

THERE are few things about which it is easier to disagree than a historical tale dealing with a period so remote that fable and fact contend for the field.

The authors of this story have taken the liberty of adjusting the uncertain calendar of the times to the necessities of art. They have not thought it urgent strictly to follow the Biblical chronology, for reasons obvious to any Oriental student and important to the movement of the narrative.

Modern Assyriology has become a rapid and complex series of discoveries. To dogmatise, is to be unscientific. The enthusiastic research of to-morrow may overthrow the theory of to-day. "The Master of the Magicians," be it remembered, is not an archæological treatise, but a novel.

H. D. W.
E. S. P. W.

THE MASTER OF THE MAGICIANS.

CHAPTER I.

IT was spring in Babylon. The ingenious clepsydra lazily marked the second division of the sultry morning. It was the month Airu.[1] The moon and the sun were balanced, and food was in the mouth of the people.

Protected by a high wall, that incloses a square of two stades each way, stands the towering temple of Bel. This holy pyramid is the glory of Babylon, and confers imperishable honor upon its royal restorer, Nebuchadrezzar the Great. The essential and conspicuous feature of the temple is the Ziggurat, or tower, which rises in decreasing rectangular stages to the height of three hundred and fifty-six feet from the level ground. This tower rears itself upward in seven courses from its platform base. The platform is considered by many the eighth stage. But such is not the case. It is a square

____

[1] April.

whose sides measure one stadium, or six hundred feet each. This is the mountain which the king —may Merodach protect him!—reared to Bel. Not even are Imgur-Bel or Nevitti-Bel, the ramparts of this eternal city, more magnificent than the stupendous foundation of the temple of Bel and of the Queen of Heaven. Upon this platform (whose sides confront the cardinal points, and under whose four corners the king hath set his seal and cylinder) rise the seven different elevations in pyramidal exactness. Each of these is sacred to its own planet. Each has a proportionate and decreasing base line, and each, with the exception of the crowning shrine, is thirty-six feet high. Is not this the square of six, the number of the lawful days of labor? The first stage, dedicated to Saturn, is painted a bituminous coat of black. This is a square of two hundred and fifty-six feet. The second is painted white; each of its four sides measures two hundred and twenty feet. The third glows in the hue of a Damascus orange. This is dedicated to Jupiter; its sides measure each one hundred and eighty-four feet. The fourth, sacred to Mercury, was burned in its building to a vitreous blue. Its sides are diminished like the rest by thirty-six feet. The fifth stage shows a bright blood-red; the ruddy clay, by order of the chief high priest, was simply burned. Mars rejoices in this scarlet token, and gives victory to the army of the king. The sixth huge step is sacred to the moon. Each of its sides measures seventy-six feet. They shine like the moon at midnight. They are coated with princely silver. The number of talents of precious metal used thereon is a royal secret, but each plate was hammered to the thickness of a thumb nail, and who dares tear it away? The seventh stage is the last. It is a cube. Forty feet is its height. Forty feet is its width. Forty feet is its length. This is the temple of the god Bel. It is sacred to the sun, and is as dazzling to the eye. The king said, Let there be naught but gold without and within. Beaten plates of gold were affixed to this shrine of Bel, and its framework was built of selected cedars of Lebanon from beyond the desert. The grandeur of this pyramid is supreme. It is likened unto the rainbow that is seen when the sesame first sends forth its shoot. There are thirty-six temples to the gods within Imgur-Bel, the outer wall of Babylon. This is of all the greatest, and in declaring it the tongues of men become confused. Planned by the astrologer of King Sargon, it rises to a mystic height. Is it not the square of sixteen, the square of four, the square of two? A broad, winding ascent, mounting from stage to stage, leads to the top; and midway there is a resting place for the people who offer at the altar of Bel.

Such is the wonder of Babylon, unequaled among all the architectural marvels of the city of the Gate of God. Within the golden shrine blaze three images of gold. They are known as Bel, Beltis his wife, and Ishtar the Queen of Babylon. Before the image of Beltis, the Queen of the Land, are two lions of gold. On each side of these gleam two serpents of silver. Before the sacred statues is the table of gold, and upon this rest the golden bowls, one for each of the deities.

No one knows the full extent of the treasures of Bel but Nebuchadrezzar the king, and no one is more beloved of the king than Mutusa-ili, the wisest of his subjects, who teaches the mysteries of the priestly lore to such pupils as the king ordains. At the base of the tower of Bel is a second chapel; this contains a sitting image of Bel, molten of gold. Opposite to this rises a statue of the king, twelve cubits in height, also of solid gold. Within are the offerings of the rich, jewels of carbuncle and ruby, and thrones of carved ivory and gold taken from the Sidonians in battle. Outside of this smaller shrine are two altars. The larger one is of silver; on it are daily offered fifty full-grown victims. Upon this great altar, at the annual festival of

the god, are burned a thousand talents of frankincense of priceless odors. The smaller altar is
of gold. Here a hundred sucklings are offered
between the morning and the evening hours.
These altars stand upon the northeast, the cool
front of the great tower of Babylon. Opposite
are the brazen gates within the wall, the entrance
to the sacred court. Here ends the road of
Nana, which the king laid out from his new palace northward to the temple. The road of Nana
crosses the Shebil canal half-way from the palace to the Ziggurat. On the right of the road
of Nana, just beyond the Shebil canal, which protects the pleasure-ground of the king, about two
stades southwest of the temple of Bel, stands the
ancient library of Babylon. Built two thousand
years before the son of Nabu-pal-usur began to
reign, it had been restored by each successive
ruler, until now, with all its additions, it has become a solemn and a stately pile. Raised, as all
public buildings are, upon a platform, it is protected by a battlement, or escarpment, that rises
fifty feet from the ground. A moat, fed from
the lazy Euphrates, surrounds·the battlement.
From the Nana road projects the only entrance
to this palace of learning. This short avenue
is paved with brilliant bricks, upon which are
painted and burned the Houses of the Sun. A
drawbridge drops across the fosse, and the way

comes to an abrupt stop before huge doors of brass that are guarded on each side by lions carved in stone. Thence there is a dark ascent until the upper court is reached. Now the maze of buildings and their foreboding look strike the searcher after truth with bewilderment; his hushed foot falls within timidly. To the right, in a wing, is the hall of instruction of Mutusa-ili, the sage of Babylon, beloved of the king.

It was the third hour of the morning watch. The water-clock seemed flooded. This common timepiece had an odd attachment. At each division of the day it dropped a corresponding number of pebbles into a brazen urn below. Three times this pleasant clatter resounded through the silent halls, on a bright morning of the second month of the fifteenth year of the reign of Nebuchadrezzar.

A little group stood in the court-yard under the shade of a tall date-palm, intently watching the gilded shrine on the Ziggurat of Bel. It was the hour of prayer, and the pilgrims on their weary ascent were seen to halt and bend their bodies low in devotion. One among this group, in the court of what was known as the royal library or university, stood preëminent for his age and bearing. From his head rose a turban, shaped like a cone, crowned with a scarlet rosette. That was the only bit of color on his attire. Cool, white, spotless linen reached to his feet. In his left hand he held a stick of choice cedar; its handle was a sphere of lapis-lazuli, upon which the sun and moon were engraved. That wand was a badge of office, and was the sole ornament which Mutusa-ili owned; it was a present from the king. His beard was long and white. It hung upon his breast in curls. From behind his turban fell what might be called a veil: it consisted of two broad linen bands; these protected his neck and back from the scorching heat of the sun. About him were his pupils. They were the pick of the Babylonian Empire. They numbered hardly over a score, and were the future high priests, astronomers, diviners, and rulers of provinces and of the armies of the king. These youths, for the oldest had not yet known seventeen years, were gazing as devoutly as boys can, and with a suspicion of curiosity, upon the iridescent temple before them. At nine o'clock precisely, a bright standard was raised from the top of the tower. This could easily be seen all over the aristocratic part of the city. It was the signal for prayer. The boys were in the habit of timing their water-clock in the court by this daily token. This morning the water-clock was almost a minute ahead of the official time, and one boy, in the midst of his profound devotion, nudged another significantly, as if a wager had been won. He that was the master stood intent. He mused, rather than adored, and seemed, contrary to his wont, to be communing with another divinity. A bright-faced youth by his side may have understood his master's thoughts, for he touched the linen robe of the teacher not irreverently, and whispered, —

"Is not Bel enough?"

"Hush, Susa!" hastily answered the sage. "Bel is not alone. There is another fount of Deity. I look beyond the veil of yonder sacred shrine. Thou knowest naught yet of these mystic things."

The lad blushed at this transcendental rebuke, and, wondering what it meant, fixed his gaze again aloft. One hand was folded across his breast, the other extended before him in the conventional attitude of devotion. Then the crimson banner that flaunted from the height was lowered. The moment of prayer had passed, and the business of the day was briskly resumed. Astrologers swarmed into the library to consult the Illumination of Bel. Historians came to verify their records; students were numerous. They had flocked from all parts of the empire to study what only this university, with its incomparable library and ready corps of instructors could teach them.

Mutusa-ili was the recognized head of this seat of learning. His word was the final appeal in the culture of the times. But his special duty was to train youths to be men, and to carry them through all the branches of learning known to the Babylonians. His term of instruction was completed when the students became fit to take the position in the world which the king commanded. The present class was not yet two years advanced. Another had almost completed its course. That was mainly composed of high-born captives who were becoming naturalized. Of these, many were Jews of the last captivity from Jerusalem.

Within the chamber of instruction the buzz of work had begun. On a high seat, or throne, sat the master. In his left hand was the wand of office. With his right he gesticulated gravely. About him, on low benches, the boys wrote diligently.

"May Nebo instruct me!" said one lad petulantly; "any fool can copy Akkadian, but who can translate the stuff?"

"Bring the tablet here," said the teacher mildly. "Thou didst well to call upon Nebo. Thou needest more of the art to learn." For Nebo was the deity of the university, the god of instruction.

The boy brought up his tablet of moist clay and stood with his stylus in his mouth.

"Surely thou canst render the fable of the ass and the lion's skin?" asked the master.

"It is easy enough to recognize the words for ass, owner, and long ears.   I cannot understand the rest; it is useless work."

The lad looked disconsolately at the neat tablet which he had to copy and translate into his own tongue; it was written in the language of two thousand years before his day, — the language of the priests and scribes, and of the literature classic to the age.

Susa's venerable teacher smiled.

"When I taught Balatsu-usur, whom the king (may Merodach protect him!) brought captive from Jerusalem, the alien learned it in one day.   Surely a stranger shall not outstrip thee.   Now get thee to thy work again.   Use the dictionary more diligently, or thou shalt never become a Rubu-Emga, a glorious chief like thy father."

The lad looked discouraged, and his teeth unconsciously closed upon and splintered the three-edged wooden stylus, — the pen which wrote characters upon the clay by pressure.   He drew another cedar stylus from his bosom and bent to his work.

When the morning work was nearly done, the boy lifted a bright face to his master, and made it known that the transcription on his tablet was complete.

" Has any other pupil finished the fable?" asked Mutusa-ili. No one answered.

" Then read what thou hast written, Susa, and the gods guide thy speech."

The lad proudly read his translation as follows.

" An ass, finding the skin of a lion, put it on with pride. Disguised, it now spread terror among the neighborhood. Some went and told the king. The royal hunt was organized. Just as the king came up in his chariot, the fraud was discovered by the master of the ass, who espied his long ears and recognized his loud voice. The master belabored the ass until the skin of the lion fell off, revealing to the disgusted king the vulgar beast of burden. In his disappointment, the king ordered the ass to be killed, and the owner to work in the brick-yard for one month."

" Let me now see the writing," said the master, as a low hum of approval was heard from the rest of the boys at this glib and perfect rendering. Susa was the quickest scholar, given to pranks, but aspiring and earnest. His family was of the best old stock in the land, and, being destined ultimately for high preferment, he had importance among the lads. His brother, a young man of twenty-five, was already captain of the king's body-guard, an office of distinction. Allit, known to many by his military name as Arioch the Tall, was preferred by the king; Amytis, the queen, shared this sentiment. Susa would naturally come before the notice of the king, who took a personal interest, when he was in Babylon, in the advancement made by each of his *protégés*.

The teacher scanned the tablet which the boy had laid upon his knee. Here and there a wedge-shaped letter was written indistinctly through inexperience, but the transcription was correct.

"See," said the pleased master. "I will stamp it with my seal, and do thou put thy mark upon its edge. It shall be stored in the vaults where thy father's and thy grandfather's first perfect exercises are kept for all time and times and a day."

The lad's face quivered with joy at this great honor; for it was the custom to preserve the first perfect translations of the old Akkadian in the library. This acted as a powerful stimulus on the student, and it became a matter of honor in a family that such exercises should date back a thousand years or so in direct descent.

While the teacher was yet speaking, an unusual commotion was heard in the halls of the building. The master, with the composure of age, exhibited indifference, but the boys became restless. There was a shout, followed by another. The lads could stand it no longer. At a nod from Mutusa-ili they rushed to the terrace without.

The cry now rang out distinctly: "The king! It is the king! The favorite of Marduk! Nebuchadrezzar the king!"

CHAPTER II.

It was true that the king had returned to Babylon. He had been on a military expedition — one of a score — organized against the mountain tribe that happened at the time to have revolted and refused tribute. Like the majority of such excursions, it had been only a matter of days to punish the offenders and bring captive thousands of rebels. Nebuchadrezzar had approached his royal city at the northern gate, and now, palpitating with triumph, advanced to offer his booty before the altar of Bel.

In his chariot of state the king rode. Beside him the charioteer drove the restless horses. Behind him stood a bare-headed eunuch, who held the gorgeous parasol, the emblem of sovereignty, above the monarch's head. Behind the king rode the generals of the right and of the left, each in his chariot. Allit, the brother of Susa, followed upon a mighty horse. After him were his men in rank, their hands upon their javelins, ready to start at the king's command. Then came throngs of prisoners, about to be branded as slaves. These marched sullenly, their hands behind them, their heads in halters. In droves, like cattle, they staggered along. Among them were women and children. The weakest of these were carried in carts. This procession was miles in length, and as it wound its way through the crowds of hooting citizens, the captives looked in vain for sympathy. In such a piteous procession lay the source of the nation's wealth and weakness, for the captive force must be recruited whenever gigantic building enterprises were undertaken. It was rumored that the king had himself fomented this last revolt, so as to have at hand sufficient laborers to build some elaborate gardens for his Median queen. However that might be, the people did not trouble themselves as long as their king was successful and the trade stimulated.

The boys had run swiftly to the Nana road to meet the procession. The streets were crowded with excited people who came out to greet the pageant. The greater part of the mob were of the lower class, who always traveled on foot; many were slaves; but here and there a chariot revealed an arrogant noble, or from a brilliant litter, carried by Egyptians, peered the uncovered face of a woman decked with embroideries and jewelry. As Susa ran along, he jarred against a girl. She was young. She could not have been **over seventeen.** She turned, with a motion of annoyance, but when she saw the lad's guiltless face she smiled pleasantly upon him. In the rush of the throng Susa noticed only two things about this girl: a soft, dark look, and crimson fringe upon a white robe. The boy was a young observer, but he was conscious of a startled, truant expression that played prettily over her face, as if a home-keeping girl had snatched a forbidden pleasure, a moment's glance at a world that was not hers. Susa, with the chivalry of youth, hastened to make such reparation as he could for his roughness. He nodded brightly to the maiden.

"Come after me. We 'll get the best view of the procession."

Then he plunged forward in a lordly way. He bellowed to a slave, and nudged a portly citizen aside. The girl followed closely, and Susa escaped many a hard word as she smiled apology here and there for the ardor of her young protector. It was not long before the two, panting with exercise, had skirted along the lower wall of the temple and faced the procession as it was about to pass within the sacred inclosure.

" Yonder rides my brother," said Susa proudly. "He is captain of the king's guard. He is a fine fellow. I came out to see him. He has been at the wars. I shall shout to him when he gets near enough."

"Where?" asked the girl. "Quick! I must get homeward. I ought not to be here."

"Have you run away?" suggested the lad comfortably. "That is excellent. I do that — when I can. I ran away from school once. But Mutusa-ili knows how to make you sorry you did it, I can tell you! It is a poor bargain to play truant at the king's school. But it is fun while it lasts."

The girl nodded, with a twinkle in her eye.

"I *can't* play truant," she answered confidently, "for I may not go to school. I have only run away from home to see the parade. That is very tame, you see. I am only a woman."

"Women are very useful," observed the young lord calmly. "But there comes my brother. See! His name is Allit. He is brave, I tell you. *He* never surrenders. *He* is never captured. Yonder he rides, like a king behind the king. Is he not a handsome fellow?"

Susa pointed to the procession, and the maiden's eyes demurely followed the slow motion of his finger. The parade was an imposing affair. The king rode first, haughty and splendid. His chariot was covered with plates of gold. The wheels and the harness of the horses were studded with gems; these were of differing colors, — turquoise, garnets, and emerald. The horses were cream-white, caparisoned in cloth-of-gold.

The monarch was arrayed in his royal robes. The tiara glittered upon his head. The charioteer checked the pace of the impatient horses as they approached the brazen entrance to the temple. Nebuchadrezzar motioned, and the well-trained horses came to a full stop. They might have been carved from marble, so still they stood. But for the tinkling of the bells attached to their collars, they gave no sign of life. Now, not even the king could ride into the sacred court. Like the humblest of his subjects, he was proud to walk and bow the knee to his protective divinity.

Thus it was natural that when the king halted the procession should crowd up. The mass pressed closer. Bearers of shields tried to calm restive horses. When the sovereign alighted, the shout of welcome rent the air.

The throng had now become so great that Susa and the girl had been forced apart. Susa had been jammed into the front rank of the spectators, while she was looking at the captain of the guards, — the king behind the king. The boy searched for her in vain, but she had disappeared. Wild songs of joy burst from the people. The horns, the timbrels, and the harps resounded shrilly. One looked, and the faces of the musicians were sad. They were out of tune with the universal joy, for they were Hebrew captives playing at their master's nod. This was the song with which the people greeted Nebuchadrezzar : —

> " Mighty legions which devised against thee,
>   Before thy feet
>   Thou cuttest them in pieces.
>   Thou, thou,
>   Art king of kings! "

As the last triumphal sound died away, two horses that their attendants had vainly tried to hold, became maddened. Hemmed in by a wall of people, they communicated a contagion of fright to the horses of a chariot at the immediate left. The four infuriated steeds charged the mob. Cries of terror and warning rang out from the occupants of the two war-chariots. The mass melted before this onslaught. One slave, caught by hoofs, was crushed, and the heavy chariot passed over him. No one paid attention to this incident. It was only a slave.

Susa was in direct line of the path of destruction, but with the alertness of youth he had dodged, and now stood safe. As he watched the people parting before the shock, he saw that one was left behind. In his confusion, he noticed

nothing but a waving drapery of white touched
with crimson, which looked to his excited imagination like spots of blood. The horses were
upon her. He fancied that she was struck, and
in an agony of terror cried above the universal
shriek, —

" Allit, Allit! Save her! Save that girl! "

During this, to say the least, unusual commotion, for these horses were by far too well trained
to lose their composure, except under extraordinary provocation, a young man sat disdainfully
observing this disgraceful lack of equine discipline, lightly checking his own impatient horse.
The youth had an unconscious but proud air of
command that was exceedingly becoming. It
bespoke high birth and a manly training. He
wore a brazen helmet, with its curved crest
carved into the head of a horse ; it glittered in
the morning sun. Beneath it appeared a face
that might have belonged to Adar, god of
strength, the champion warrior himself. It was
large, but not coarse. The bones of the head,
like those of the rest of the young man's body,
were massive ; yet the skin, tanned by a hundred
expeditions, was as soft as silk from Shushan.
His deep, luminous eyes had a boyish sparkle.
Dark lashes gave them a happy look. His thick
but finely shaped lips curled as he watched the
confusion. He grasped his sword and looked

towards the king, as if awaiting an order to punish the unskillful charioteers. When he looked back, the four horses had begun their mad plunge. The rabble was scattering before them. The charioteers were pale with fright at the coming catastrophe. The young warrior nonchalantly prepared himself to view the disaster. He was as composed as if in his own apartments. This indifference, which was either acquired through soldierly discipline, or affected to conceal habitual and deep feeling, had a marked influence on his men, who glanced at him, and stood still. As the young man watched the dispersion of the crowd, his heart gave a sudden upward start. The receding wave left one behind. She stood with her hands clasped across her breast, swaying this way and that, in a stupor of indecision. Crimson trimming flickered like flame upon a snow-white robe. Allit was at right angles to her, and to the dashing horses that bore down upon their sacrifice. The young man spoke one word to his horse; his heel enforced it. There would be only a hundred-yard dash. Susa's cry of distress reached the rider's ears. The horse entered into his master's spirit, and flew at an unprecedented speed. All eyes turned upon the captain of the guards. Did he not ride to certain death? Allit and the chariot with the uncontrolled animals drew together. The horse was as true to the will of his rider as an arrow to the aim of an Assyrian archer. No power could now stop the impetus of trained brute speed. The young man bent from his embossed saddle. Was it to escape the pointed pole of the chariot? The girl seemed unmindful of her position. She was in a trance of fear. Every motor muscle had been struck with nerve paralysis. She drooped and fell. The people could not see the arm that enveloped her, for the action was too quick. But they saw a white form rise like a whirlwind in the air. Her feet swung far behind. The sharp pole that bound the horse to the chariot was afterwards found to have impaled a sandal which it had pierced through the heel. There were also a few shreds of cotton, and one drop of blood.

The deed was done, that all Babylon rehearsed for many a day. The girl was saved. Allit at the last moment hardly doubted his own destruction, but the maiden must be saved at any cost; this was the duty of a soldier and a gentleman. He spoke a final word to his horse, lovingly, as a true horseman does, and galloped on. So close was his escape that, as he thundered across the course of the runaway chariot, its sharpened pole tore a furrow across his horse's flank, and wounded the girl in the foot. She had fainted.

She did not hear the king speak. The cries of the court, and the people shouting applause at Allit's superb deed, passed over her unconsciousness. She did not know that this rescue disconcerted the flying horses, and resulted in their capture. Susa's hand clutched his brother's bridle, and the two spoke affectionately. It was Susa's arm that helped her down and placed her on the pavement, and the boy's voice that kept the curious mob back. After a few moments, her eyes opened languidly. A handsome, unfamiliar face bent over her with a smiling but critical look. A cup of palm wine soon restored her to herself. She turned from the stranger to Susa, her boyish friend.

"I don't know where I am," she said faintly.

"You are safe enough now," answered the boy briskly. "What a narrow pull you 've had! My brother did it. Speak to him. He saved you. Is n't he a magnificent fellow?"

A blush stole over her pale, olive face, giving her the complexion of a pomegranate when its core is ripe. She regarded for the first time "the king behind the king."

Allit saw this beautiful color transformation. He had only a moment to stop. The procession was already moving, and he must keep his place. The girl was agreeable to him. He was glad she was not ugly or old. How they would have laughed at him — his brother officers — for risking his life for a wrinkled woman or a common slave! He had known many loves, after the manner of a Babylonian noble, and thought lightly of women. The maiden attracted him. It would be easy to see her again.

Susa now thought it time for him to speak.

"Come, Allit, don't be bashful. She wants to thank you. Then I will see her home in a litter. For a few shekels, the dogs shall fetch one." The boy pointed to a batch of curious eunuchs.

The girl, supported by Susa, had now struggled to an upright position. Allit approached her, and gave an unconscious military salute, as if before his superior. She made a pretty motion with her lips, and said, —

"My young friend says you are his brother. He must be happy to own such a brave and noble brother. I thank you, and my father will express to you more fittingly my feelings. He will call upon you."

"It was nothing," said the captain. "My men wait for me. Tell me, who is it I have saved this day? Who is the father of so fair a child?"

"I am Lalitha," answered the maiden, with slight embarrassment, "the only daughter of Mutusa-ili, the sage."

" Why, that 's my master ! " began Susa.

At this juncture the trumpet sounded. Lalitha gave a little start at the peal, and tottered,
moaning, —

" My foot!   Oh, my foot ! "

The sandal had been torn away, and drops of
blood now stained the bricks beneath. Hastily
drawing forth from his robe a silken cloth of fine
texture, Allit stooped down to bind the wound.
The second call sounded. The soldier dared
not wait. With one of the too significant looks
he knew so well how to give, he gently said, —

" Maiden, Lalitha, daughter of Mutusa-ili, we
will meet again."

Susa was busy trying to bind the wounded
foot, when the captain of the guards galloped
off and appeared at the head of his command.
When Lalitha was lifted into the litter which
Susa had ordered, she did not see the captain,
but her eyes encountered the piercing glance of
one surrounded by a hundred eunuchs. She
shrank from a woman over whom a golden canopy waved, and behind whom royal fan-bearers
performed their meek attentions. Well might
Lalitha hide her face; she beheld, for the first
time, Amytis, the daughter of Astyages, the
dreaded Queen of Babylon.

CHAPTER III.

When the brazen gate had closed upon such as the King of Spirits allowed within his sacred court, a young man was seen to disengage himself from the crowd, and walk briskly away. He had been a spectator of the pageant. He had witnessed the rescue, and he had strained his eyes to note the features of the girl. His face had taken on an expression of benevolent satisfaction when the deed was accomplished. But when the excitement was over, and the procession had disappeared behind the wall, the young man, with a sad and thoughtful mien, left the place, and walked back over the same road towards the palace of the king. People whispered to each other as he passed. Some bowed reverently, and many a maiden put on a coquettish air to attract his attention. But he passed indifferently by; his robe swayed behind him as he strode the tessellated pavement.

His garment was not dyed, according to the custom of the place, nor was it marked by heavy embroideries. Cleansed to a curious whiteness by the fuller, its sternness was relieved by a scroll-work of gold along the border. If one had looked nearer, he would have recognized characters within the pattern. The scholar would have pronounced them Hebrew. A handkerchief of the finest linen was worn loosely, like a turban. At this season of the year, a light covering was ample protection from the perpendicular rays of the sun. The youth wore shoes that curved upward at the toe. These were colored a dull red and had no latchets. He was conspicuous as the only one on the street without a cane. Every movement of this young man's was aristocratic. The refinement and intelligence of his face revealed high birth; his grace, the courtier; but his simplicity and utter disregard of all the frippery of the day gave an unconscious rebuke to the *jeunesse dorée* of Babylon. This man was no free Babylonian. He was a captive and a Jew; since the last conquest of Jerusalem, the most distinguished prisoner-of-war known to Babylon. This captive, who had already made such a stir at court, was known to his countrymen by the name of Daniel. They called him the representative of God, the most beautiful of all the sons of Judah. But Babylon had given a title of its own, half affectionate and half sarcastic, to this upstart whom the king honored. They named him Balatsuusur, "May Bel protect his life."

When Daniel came to the Shebil canal, he
was challenged by the guards who protected the
drawbridge, but in giving the sign with his left
hand he was as usual passed with a salute, which
he courteously returned. He was now within
Nebuchadrezzar's private pleasure - grounds.
Two large palaces glittered before him. Fountains abounded ; streams of water dripped with
a pleasant lisp into cool basins. Well-culti-
vated trees stood in groups, with a stately air,
like princes ; in their luxuriant leaves the breeze
stirred deferentially. The hot air was moistened
and grateful. The broad avenue of the gardens divided into three parts ; one went straight
through a wall into the court-yard of the great
palace. This wall was a hundred feet high
and fifty broad, and was calculated to impress
the visitor with his own insignificance and the
supremacy of the king. Another way skirted
to the right among cool shrubbery, and then
mounted by steps to the embankment of a huge
reservoir with a long name (the Yapur Shapu),
that protected the grounds upon the east, and
afforded continual refreshment against the terrible summer heat. The third arm of the avenue passed westward a few hundred feet, until
it reached the Euphrates itself, the god-given
river of Sippara. Daniel chose this latter road,
and soon reached the brick quay that protected

the banks from encroachments by flood. This brick wall formed an important feature of the defenses of the palace fortress. Military watchtowers frowned upon it. The wall was used as a favorite promenade by the king and those whom the king honored. Many feet beneath flowed the river. Boats shot across it like busy thoughts.

Daniel walked on until he came to the stone bridge spanning the river which separated the greater from the lesser palace. His eyes looked over this long masterpiece of engineering towards the west. They had a pathetic expression. Beyond the river was the desert, and beyond the desert was home, his birthplace, the city of Jerusalem. He loitered on the bridge sadly. A carved lion arrested his attention, and he stopped and mused before it; it was an excellent piece of sculpture, and he gave to it the naive interest of the Jew, to whom " graven images " were forbidden sources of culture. The beast was bending over a man held in a mighty clutch: one paw tortured him; the other was raised to strike. Daniel's homesick imagination saw in this painted carving the emblem of Babylon, which had crushed his country underfoot, and was ready to smite it again.

" How long! How long !" murmured the captive. As he leaned over the parapet, hot tears of impotent bitterness fell into the water below.

Daniel was one of the very few Jews who at the court of Babylon had preserved their national characteristics unscorched by the splendor and luxury to which their sensuous natures deeply responded; and who had kept their religious spirit unsullied in the midst of a ceremonious devotion to any one of a thousand gods one felt pleased to choose; who were fiery patriots, ready to disregard a royal command for conscience' sake, at peril to position or to life. It was a well-known fact, the talk of the court, the thing which first brought him into prominence, that he refused to eat the dainties and wines served directly from the king's table; he lived upon fruit and vegetables alone, to the extreme fear of Allit Arioch, the captain of the guards, who, by reason of his position, was responsible not only for the health but even the good looks of the Jewish prince. But Allit the Tall was bound to acknowledge that the young vegetarian grew fairer and fatter than all other youths fed richly from the king's table. In point of fact, Daniel had an abhorrence for the practice of the court in the dedication of food. Not a mouthful appeared before the king but had been consecrated to some heathen god or other. Daniel would not eat idolatrous banquets; he preferred vegetables and hunger; and the jeers of his fellow-captives did not swerve him by the length of a grasshopper's beak from his strenuous purpose.

Now, Daniel had unconsciously won recognition in another way. For so young a man he was eminent as a scholar; quick in acquiring a difficult language, and the science of the observation of the stars contained therein; adapted general culture by an intuitive graciousness; ready to yield to foreign customs when a matter of religion was not involved. In addition to these qualities, which commanded the highest esteem in Babylon, where learning and *savoir faire* were more highly prized than at any other court, Daniel was a dreamer. Like Joseph of old, he had strange visions and told them to no one. This habit of communing with a world beyond the visible had given him peculiar eyes. They were un-Jewish; they were long, and at once full and narrow; they were gray, one might almost say green. They appeared unobservant of passing detail. When they looked at one, they seemed to gaze upon the image cast within. They were not sparkling, but had an iridescence. The pupils were always dilated, as if they groped in the dark. In contrast, the bright color of his face was impressive. His aspect gave significance to a phrase in the writings of his people, "the light of his countenance;" for in the company of other men he shone like a torch.

As Daniel stood leaning over the bridge, he fell, not for the first time nor the last, in his nervously excited history, into a state which was nothing more nor less than a trance. He was looking at the motion of the water below. Its quiver fascinated him. The sparkle of the water flooded his brain as a crystal ball swung in the air affects a mesmeric subject. The light grew within him until he was faint. Daniel was in another world, although his eyes were open, and he seemed to be altogether in this. To a casual observer, nothing unusual had taken place; probably the young seer could have explained the mystery of such a vision no better than we.

Now, as Daniel stood entranced, a fat man waddled toward him from the king's greater palace. This creature was short, puffy, and held a stout stick in his right hand. His fingers were covered with rings. In his left he grasped a long fringed scarf, which hung loosely before and behind, passing over the left shoulder; tassels of dark Tyrian purple swung from each end of this scarf. His dress was highly colored, and conspicuous for an embroidered cross-belt, that passed under the right arm and over the left shoulder, and also for an exquisite girdle about the waist. His face was beardless, and his head and feet were bare. Such was Ashpenaz, the prince of eunuchs, as he salaamed before the dreamer. At that moment he had an air of lordly command that would have been ridiculous in any other eunuch but Ashpenaz. His head wagged solemnly. He was theatrically conscious of his official importance. He was perhaps a bit embarrassed as he stopped behind Daniel, and his **fat** fingers tightened on his scarf, his badge of authority, with a resolute grip.

Ashpenaz gave an important cough to attract the attention of the absorbed Jew. There was no answer. The eunuch tapped his cane on the pavement impatiently, but no response came. He glanced over his shoulder to see if any one were looking, advanced cautiously, and touched Daniel with his stick. The seer did not stir. Ashpenaz was out of temper at this delay. He plucked up courage, and, taking the prince of Israel by the arm, gave him a vigorous shake. This interruption had the desired effect. The young man turned, towered above the chief eunuch, and bent upon him sightless, open eyes. Ashpenaz shuddered and grew pale. He was in the habit of saying that he did not believe in seers ; which meant then, as it is apt to in all ages, that he was particularly afraid of them.

Collecting himself with a spurt of bravado, Ashpenaz made out to mutter, —

"The queen — Amytis the queen would see thee immediately."

This word had a marked effect upon Daniel. He stretched out his hands in a warning gesture, and, in a low tone that struck awe to the heart of the now thoroughly uncomfortable eunuch, exclaimed, —

"The queen? Amytis the queen? *She shall meet her doom between heaven and earth.*"

The young man stopped, put his hands before his face as if brushing away an unwelcome sight, tottered, sighed, and then awoke. Looking about in amazement, he recognized where he was. Ashpenaz stood before him in an attitude of unusual deference and fear.

"Ah, my friend," said Daniel courteously. "I am afraid that I wandered for a moment. What can I do for you to-day? The king has returned, I see. There will be gay times and much building now. Is he well?"

"My Lord Balatsu-usur! Why didst thou give me such a fright? When I gave thee the message of the queen, thou didst look and say — but I dare not repeat it. The queen wishes thy counsel immediately. I am ordered to summon thee to her presence."

Ashpenaz stopped with a wheeze, and looked

at his companion cautiously, as if in fear of another ill-omened retort. Daniel only said —

"Let it be done ; I come."

But as he strode along his face darkened and his lips tightened. Daniel had a genuine affection for the king, and but scant respect for the royal consort. Amytis was not a Babylonian, but a Mede. She was the price of peace between the two great empires that divided the Assyrian spoil. She had come willingly, for she was then but a child. But now she was in the full sway of feminine caprice. Beloved after a fashion by Nebuchadrezzar, who cared more for the construction of memorable temples and palaces than for the lures of women, and more for the gods than for either, she was restlessly dissatisfied with herself and all about her. She had been reared in the cool mountains ; she hated the lowlands and the heat. Her home-sickness, or what passed for such, served as an excuse for every fit of petulance or flitting freak. At present she was wearied, and desired to be amused. Daniel was the latest craze at court, and so he was summoned. This was no secret. The young captive understood it perfectly. Though but twenty-two years of age, he had learned to keep his social discoveries to himself. He had met Amytis frequently, but this was the first time that he had been ordered to a private audience. Her mood might load him with chains, or exalt him to dangerous honors.

The two had now left the bridge, and were passing through the garden. It was about mid-day. Had it been two months later, the heat would have been unendurable. As it was, the sun burned furiously, and both men were glad of a halt to refresh themselves at a stream that was carried artificially beside the path, beneath a cluster of orange-trees. Neither spoke, and after a brief rest Daniel made a silent motion indicating that he wished to proceed through the bronze gate that swung against the wall. This huge wall was the last fortification to the inner palaces of the king. Within the inclosure another large garden blossomed gayly. Two palaces glittered down upon the flowers. The most famous of these was built by the king in fifteen days.

In the garden of the king was a beautiful shrine dedicated to Bel-Merodach, Nebuchadrezzar's favorite divinity. Daniel and Ashpenaz passed through the guarded wall, and mounted the platform of the palace. Entering, they walked rapidly by halls of state and private apartments until they came to that portion of the new palace which contained the apartments of the women of the court. This looked directly down upon the queen's private gardens and over into the Shebil canal. Ashpenaz now left Daniel in a vestibule, and hastened to announce his approach. This was Daniel's first introduction into the harem of the king. He did not wait long. In a moment the eunuch appeared, put his fingers to his lips, and said, —

"The queen awaits thee; follow me."

CHAPTER IV.

Susa was almost beside himself at the dignity
of his new position. Boys of his age were
thrust aside in Babylon, and treated as mere
infants until they assumed the flowing manly
robe, and brushed their forelock aside in token
of their having come of age. Whether they
were teething or studying astrology, they were
as subject to their parents as the meanest slave;
life itself was at the disposal of the child's father.
This was Susa's first responsibility, and he
strutted beside the litter of the faint girl impor-
tantly. Every now and then he pushed his head
with boyish familiarity, but quite respectfully,
behind the curtains and asked her how she was.
Lalitha answered cheerfully; the boy was not
old enough to know whether she were really
hurt or not. As he walked beside her he chattered continually; he told her about the prowess
of Allit, and assured her that his brother was
in the habit of doing just such favors to pretty
maidens every day.

"Indeed?" said Lalitha demurely.

It was not far to the modest house of Mutusa-ili, but before they were there a cry of pain was heard from the litter. The motion, gentle as it was, had been too much for the wounded foot. The bandage had slipped, and blood was slowly trickling from an ugly wound in the heel. The girl was evidently suffering. Susa held her quivering hand with pleasant boyish kindness. He ordered the bearers to push on and up to the house unceremoniously. The door was flung open, and the venerable figure of Lalitha's father appeared. His white beard flowed to his waist, and his long hair waved in the delicate breeze; it lay like a nimbus about his dark, emaciated face. He was pale with alarm. Lalitha reached her arms out of the litter toward her father with a pretty, courageous gesture.

"Dear father, I have only hurt my foot a little; I am well and safe. I almost can walk. See!"

She tried to place her foot upon the ground, and gave a low cry of anguish. Mutusa-ili did not speak a word. With the self-possession of his race and his experience, he gathered his daughter silently into his arms, and bore her to the house. Love put strength into his spare frame. He was father and mother to Lalitha.

As the girl passed from sight over the threshold she waved her hand to Susa, who stood disconsolately beside the litter. But Mutusa-ili noticed him no more than if he had been one of the slaves; he was so used to the boy.

When Lalitha was laid upon a couch in an inner chamber she turned her face to the wall, and the scenes of the past hour rolled like a ball through her brain. Her father did not discuss the accident. He gave her a cooling drink, and proceeded to investigate the wound, and by an application of pounded roots to relieve the pain. The hurt was severe. Lalitha would not be able to walk for a long time.

"How didst thou happen to meet my pupil, Susa?" asked Mutusa-ili, when he had come to the end of such surgery as he knew. It was his first question.

"His brother, the captain of the king's guard, snatched me from under the hoofs of the horses, and Susa brought me home," said Lalitha. It was her only answer. It seemed to her as if she said a great deal. It seemed to the old man as if she had said more than she had. He regarded her piercingly.

"Dear father!" said Lalitha, laughing. "What have I done?"

"Thou hast lived to bless me," said the old man tremulously.

With moist eyes he sat by his daughter's couch. She kissed his withered hand, while he played with her hair and stroked her cheek.

As he fondled her, his dark eyes seemed to the girl to dilate. She could not take her own gaze from his. As he lightly waved his hand over her forehead, he muttered words in a strange tongue. Her eyes closed. When he stooped and kissed her forehead the pain was forgotten. The excitement had passed. The girl slept.

Mutusa-ili, teacher, student, astrologer, and seer, an unworldly man, had family connections of the most worldly sort. He was, in fact, no other than own brother to the great Egibi, head of the banking firm of Egibi and Sons, famous to all Babylonian history, the richest bankers of their age. At present, Egibi was the treasurer of the state. He lived in a lordly mansion, that compared well enough with some of the king's palaces; it had, in fact, been at one time used as the residence of the governor of Babylon, and was the most imposing private house in the gorgeous city. But the poor relation, like the poor relation of all ages, was none the better for the wealth and importance of his brother. The two men had gone their several ways: Egibi to his fortune and fame; Mutusa-ili to the scant luxuries and severe seclusion of the scholar.

The home of Lalitha was a simple place, only one story high. It stood in a quiet court, and had a little tower. In the daytime an awning protected the tower from the sun, and night found it a cool retreat. Bright flowers and vines grew luxuriantly over the tower, which had a gay, jaunty appearance, like a well-dressed girl. Here was Lalitha's private garden. Beneath was her own room, and directly adjoining that the room of the elderly woman-servant, Kisrinni by name, who played duenna to the motherless girl. The walls of the house were thick, and the bricks were large, each stamped with the name of the king. For the king owned many of the brick-yards, and part of his revenue was made by selling bricks to his subjects at cheaper rates than any one else could manufacture them. There were no windows in Lalitha's room, but light was diffused from a square opening in the roof above. During the heat of the day this was covered, so as to exclude the sun, but not the light.

The other part of the house was the master's. Ever since his wife had died, Mutusa-ili had lived in secluded rooms alone, and only his daughter approached them. In one he slept; in another he kept his library, carefully stowed away in earthen jars; his astronomical instruments were there, jealously guarded. The roof of this study, or laboratory, rose in a cone. Steps of bricks jutted from the wall, leading to the top of this cone. The steps protruded by less than two feet, and there were no banisters to support the hand. It looked almost impossible to a stranger to mount these stairs, but they were as sufficient to the aged scholar as the stone steps that led majestically up the platform of the temple of Bel. The top of the cone, which was barely large enough for two or three persons to stand upon comfortably, was the watch-tower of the sage. It was here that he observed and calculated the stars and their courses. It was here that the devout seer knelt in prayer. It was here that the mystic received those revelations that gave him his coveted influence in Babylon. It was to this secluded spot, screened from view by a high terra-cotta railing, that Mutusa-ili mounted on the night of his daughter's rescue. He held in his hand a disk of black stone, on which quaint figures were inscribed. In the centre of the diagram were carved the sun, the crescent moon, the star Venus, and the thunderbolt of Mars. The edge of the design held the scorpion, the bull, the ram, the serpent, the dog, the arrow, the eagle, each surrounded by its mysterious sign, known only to the initiated student of the constellations.

When Mutusa-ili had reached the platform, he laid the precious planisphere upon a small table, and took from his pocket what looked like a wooden tube. This he leveled upon the heavens with diligent search. After a time he took his eye from this strange instrument, and began to trace some curious figures carefully upon soft clay. Mutusa-ili was an ardent astrologer. Brought up under Chaldean or priestly instruction, he had far outstripped his contemporaries in astronomical researches. No one understood how to predict an eclipse better than he. He had made the most valuable discoveries of his time by means of this instrument which he was now holding in his hand. Pondering upon the properties of the magnifying-glass, he had naturally discovered its opposite. Mutusa-ili had, in fact, invented the telescope.[1] By its aid he was now making a new chart of the heavens. When he had shown to Nebuchadrezzar the satellites of Saturn and of Jupiter, the delighted monarch would have raised him to a princely rank, but the scholar declined to leave his simple life. For Mutusa-ili was a mystic, and what mystic can be a courtier? The young seer, Daniel, was trying to solve that problem. The old man abandoned it outright.

Mutusa-ili believed implicitly in his own ability to predict the occultation of a planet; he was no less assured that the stars were the infallible heralds of fortune to men, be it good or ill. It was he whom Nebuchadrezzar had been used to consult in every expedition or great un-

---

[1] Rawlinson's *Fourth Monarchy,* chap. 5.

dertaking. Mutusa-ili was at least an honest diviner. He trustfully regulated his own life and that of his household upon the results of each night's observation. These he carefully wrote down, and the records were kept in sealed jars until the fall of the holy city.

Mutusa-ili was now casting, for the fiftieth time, the horoscope of his daughter. He was unmanned by the events of the day. They had found him completely unprepared. Why had his art failed him? Why did he not know that his darling was at the point of destruction? "Surely the night-hawk troubled my soul yesterday," muttered the old man, as he bent nervously to his occult calculations. Would Lalitha recover from her wound? Did the presence of the astral house of Allit foretell peace or war, power or love?

Astrology was Mutusa-ili's hobby, nay, his weakness. In his way, he was a powerful skeptic. He repudiated the prevalent belief in omens that directed one's hourly acts. He laughed at those who were controlled by the presence of a white dog in the house or the position of a mule's foot in death. He held these superstitions as degrading. There was no science in them, and that was the end of it. But astrology was the bride of a great intellect.

Mutusa-ili was of Jewish descent. His family

had been in Babylon for two hundred years. After his ancestors had been torn from their country and transplanted to this hot-house soil, they had gradually succumbed to the Babylonian customs and religion. Yet these apostate families had religiously intermarried, preserving the purity of their blood and some of their traditions. Probably not a dozen people knew that Egibi, the powerful banker prince, was a Jew, and that Egibi, being translated, meant Jacob. Surely not five understood that Mutusa-ili, the Babylonian sage, the interpreter of the mysteries of the heavens and of the gods, was of the conquered race, and that his honored name was but the Babylonian synonym for Methuselah. Not even Lalitha, his only child, had suspected, until less than a year ago, that her father was not of the priestly class, a Chaldee of the Chaldeans. One day he told her. For, he said: " Thou art no longer a child, and I may not deceive thee."

Mutusa-ili was a wavering man, in a strange position. A Jew, and yet not a Jew, in a thousand ways he, like his influential brother, lightened the load of those who had recently come as captives from Jerusalem. The Egibi had not the paltry nature of those who, when alienated from their nation, sink into its habitual foes. These good men were the greatest benefactors that the poor Jewish slaves had in Babylon, and it was through their persistent and diplomatic intercession at court that the burdens of the mechanics were lightened. Some prominent captive families were even granted land outside the city gates, for homes.

Daniel had been a fortunate captive from the first. When, with hundreds of others, he arrived in the city, homesick, forlorn, and friendless, he had attracted the attention of Mutusa-ili. Through the scholar's mediation, the young man and three of his companions were educated at the university of the king. Mutusa-ili had been enthusiastic in the matter of Daniel's culture, and the result had justified his benevolent whim. Daniel had come to Babylon thoroughly equipped for new instruction. Young as he was, he had already exhausted the wisdom of the rabbis, whose knowledge consisted in the interpretation of a few books of law, barely large enough to cover a hundred tablets of clay. Mutusa-ili had devoted himself, body and soul, to this lovable youth. At the end of a three years' course of instruction, Daniel stood preëminent among his fellow-pupils.

But the teacher was afraid of his scholar. Daniel probed him too deeply with questions which he could not answer. The sage of Babylon had to acknowledge to himself that he was as a babe before that Jewish youth, whose un-youthful eyes read right through his head into his heart.

One day, when the teacher had been expounding to his pupil the grandeur of the temple of Bel and the power of Merodach, the young man interrupted him : —

"What is Bel-Merodach, O my master? He lacketh the proof of godliness. Jehovah is not made of gold, but he could lead my people out of Egypt, as he can out of Babylon, in his own good time. What has Bel done? What can the golden god perform?"

Mutusa-ili was silent. In the voice of the lad, his own conscience, dormant for seventy years, awoke. What *could* Bel do?

At another time, in the midst of a heavy discourse upon the nature of the worship of Ishtar, Daniel gravely propounded a startling query : —

"Do the groves of Ishtar keep a maiden pure?"

Mutusa-ili shot a fiery glance at the young man.

"Thou speakest," he said sternly, "of matters which are beyond thy years and the understanding thereof."

"I can understand the whiteness of woman," replied the youth, with a gesture of beautiful obeisance, "and I perceive that the worshiper of Ishtar respects it not. The shekels, or the land, or the ass of his neighbor, — these he respecteth; but not his wife or his daughter. Babylon has become a reproach among nations, and a dishonor to all mankind, in that her daughters are not chaste. Wouldst thou, Mutusa-ili, my best beloved teacher, allow thy daughter to enter the grove of Ishtar?"

The scholar bowed his head, and for very shame made no answer to the pupil. How could he? For thus stood the shameful law of Babylon: that every woman in the land, for once in her lifetime, should subject herself, in the name of religion and of the custom of the country, to dishonors of which the pen may not write. And when the daughter of Mutusa-ili came to woman's estate, the priestess of Ishtar had sent for her, that she should visit the splendid and abominable shrine of the goddess. The pitiable fact was that the girl's father, Babylonianized Jew that he had become, for very lack of courage to resist the current of society on which he drifted, might even have yielded to the stream, and accepted the dishonor of his house, as he did other incidents of captivity. But Lalitha had settled the question in a very simple way. The high-spirited and pure-minded girl had flashed a dagger before the old man's face, and vowed to plunge it in her heart, if a deed like that were mentioned in her presence by either gods or men. Then Mutusa-ili asked his first favor of the king, — that his daughter might be spared by the law of the land ; nor did he plead his alien blood.

Daniel had scorched the soul of Mutusa-ili. The young man's high look blazed like a pillar of fire before the life of the morally feeble, in- tellectual man. The two loved each other. Yet Daniel made no effort to proselyte Mutusa-ili, whom he supposed to be a Babylonian of the Babylonians.

Mutusa-ili was troubled in spirit. The wor- ship of what Daniel called " a litter of gods " was becoming more and more unsatisfactory. In his old age he yearned for the stern, un- compromising spirit of the young captive. He cursed his father and those before him that they had departed from the worship of the one only God. Each night he consulted the stars for an- swers to impossible questions.

What had Bel-Merodach to say? What was Ishtar's whim? Did Jehovah hear? When should he, Mutusa-ili, find a way out of his diffi- cult position? What planet departed from, or defaulted to him? What sign of the zodiac kindled toward him? Should he renounce? Should he advance? Could the denationalized

exile become a patriot? Must the man of books,
and dreams, and social importance sacrifice himself for such a common thing as religious truth?

Mutusa-ili substituted astrology for conscience, and made the stars do the work of common sense. As he leaned over his calculations,
on the top of the conical tower, a solitary, struggling, picturesque old man, the full moon threw
pale fires upon his head ; the locks that escaped
from his turban seemed phosphorescent. He
looked like a spirit beating out its destiny from
fate by forces that might become his slave or
his master.

CHAPTER V.

WHEN Ashpenaz, the conductor of Daniel, had impressively enjoined silence upon the young man, he bade him follow. They passed through an entrance guarded by fierce attendants. These bowed low and grounded their javelins; a deaf-mute preceded them. The three halted before a *portière*, colored yellow, red, and blue, that hung from the high ceiling above, and touched the floor with brilliant rosettes of purple and gold. Here the deaf-mute struck a bell; this was soon answered from within. The deaf-mute averted his face and drew the hangings apart, that the two might enter.

When Daniel passed between the heavy folds he started back, as if he had been smitten in the face. He was in what seemed to him a long garden. The intoxicating fragrance of a thousand flowers puffed in his face. Added to this stole the overpowering odor of frankincense, precious and penetrating beyond compare. His senses were staggered. The warm breath, laden with spices from Arabia and cinnamon from Ceylon, mounted to his brain. Before him he saw, through the haze, palm-trees rise, and beneath them shrubs, with flowers of burning hues, waved amorously towards fountains that tinkled and cooled the air. Rich draperies hung sumptuously where they could, while hidden music of the harp and flute calmed the listener to languor. Color, scent, sound, and beautiful form had played the witch to make the spot alluring.

Daniel was familiar with the luxury of courts, but of such a sight as this he had never dreamed. This unknown life was jealously guarded from the outer world, for whom it was death to enter unbidden by the royal hostess. Daniel might have surrendered to the scene in a dreamy way: it was a fair sight; he was weary and disheartened; for once in his life he would have been glad to clasp a lotus blossom to his breast in heavy-lidded revery.

But, at the sight of the queen, the ascetic started. He had seen her before. All Babylon was familiar with her beauty, when she sat on the throne before the people, beside the king, clad in her robes of state, and looking down haughtily like a handsome sphinx. But this was Daniel's first private audience with the queen. As he entered the presence chamber, Amytis had turned her head, looking backward from the couch on which she lay, and motioning her fan-bearer to cease. Her hair swept loosely to her waist. Her bare arms curled above her head, showing a golden serpent that wound itself about her wrist. Her only garment was a leopard-skin, caught about one shoulder, and extending almost to her bare feet. The blood surged into Daniel's face. He would away, and flee this polluted atmosphere, and defy the Median and her wiles! The young Jew held back; but Ashpenaz whispered: "On my head, thou must come." For now the queen, waving Ashpenaz back, raised herself languorously, moved her blood-red lips, and said,

"Come hither, fair stranger; or art thou too wise to talk to so frivolous a woman as I?" As the queen spoke, she slid farther into the leopard covering, as if in deference to the stern look of disapproval from Daniel's eyes.

"The queen has commanded, and I am here," answered the young man coldly, averting his eyes from the dangerous sight before him. The ear-rings of the queen glistened merrily. This evident lack of adoration was new to her; it amused her, and she spoke good-naturedly: —

"Ah! So? Well — Did I not spy thee watching the procession to-day? Didst thou see the king? He looks weary after so hard an expedition. And " — Amytis ·blushed slightly — "and what thinkest thou of the victory? Was it well snatched? And, prithee, dost thou know who saved that girl from the chariot?"

Daniel hardly knew which question to answer first. It was his instinct, not his knowledge of women, which led him to say enthusiastically, with brightening face, —

"Verily, O queen, that was a fine deed! The young man performed what no other in Babylon could have done. The king is honored by Allit, his captain."

"Oh," said Amytis, casting her eyes down, "any one of the guard could have done as much, and better too, perchance. And why give the quiver of an eyelash to risk one's self for the sake of such vulgar clay?"

The queen angrily tossed her head. Her heavy perfumed hair gave forth a scent, new to Daniel in the overpowering catalogue of sweet odors that greeted him on his first entrance. He turned abruptly away to hide his displeasure. This woman before him represented to his mind all the luxury and glamour that enchained his people to magnificent Babylon, and made them traitors to their country and their God.

Amytis, observing the preoccupation of her visitor, made sign to a slave to fetch two goblets of Damascus wine, cooled with snow from the Zagros mountains. The Jew remained standing, absorbed in thought.

"The maiden is a woman," he said at length, "and the captain did but a soldier's duty towards a gentler citizen."

Daniel spoke firmly and very respectfully, but with a gentle hesitation. His cheek, generally so pale in comparison with the rich and swarthy coloring of the Babylonian, flushed brilliantly for a moment, and then the color died away, leaving him as white as a lily. Who had ever spoken to the queen like this before? Only sweetmeats dropped from the lips of others upon this pampered woman. Nebuchadrezzar loved her: that was the beginning and end of the matter. Who rules the king rules the kingdom. A thousand lives like Lalitha's might be sacrificed to the whim of Amytis with scarce a comment. Daniel was half alarmed at the probable effect of this interview upon the helpless girl. But the queen proceeded, with pretty, well-bred softness: —

"So? Bold Balatsu-usur! The girl is young and handsome. That accounts for it, for Allit is ever cavaliering after a pretty face. Who is she? Knowest thou?"

The queen leaned far over to look into the young man's face. Hate and jealousy gleamed for an instant in her eyes, and then died away, leaving only a look of girlish eagerness. The leopard-skin had slipped from her breast; a cincture of gold shone against her rich red skin. Her feet glistened upon a many-tasseled shawl, dyed ruby-red and embroidered cunningly in a quaint pattern. Her nails were dyed black and polished, after the latest fashion of the hour. Daniel tried not to look at them. Luckily a diversion came. The slave approached, bearing the wine. At another motion from the royal mistress, a girl drew near with an armful of flowers, which she strewed upon the inlaid pavement at their feet. Amytis gathered the orange blossoms, and, as she took the goblet, crowned it with a spray.

"Drink," she said softly. "The wine came hither but yesterday. I will crown thy cup, if thou tellest me the name of the maiden."

"If that be the condition, O queen," answered Daniel, glad to escape again, "I could not tell thee, though thou slay me. I drink no wine. When I was brought hither I vowed that naught but water should quench my thirst."

The queen's eyes now shot a look of open anger that would have caused any other man in the kingdom to shiver with fear. Two slaves instinctively tightened their hands upon their weapons. Daniel stood as if unconscious of the storm that might burst upon him. But an expression of amused sarcasm quickly followed on the countenance of the queen.

"Are not the wines of Babylonia fit for Jewish taste? Is the juice of the Galilean grape sweeter than the goblet before thee?"

"Not so, great Amytis," answered Daniel truthfully, with a view to conciliation. "But Babylon, with all its splendor, is so seductive that, lest I should fall from favor with my God, I have vowed unto Him abstinence in food and drink."

The young man bowed like a courtier. The queen's face brightened. She observed his grace and modesty; secretly she felt awed by his undaunted manner. She knew a handsome man when she saw one. Daniel's beauty was not lost upon her.

"Pity that so handsome a fellow is a Jew!" she thought. The queen, being of Median birth, could not understand the tolerance and affection felt by the Babylonians towards the Jewish prisoners of state. In her eyes Daniel was but a captive; by a native Babylonian he was regarded as an imported citizen, a *protégé* of the king, and eligible to any office in the empire.

"Canst thou ride, O Jew?" asked the queen, suddenly glancing at the slender but compact nervous physique before her.

Daniel smiled. "I am a prince in my own land, and bred to arms as to the law. As a pupil in the palace of Babylon, I exercise in mimic battle, on foot, on horse, or in the chariot, every day."

“Then perhaps thou wilt accompany us upon the hunt — after the Seventh day?” The queen had a mocking air; these words dropped in a light, sarcastic ripple; with a saucy nod and playful twist of the orange blossom, she added, —

“I should like to see you two ride together against the roaring lion.”

“I have hunted the lion, O queen,” said Daniel composedly, though his hands, hidden in the folds of his robe, clutched at the insult, “and I have bearded the lioness and her young. But when does the king hunt?”

“Next full moon.” Amytis lost her vivacious air when the name of the king was mentioned.

“The king is much disturbed by dreams, and the seer has prescribed a moonlight hunt on the plains of Doura to blast away the evil spirit. Nebuchadrezzar is moody and weary with fighting. The hunt will favor him. It will be a fine affair, for Allit leads it. And canst thou answer this riddle, O Jew? Who is the best horseman in Babylon?”

The queen had suddenly become stern, as befitted any judge who sat within the city gates.

“The king,” answered Daniel simply.

“I mean next to the king,” replied Amytis petulantly.

“That riddle, O queen, is not easy to answer, for many an obscure horsemen there is, who can tame an ostrich for his steed. But of such as are known to the queen, Allit is the chief by far."

Another warm blush rose to the passionate face of the queen at mention of the warrior's name. Was it love, or hate? Suddenly an expression of intense fury spread over her brow.

"By the gods of my father! would that that shameful slave had died by fire, rather than the captain of the king's guard had risked but the nail of his little finger to save her! Who is this woman, who is doubtless even now weaving subtle nets to entrap our Allit? Who is she, captive Jew?"

But scarcely had she allowed herself this outburst, when Amytis drew back as if struck by an arrow. The eye of Daniel encountered hers sturdily. A fathomless light blazed upon her. The youthful form had expanded, until his stature seemed to reach that of the mighty gods. His face shone with a strange radiance that blinded her. His words came forth slowly from pale, stern, unyouthful lips : —

"O queen, live forever. Thou knowest not thyself, nor will the king lend the countenance of his bidding to that which the gods deny. But if ·Bel-Merodach and the gods of Babylon punish not the thoughts of thy heart, behold, Jehovah, the God of Israel, liveth."

The young man stood for a moment as if wrapt in prayer, while Amytis regarded him more in awe than anger.

Hardly knowing what she did, she motioned to the girl who brought the garlands, and, with something like embarrassment, said, —

"Mariamne, sing us one of your songs. The prince of the Jews is ill. Methinks, fair sir, thou hadst rather hear a slave of thine own land sing than talk with the courtesy due from subject to queen. Come, girl, get thy lyre, and soothe this caged leopard with thy melody."

The Jewish girl cast an appealing look at Daniel; her eyes were hopelessly sad. She struck a few preliminary chords that rang plaintively across the garden-court, as if they sought a concord among the listening trees. Then she lifted up her pure voice and sang, —

<blockquote>

A wind came out of the west
  At the cool of the day,
  Close a lotus blossom lay
Upon my breast.
Silken is my vest,
And soft the bed
On which I hide my head.
  Carven is the cup
  From whose lip I sup.

But a wind came out of the east
  At the dip of the day,
  And carried my heart away.
  Oh, it bore my soul away,

</blockquote>

And bore it home.
For the wind is free
To rise and roam,
Out of the east,
And into the west,
And home!
Ah, me!

The low wail died slowly away, and was lost in the key sounded by the waterfall near by. The maid had sung resting one knee upon the ground, half leaning against the trunk of a fragrant citron. Shadows played across her face, and her eyes were cast down.

When she had finished she seemed scarcely to breathe, but stole a quick glance at the countenance of Daniel, which was reverently turned towards the west. Tears welled from his eyes; his heart was borne on the wings of the setting sun to Jerusalem.

The queen dismissed the girl with a gesture of great displeasure, and would have done the same to Daniel had not an officer announced the coming of the king. There was immediate bustle in the court. Opposite the couch of the queen stood an ivory throne, finished with Sidonian carving and studded with precious stones.

The king walked alone, followed by two fan-bearers. He motioned to Ashpenaz to stay behind, and eagerly approached the queen. He was still clad in his garments of state. The odor of frankincense from the altar lingered about his person. His expression was noble and benevolent. His eyes were of the sort one might call visionary. They had a reverence in them, as if he felt himself the viceroy of the gods. Two deep furrows ran upwards across his forehead, the only indication of the moroseness and ferocity that often characterized this great monarch. His robe was resplendent in embroidery. Upon his head he wore the high, conical tiara, emblem of royalty. He carried his bow in his hand, in right warlike fashion. With real affection he approached his favored queen, whose eyes had not left him. She bowed her head deeply, but did not rise from the cushions. Nebuchadrezzar regarded her, as she lay like a tamed tigress on her couch. The queen pleased him. He was at first unaware of the presence of Daniel, standing respectfully at one side.

"Thou art not alone, my fair mountain queen," he said, turning with slight displeasure. "But we are pleased to know that thou conversest with so learned a youth. Come hither, my fair prince. Didst thou teach thy queen aught of the stars, or of the secrets of the gods?"

The king smiled pleasantly at the young man, who knelt for a moment respectfully before his conqueror and protector.

"Nay, indeed," laughed the queen, "nothing so solemn. I leave the stars and the gods to thee. We were discussing nothing less than the new mountain garden thou didst promise me on my return."

"And what I promise I will perform. I will rear thee a garden to the skies. Thou shalt forget thy mountain home in the cool breezes that shall soothe thee from the summit of the wonder I shall erect for her whom my heart loveth. May Merodach judge me and be my witness, thou shalt dwell in thy mountain garden, as thou callest it, in thirty days. What I have said I will execute."

The king indicated by a paternal gesture that he was ready to dispense with the company of the favorite captive. Daniel arose quickly from his knees to leave the royal presence.

"Go thou in peace," said Nebuchadrezzar. "Thou art continually in my favor. Increase in learning. The king forgets not the wise. I would speak alone with the queen."

CHAPTER VI.

THE captain of the king's guard was on duty. He sat in a chamber within the broad gateway of the wall that protected the palaces and shut them off from the city proper. Allit was alone. The other soldiers were more social; they played at games to while away time, or burnished their trappings leisurely, after the havoc of the campaign. A selected number patrolled the fortifications, and kept to their stations on the citadel. The sun was declining, and the multitude that had sought shelter from its fierce gaze now flocked in the streets and about the bazaars and gates, gossiping, and bartering their goods. It was now three days since the army had returned, and the citizens were wondering at what enterprise the king would put his myriads of slaves to work now. It was rumored that he would finish the temple of Nebo at Borsippa; it was said that the fortifications at Cutha were to be enlarged and repaired; it was whispered that a huge and curious garden for the alien queen was newest in the king's fancy.

The rescue of Lalitha by Allit, being a piquant

adventure, occupied a large share of the street chatter. Give your ordinary gossip a chance between affairs of state and an event in which a man and woman are concerned, and he makes no delay in his choice, which is as inevitable as love or scandal.

"He is a brave fellow, of the true stock of Akkad," said a seller of lentils to a woman who had come with provisions from beyond the outer wall.

"Say you so?" asked the market-woman indifferently; she was absorbed in selling a measure of last year's barley at double its quoted price. She continued with more vivacity when her shrewd sale was effected: "Would that he had saved my daughter! He could have had her to keep for two maneh."

"Thinkest thou the captain of the king would trouble his fine head to look at thy girl?" sneered the lentil merchant. "But by our lady Ishtar! —nay, sir, it is impossible that the palm wine should be fermented; it came from the press only yesterday. By Nebo! there goes the only customer I 've had this morning, — but, as I was remarking, by our lady! it is my belief that Allit Arioch would have ridden to his death to save any girl in Babylon, if that were the end of the matter. Come, neighbor, let us drink my new wine to this brave Babylonian!"

But a toast that had to be paid for was too much to contribute even to the popularity of the reigning lion.

The barley woman turned the subject of conversation — to the barley crop.

But Allit, like many another hero, thinking less of his deed than of the complications into which it brought him, sat with troubled look. His gay appearance was curiously at odds with his dismal expression. His head-dress was of a brilliant color; his locks had been carefully pomaded; his black beard dropped in straight set curls from his chin; and his cheeks glistened with the latest fad in ointments. The daring captain had changed into the luxurious man of fashion. In his delight at getting back to the city after an arduous campaign, he had given himself over to all the pampering ease that the metropolis could afford and that his profession would allow. But Allit was not happy. Outside of the door the human-headed bull, the gigantic winged cherub that adorned the entrance of the gate, regarded him: it had the impenetrable solemnity belonging to the sculpture of the times. For the first time in his life Allit observed it attentively; the winged cherub eyed him like a sphinx; it seemed to ask questions and to answer none.

Allit was in a fermentation. A civil conflict

was agitating him. He had long since learned how to obey. It was easy for him to command; but now the art of thinking and of planning for himself was forced upon him. Allit was not used to reflection; it was like a new science to sit there, while the other soldiers were amusing themselves, and seriously consider himself and his relations to the finer aspects of life. Allit was young. He was extremely handsome, and a great favorite with women. He was a man who had always adopted the fashion as a matter of course.

Brought up from youth with his king, he had blindly followed Nebuchadrezzar's fortunes, his wives and his gods. He had done this carelessly, rather than with an eye to royal favor; and his establishments and horses, his escapades and intrigues, were the despair of his fellow-officers, as well as the gossip of the court and town. It had been no uncommon thing for him to buy two or three beautiful daughters of some prosperous land-owner in the vicinity, tire of them in as many weeks, and then distribute them to his friends. Such was the state of morals in Babylon at that time that no one thought the worse of the king's captain for adopting the custom of his people, nor did it occur to him to think the worse of himself. Open-handed and ardent, proud and courteous, soldier and aristocrat, he represented the old stock of the earlier Babylon, before Assyria smote and conquered the province, which, revolting in turn, under the control of the father of Nebuchadrezzar shot into a second glory, now known as the proudest of the world. Allit had the full benefit of the highest social glamour to transfigure his attractive *personnel.* He was implicitly trusted by the king, and madly adored by the ladies of the court. Just now the golden thread in the intricate pattern of his life was woven by the jeweled fingers of Amytis the queen. Conqueror of the proudest man who ever lived, the wife of Nebuchadrezzar stooped to court the admiration of her eminent subjects.

The king was loving, but blind, and the excitement that nourished Amytis first intoxicated, then withered, her victims. The predecessor of Allit had paid for the queen's favor by the loss of his head. It was now the turn of Allit, and the court wondered how long he would last. But Allit was too fine a tactician. He played for the game, not for the stake. The queen was unscrupulous in her pursuit, but Allit was honorable and even playful in his evasion. He enjoyed being put upon his mettle. It interested him that he could successfully steal an interview with the queen, and not even allow his royal mistress to suspect that he was carrying on the same strategy with twenty other women from Sippara to Eridhu. But for the first time the jealous attention of Amytis had become irksome to him. Since he had cast that hurried look into the face of the girl he happened to save, his fancy, ready to fly at the first touch, had taken a new turn. For the life of him he could not forget her. True, his fellow-officers had amused themselves considerably at his expense, and already high wagers were offered as to when the fortunate girl would swell the list of the captain's victims; but the badinage of the court did not seem as important to him as usual. The girl haunted his imagination; he tried to throw her off; he refused, on plea of official business, to see her father, the venerable Mutusa-ili, who came to thank him. He had roughly rebuked the boyish prattle of his brother Susa; but the lad's enthusiastic praises of the stranger whom he protected but for an hour had their effect. Amused and annoyed at the persistence of an interest his intellect repudiated, Allit was glad when his solitary reflections came to their natural end. He started with pleasure when the gnomon marked the hour of his release, and his duty for the day was done. He glanced at the colossus by the gate.

"Remain thou in solitude, if thou likest it, and answer thine own questions!" he muttered.

He straightened himself with military alacrity, received a report or two, gave a few final orders for the night, and sauntered slowly toward the temple of Bel, whose seven brilliantly colored stages shone with a sacred softness in the twilight. Allit walked abstractedly, and hardly noticed the greetings of the people. Two incidents only clearly arrested his attention.

A foppish-looking man reined up his horses and invited the captain to a private carousal in honor of a god, to be held next week.

"Nay," replied Allit gravely. "Thanks for thy courtesy, but I am preoccupied."

He had scarcely refused the invitation, when he was summoned by a glance to a litter borne by four Egyptians. Within this litter reclined Ina, the acknowledged beauty of Babylon. Ina was the daughter of Egibi the banker, who, it will be remembered, was the wealthiest untitled citizen of the province and treasurer of the state. She affected the softer hues of red, because they became her peculiar complexion. This was of a coloring lighter than that of most of the Babylonian women, but it preserved the rich olive tints that were frequently found among Jewish maidens of distinguished birth. Her hair was wavy and dark, and was looped behind on the top of her head. A fillet of gold confined it in front, and rubies shone from arms, ears, and

throat. She lay in her litter plunged in red and
silver, and poutingly beckoned Allit to approach.

"And why, noble Allit," she immediately began, "hast thou not numbered thyself as one of
our guests since thy return? Does the favor of
the queen turn thy heart to forget old friends
of humbler station? Or dost thou search the
streets for another maiden to snatch from death
to life?"

For the first time, Allit, to his own inward
discomfort, was betrayed into a blush, which
Ina, daughter of Egibi, was delighted to see.
Needed a woman better proof that her charm
worked well?

Allit bowed without smiling, and looked Ina
so steadfastly in the face that she cast down her
eyes.   Allit at this moment was indescribably
reminded of Lalitha.   He remembered a glow
of red upon white, a mass of waving dark hair
against an olive skin, and a smile.   That was all.
In Ina he saw the same type of feminine beauty;
but he missed — and valued the more — the un-
decorated, unassuming expression of the modest
stranger.

"Nay, my Lady Ina," he said gallantly, "I
have by no means forgotten thee. How could
any man do that? But I have been busy with
affairs. The king is about to put ten thousand
captives at work upon a new garden he buildeth

for the queen. I am well occupied. I will come soon to thee, perhaps to-morrow. Is thy father well? He is a very busy man. I have need to convert some spoil into well-coined silver shekels, and will consult him. Farewell. May Ishtar be thy guardian!"

Allit walked away, twirling his cane comfortably; he fancied that he had got out of that very well. The lady looked after him with a troubled expression, sighed deeply, and sternly ordered her slaves home.

The captain walked on fast and faster. The vision of a girl dashed to her death beneath a chariot flew faster than he; he could not outstride it. He felt as if he were gathering himself together again for the dangerous rush.

"May Nergal sustain me!" he muttered. His pace had quickened almost to a run; and, the street being crowded, he paid for his dreaming by a collision with another foot passenger, who was going in the opposite direction. Allit, in short, bumped into a very venerable man, and fairly knocked him down. He quickly recovered himself, and proceeded to pick up the person whom he had so unceremoniously overturned.

The old man was groaning, more in anger than in pain.

"Has Raman in his anger blasted me, or has

a scoundrel committed an assault, deeming me unprotected?"

He glanced fiercely upon Allit, whose apologies he did not seem to find impressive, adjusted his turban, regained his stick, and now carefully scrutinized the luckless offender. Allit had recognized the subject of his awkwardness immediately, but he waited for Mutusa-ili to do him a like honor.

"By my faith," said Mutusa-ili, in a changed tone, "it is Allit, the king's captain. Truly, Adar, the lord of the brave, hath given thee strength as well as clumsiness. My bones feel as if a battering-ram had smitten them. But, gallant captain, for the sake of my daughter, thou art forgiven; thy penalty is that thou be my right-hand staff and accompany me home."

Thus it was. Fate had stepped in, and Allit, with no slight feeling of embarrassment, urged Mutusa-ili to lean heavily upon him; he fell slowly into step with the old man.

"I have endeavored to thank thee," observed Mutusa-ili, with the scant effusiveness of age, "for the service thou hast done my house. I was denied entrance to thee at the palace. Enter now with me, and grant me the opportunity of a host to express my obligations. Partake thou of our evening meal. We may not furnish Libyan wine, but I have a skin from

Shushan not yet opened, and my daughter would gladly greet thee, though she walketh not as yet, poor maid!"

There was clearly nothing else to be done, and Allit accompanied the scholar, with an eagerness to which he tried to give the name of reluctance. As he was about to enter the gateway of the old man's home, he noticed a stir upon the street. Slaves in royal livery loudly ordered the populace aside. Then came the cry: —

"The queen! The queen!" Involuntarily the two men halted. A covered chariot approached. There was a flash of footmen, horsemen, and brilliant metal standards. Allit did not see two angry eyes resting upon him, and with a torrent of jealousy regarding the house. People rose from their humble postures. The procession had passed. The two men turned and entered the house. The queen, Ina, the hundred loves of the man of pleasure, — where were they? What were they? When Mutusa-ili led Allit to the couch of the wounded girl, there seemed to exist no other woman in all the world.

Lalitha, very pale but very sweet, looked up at her visitor like a contented bird viewing a new land. If she had not been lying down, one would have expected her to turn her head sideways, twitter a little, and start a pair of pretty wings. Allit stood in a constrained attitude, but his eyes leaped toward her adoringly. The girl spoke first.

"Thou art come," she said simply. "It gives us pleasure to bless thee, kind sir. My father and I are thy debtors for all our lives."

"Thy preserver suppeth with us to-night," said Mutusa-ili. "I will summon our slave Kisrinni to prepare the evening meal. Do thou entertain our guest until I return."

In this natural way the old man departed, leaving the two alone. Allit found this more comfortable; but Lalitha thought it strange that she began to feel embarrassed. She dropped her eyes and played with the fringe upon the coverlet of her couch. Lalitha was charming in a white robe, but the draperies about her were of crimson silk and wool. She gave to the young man the same vivid impression of white and red that he had snatched from that vision of her as she stood, swaying to her death, before the chariot; but now, as before, the whiteness overcame the redness in his fancy. He noticed that the girl's garment was fastened at the throat, contrary to the fashion of dress among Babylonian women, who wore the robe caught over one shoulder and under the other arm, freely unveiling the breast. But Lalitha was modestly draped from her fair throat to her wounded foot. Her eyes had nothing of the

boldness which Allit expected to find in a woman, and took as a matter of course. She regarded him timidly. The king's captain looked
at her with a frank, critical glance; it deepened
to an expression perfectly new to Allit's gay
face.

"Thy brother, the lad Susa, comes here every
day to cheer me, for I am a prisoner," said Lalitha suddenly.

It was an abrupt, awkward little speech, but
Lalitha felt as if she must say something; she
could think of nothing else.

"Would that I were Susa!" observed Allit
quickly. He had no sooner said this than he
felt ashamed of himself for bringing the paltry
gallantries of the court and the world into this
nest of peace and purity. Lalitha shot a quick
glance up his tall height; she looked startled;
one could almost hear her rustle her invisible
wings to fly. Evidently she believed what he
said. Well; why not? Was it not true? Allit
watched her. The man of the world was overcome with the intoxication of a perfectly new
sensation. She looked at him so fearlessly, yet
with such an expression of shrinking delicacy,
that he was stirred toward a respect he had
never felt for any woman. All the unexercised
honor of his manhood was challenged by her
chastity.

"Thou art a white bird!" he murmured impulsively. "May the gods guard thee! Thou shouldst receive the homage of a better man than I."

"Art thou not a good man?" asked Lalitha, in wide-eyed wonder. "I have thought kindly of thee . . . all this while."

"Think of me as little as possible," protested Allit, stung into a downright honest effort to protect the girl from herself, —from himself. "Think of me no more."

Lalitha laughed merrily.

"Is that the way they talk at court, kind sir? Such humility hath no good place, to my mind, in the life of a man who hath wrought a deed like thine. Why, I *have* to think of thee. Thou gavest me back to my father and to life. I was not educated to be a discourteous, ungrateful girl. . . . But perhaps," added Lalitha, with a sudden cloud upon her charming face, "perhaps thou hast already had enough of the affair and thou wouldst not be annoyed by even the gratitude of a lowly maiden; perhaps it incommodes thee, sir, to be reminded of me, and of the trouble I have been to thee."

Lalitha faltered out these preposterous words so ingenuously that the man of pleasure could have fallen on his knees before her innocent soul.

"Thou art ridiculous!" said Allit savagely. "Any other woman in Babylon, in thy place, would see — would know — would understand."

The courtier hesitated. The girl's clear eyes seemed to burn upon him like two soft altar lamps.

"I do not know many things," said Lalitha gently. "I live alone, with Kisrinni and my father. I go not abroad; I did very wrong the day of the procession; it was the only time. I shall not be so naughty again; I have promised my father. I do not understand a great deal that perhaps I ought to know; when I am older I may do so."

"May Ishtar forbid!" cried Allit; "but at least thou mayest understand when a man says he is afraid of thee."

"*Afraid!* Of *me?*" cried Lalitha.

But at this moment Mutusa-ili appeared, with Kisrinni salaaming behind him.

"We will spread our simple board," said the old man, looking very happy, "in my daughter's apartments, that she may sup with us, in honor of her preserver and of her dear life."

"Be it so," said Allit devoutly.

CHAPTER VII.

Nebuchadrezzar had an extraordinary position in the Babylonian court. No law restrained the king. He was the monarch, he was the nobility, he was the priesthood, he was the law. His whim might condemn subjects by the thousand to be cut into inch pieces; he was accountable to no power in earth or heaven. He raised and he dashed down. Commanders, chief eunuchs, high priests, and captains rose and fell before his will like grain before the wind. The king claimed divine descent, and devoutly believed in his own claim. For, he said, " Hath not Merodach begot me of my mother? "

Was the son of Heaven to be resisted in his most intolerable commands? The nation never disputed an authority that often partook of the most despotic tyranny. The king was of an odd, composite formation. His character was as capricious as a child's, and as undecipherable as a prehistoric tablet. He was energetic, and apt in turning energy into affairs. This leader of armies and conqueror of nations had a rebel in his own nature, — he was born with a rash temper. Many acts of cruelty resulted. The man was not by nature relentless. but it was so easy to cause the massacre of a score of chiefs by the mere wave of his hand that his royal carelessness led him lightly.

With all this, the king was the most religious of men.. Believing himself to be the child of the gods, he dedicated to them the spoil of his successful campaigns. The most magnificent temples ever enjoyed by the Babylonian deities rose like splendid prayers at the beck of Nebuchadrezzar. It was a fact which his treasurer alone knew, and secretly grieved over, that three fourths of the monarch's wealth went to the glorification of the gods, whose shrines he repaired, and whose worship he stimulated throughout the length of the land of Shinar. From Sepharvaim to Teredon, — a fortress on the Persian gulf, which the king was building, — the priests burnt incense, and praised the name of the son of Merodach, their lavish and beneficent lord.

But, although the king ruled with a hand of bronze, he himself was an humble subject. A master who mastered the king swayed every Babylonian, high or low. A power more arrogant than that of the sceptre ruled the ruler. In these days we give to this autocrat the name of Superstition. The people were divided into two classes: the Chaldeans, or priests, and the commonalty. The masses of the people lived in alarm. They feared each day of the week. They quaked every hour of the day. They blinked with restlessness at the light, wondering what it might bring forth. They started with ague at the darkness, shrinking from the fever or the pest that lay in wait for them. They shuddered at the vampire that would feed upon their blood. The sacerdotal caste concentrated in its ranks all the science and all the learning of the times. The priests were the physicians of the trembling body and of the throbbing heart. They prescribed philters, incantations, and talismans for a cough or for a panic. For a fixed price, they consulted the auguries of the stars, or studied the prophetic position of a wand.

To the Babylonian the universe was filled with spirits, good and evil, who were directly the cause of every phenomenon of nature. The blast of the sirocco or the loss of a tooth had a supernatural explanation. Projected by a blind fate into the midst of a mad contest between these spirits, the sufferer feels himself involuntarily drawn into the combat of which he is the unwilling battle-ground. His escape is only through mysterious incantations, of which the initiated alone know the secret, and by amulets which they only can consecrate. But

life itself is one long pæan of despair.   The
gods command men to eat and drink, and be
merry.   Well they may, for men are doomed at
death to the lowest depths that yawn in desert
places.   The earth carries them away

> " To the house of darkness, the seat of the god Irkalla,
>   To the house from whose entrance there is no exit,
>   To the road whose course never leads back,
>   To the house whose inmate is shut off from light,
>   Where dust is their sustenance, clay their food.
>   The light they behold not, in darkness they dwell."

Virtue is rewarded only by earthly happiness ;
it has no future.   Pain is the beginning and
the end of life.   At resurrection, the dead start
into coarse birds, frightful griffins, or horrible
vampires.   This superstitious slavery was more
frightful than the bondage of the Jewish captives.   It eroded private life to an incredible
extent.   A man could not undertake a journey,
he might not call upon a neighbor, until intricate tables of lucky and unfavorable days had
been consulted, and all the omens proved propitious.

It was to be expected that a system of coin-
cidences between certain appearances of the
sun, moon, or planets, and personal or political
changes, should be eagerly uplifted to high intellectual rank.   Thus, by the marvelous sympathy which the Chaldeans thought they recog-

nized between celestial phenomena and terrestrial events, their religion became subordinated to astronomy. Astrology developed into the ruler of life. The destiny of the people was controlled by priests, who took good care to exact what might be called a toll for passage on the sidereal turnpike. Omens were as numerous as diseased imaginations, and demons were as plentiful as priests. Phantoms and spectres made virulent assault upon unexorcised men, in magical droves of seven. Disease was always the personal work of an evil spirit; it could not be conjured away unless a propitious genius was guaranteed to take its place. It was the habit in Babylon to carry sick people to the open street, where all passers-by, in courtesy, stopped and prescribed a remedy. Besides astrologers and exorcists, there was a powerful sect of diviners and soothsayers that carried on a lucrative trade. Prophetic arrows and wands, each with an omen written upon it, were drawn from heaps. Nebuchadrezzar is known once to have chosen his route against an enemy by the tactics of a magic arrow. The flight of a bird foretold the future, and the entrails of victims opened ghastly pages to inspection. It was well known that if the intestines of an ass turned to the left, were twisted and of a bluish color, wailing would not enter the land.

Presages were drawn from the clouds, from thunder and from lightning. Serpents, being considered shrewder than most people, were elevated in some of the temples of Babylon to reveal the will of the gods. Dogs played principal rôles in the system of portents. Stray dogs acquired an awful importance in human affairs. In weird incantation the king heard once a year that if a red dog enters the palace and crouches under the throne the palace shall be burnt, and if a white dog enters the temple its gods shall desert it. A prominent official at the palace and temple was, consequently, the dog-catcher, who religiously disposed of unclaimed, unkempt animals. And alas, if a piece of furniture fell, or the timbers of a house cracked at night! The omen was prodigious and dark. It was a well-known fact that before Nebuchadrezzar was born, a peasant woman gave birth to a boy with the ears of a lion. That foretold the hero. Mothers feared to bear a son with no right hand, for then his family would be blotted out, but there would be prosperity in that of his neighbor. Two years before the overthrow of Babylon, a mare dropped a foal with only one eye. The secret was not well kept, and the demoralization resulting from that disastrous circumstance was instrumental in bringing about the destruction of the eternal city and the devastation of the land of Akkad.

There was still another class of priests, whose business was the interpretation of dreams. There were moreover professional dreamers, whose visions were recorded, and followed with great anxiety by prince and people. As an astrologer, an interpreter of the stars and their import to man, Mutusa-ili was eminent; but as an interpreter of dreams he had long easily stood without rival in the land. This art was the favorite at court. Every one had dreams sent by Ishtar of Arbela in the middle of the night, and although special dreams had their codes of interpretation, uncatalogued visions were numerous, and required a classifier. A dream was the occasion of the sale of Joseph the Jew, and of his subsequent power over his brethren. A dream influenced Gyges to pay tribute to the king of Assyria. A dream announced to Crœsus the death of his son Atys. The future royalty of Darius, son of Hystaspes, was revealed to Cyrus in a dream. Did not Isaiah reproach the Jews for sleeping among tombs to dream prophetic dreams?

Thus the Babylonian passed his daily existence, struggling to ward off evil and to propitiate the good. The priest was the only resource or relief. He became an absolute power in the land; even the king must bend to him. Yet it is noticeable that the Chaldean sorcerers did not pretend to order the gods, like many a more modern believer. They implored. They did not presume to fathom the knowledge of the divine and all-powerful word, which was to them the source of life, the panacea for every misfortune. That mysterious word was the secret of Ea, and Silik-Moulou-Ki, who dispensed good to man, and who was the mediator between Ea and suffering mortality.

The city was aghast. The palace was in a ferment. Citizens went to their business with averted faces, and spoke below their breath. The soldiers within the citadel sombrely shook their heads, and attended to their duties with an unusual military precision that was ominous. The treasurer, the Rab-daiku, the lord executioner, and Ashpenaz, chief of the eunuchs, were in stately and mysterious conference. Allit, the captain of the king's guard, had been imperatively summoned to attend upon the monarch. The queen was invisible. But by far the greatest consternation took possession of the soothsayers, the astrologers, the interpreters and diviners. A deputation of the most august in their profession were sent in hot haste to bid Mutusa-ili, their acknowledged chief, to a solemn convocation. With bleached faces this sacred body discussed the news that had startled

them from the dignified routine of their daily
duties. The temple of Bel-Merodach was in a
state of distraction. The chief astronomer, who
occupied the observatory at the summit of the
Ziggurat, was said to be almost unconscious with
terror at his failure to predict the misfortune
that had come upon the sacerdotal caste.

What was the calamity that agitated Babylon? The king had dreamed a dream. That
was all, and enough. Nebuchadrezzar had seen
a vision. The omen disquieted his soul, and he
had passed an uneasy night beneath the royal
canopy. The next morning, for the first time
in his life, he forgot, on rising, to perform his
usual devotions and religious lustrations, and
called for his captain in tones that betokened ill
to somebody. Allit, perceiving from the terror
and haste of the messenger that something was
wrong, stopped only to throw a robe about his
shoulders, adjust a sword to his side, and take a
poniard in his hand. The young man lost no
time in appearing before the king, who lay upon
his gold and ivory couch. Nebuchadrezzar
awaited his favorite with impatience, and greeted
him with a scowl.

" By Nebo, the sustainer of my house ! thou
takest thy time to answer my command ! "

" Nay, my lord, deign to behold me. I came
hither even as I was, with but this robe, a scant

protection for my body, but with my sword to defend the king."

The soldier flourished his sword with such vigor that the royal fan-bearer jumped back, in terror of his life. The king seemed appeased at this evidence of devotion, and raised himself slightly to scan the face of his officer. Allit took advantage of the softer moment to drop reverently upon his knees and touch his forehead to the carpet of the royal footstool. This was, in form, a precious tapestry, woven to set forth the contest of Bel and the dragon. Allit's eyes were on the dragon; it was a yellow and black dragon, but Allit saw neither black nor yellow. All his senses had gone to swell the power of hearing with which he listened to the king. Allit was courtier enough to know that the monarch's mood betokened ill effects in some direction.

"Nay, my good friend and captain, I doubt thee not," said Nebuchadrezzar slowly. "Would that I could depend on every officer I have raised on high as I trust thee! Thou hast my favor; for I am sad. He who hath made Babylon the metropolis of the universe hath dreamed this night a dream."

The king sighed deeply, and lay back upon his couch. The two looked each other gravely in the face after this momentous confession.

Allit, who felt the depression of the unknown quantity, was bound to cheer the royal dreamer.

"Perchance thou hast seen the body of a yellow dog" —

The king shook his head contemptuously.

"Then," proceeded Allit hopefully, "thou didst see a bear, whose feet" —

The king, with a superior smile, waved off this vulgar insinuation.

"May Merodach protect the king!" ejaculated Allit with growing fear. "Didst thou see a great light and the land in flames, or was the god Nergal smiting" —

"Hold!" cried Nebuchadrezzar, with an imperative motion. "The king dreams not after the manner of his subjects. My dream is strange to the written annals of the wise men of Babylon. This dream," — the king, as he spoke, gestured with unusual animation and impressiveness, — "which Ishtar of Arbela in condescension hath sent unto me, will astound the art of divination."

Allit knew not what to say. He felt that an epoch was at hand. He dared not comment one way or the other, lest he miss a guess, and his head with it. He took the safest available course, and anxiously suggested, —

"Shall I not summon to the king, whom Merodach honors, the high priest of Bel, and

Mutusa - ili the sage, and all the wise men of Babylon, to interpret this strange and wonderful dream ? "

But the king shook his head pertinaciously.

" I am resolved. The goddess hath not sent this vision to me in vain. Do thou make proclamation in my name as follows : ' In three days let all the wise men of Babylon assemble before my throne, and let them tell the king his dream and interpret the same. If they fail I will have their heads for it; yea, the head of every soothsayer in the land will I smite from his neck. Their science is a falsehood, and they eat the bread of wickedness, and shall die ; from the highest to the lowest they shall be cut off. Thus saith Nebuchadrezzar, first-born of Nabopolassar, and son of Merodach, the king of gods.' "

This was the edict which stunned the land. The king had proposed an unheard-of test. Any one could interpret, but who could conjure the dream itself ? Mourning was in Babylon, and the third day was nigh at hand.

CHAPTER VIII.

ALLIT himself was overwhelmed when he heard the incredible edict of the king. He knew that to attempt to divert the royal dreamer from his purpose by pleading was as foolish as to tear a hound from the flank of a wild bull. In a few hours, when he heard the criers proclaiming the will of their sovereign about the streets of Babylon, Allit began to realize the horror of the situation. He was not especially devout, and cared little enough whether the college of the Chaldean priesthood were blotted out or not. He had small faith in their prognostications; like a true soldier, he was in the habit of dashing at his end. What was an omen? Could it charge a battalion? "Only one man is worth a bunch of dates," he said to himself; then a blinding doubt smote him. Supposing Mutusa-ili should fail? Could he? Preposterous thought! Allit grew pale, became nervous and excitable. "No man interpreteth like her father," he brooded; "but can the stars reveal to him the dream itself?" The father of Lalitha tortured — dead? Distressed beyond self-control, Allit hastened to demand audience of the king.

"There is mourning among the Chaldeans, O king," he began impetuously. "Wilt thou not forget thine edict, and shall not an interpretation satisfy the heart of the king?"

Nebuchadrezzar bristled like a Parthian lion.

"May the dragon, whom Merodach my lord hath overcome, smite me if by a single dent in the moistened clay I remit my command!"

The courtier forgot himself and his own peril. He was not accustomed to forget himself; but then he was not accustomed to remember the house of Lalitha.

"But, O gracious king," he urged, "hast thou forgotten mercy? Who in former times hath demanded such a rare thing of any Chaldean? Wilt thou not honor him who doeth the king's pleasure, and thus perchance save the rest?"

The blaze of lightning on the countenance of Nebuchadrezzar turned, at this fearless plea, into the softness of a spring morning. The manly quality of generosity ruled in the king after a royal fashion, and the despotic side of his nature succumbed to it with moody ease.

"Ah! By Nergal! thou art the light of mine eyes. I had forgotten the balm that the gods have granted unto their sovereign representatives. Make proclamation that he who showeth me the dream and the interpretation thereof shall receive of me gifts and rewards and great honor, and moreover he shall save the carcasses of all Chaldeans unto life."

So it came about that this second mandate was proclaimed abroad in the courts of the wise men and in the temples of the gods. It did not soothe the apprehensions of the magicians and the interpreters as one might expect a balm to do. The more lenient favor of Nebuchadrezzar rather seemed to emphasize his tyranny. Nebuchadrezzar presented a problem older than Babylon, and as new as yesterday: How comes it that the most relentless of men are the tenderest?

The fears of Allit were allayed, but not removed. He paced the halls of the palace restlessly. His tall, broad figure loomed against the painted pictures of the gods that decorated the courts he strode. He stopped before one of these and angrily regarded it. "Canst thou, picture of a golden image, mighty god! — canst thou, O Bel, teach the hidden mysteries of the unknown world of sleep unto Mutusa-ili?"

Allit frowned upon the protective deity of the palace. Poor Lalitha! Poor maiden! His thoughts melted at the vision of that white-plumed bird in her bereaved nest. His heart stormed within him suddenly. He clenched his hand about his sword, and shook it at the effigy upon the wall; the god seemed to taunt him with a cold smile.

“Thou false and powerless god!” exclaimed the soldier. “If her father fail, by the seven planets, that change not, I renounce thee and all thy brood, and will follow the gods of even” — He stopped to think of the most powerless nation, the most down-trodden gods that he knew. His heretical outburst was interrupted by a low, penetrating voice, which uttered in his very ear two startling words, — “*A Jew?*”

As a javelin whirrs upon its deadly errand, the captain of the king’s guard wheeled. The rash interrupter at that moment stood scanter chance of his life than he seemed in the least aware of. He was robed in white; his complexion was of the transparency of a flower whose petals are smitten by the sun. The youth’s eyes were modestly turned down, but he stood as firm as one of those erect lions that support upon their backs the pillars of the palace.

“What! *thou*, Balatsu-usur?” Allit spoke in real astonishment, sheathing his sword.

“Yea, noble captain, it is I,” said Daniel. He slowly raised his eyes, and fixed them steadily upon the bold glance before him. “And well for thee that it is only I. As the lost traveler in the desert, dying of a mighty thirst, is led by his horse unerringly unto the water of life, so thy heart leadeth thee unto the Truth of truths.”

By this time Allit had recovered himself, and,

looking critically upon this didactic young man, shrugged his shoulders.

"Oh, every one to his own gods. The Jews have theirs, who seems to have little power to protect them; and we have ours, who at least tosses us victories, as I toss sweetmeats to a girl." He laughed disdainfully.

"Far be the day that makes a Jew of Allit! Who is Jehovah? Ask Bel-Merodach!"

Daniel did not answer this taunt; he was himself courtier enough to change the subject with graceful tact.

"The king hath had a dream," he said politely; "it troubleth his spirit. Can no one of the Chaldeans tell him his dream and the interpretation thereof?"

Allit's trouble came back to his mind at this question. He liked Daniel, and had always respected him. He knew that the sweeping order included this fair and eminent young scholar, who was attached to the University of Bel. He looked regretfully upon Daniel, whose blooming life might so soon be crushed out. Allit, like many another light nature, had at times felt the nameless fear with which this dreamy but unswerving Jew inspired those who approached him.

"No," replied Allit, in a new tone, "I am afraid not, unless Mutusa-ili, father of La—"

he checked himself—"unless Mutusa-ili," he stammered, "be the man."

"Thou art right," returned Daniel, with an inward prayerful look; "perchance we all die, if Mutusa-ili the sage hath not power to tell the dream. Thy gods Nebo and Bel-Merodach have no greater magician than he."

Allit did not reply, but only nodded, looking mournfully upon the ground. Daniel cast a keen glance at the captain. He noticed that his friend looked thin and somewhat pale. The aspect of his face seemed at war with his notorious life. Allit's expression was not that of the debauchee. The Jew was a young man; and he, too, had who knew what private views of Lalitha? whom he must often have seen. It needed but the divination of youth and sensitiveness to interpret the courtier's condition. But what superhuman wit reviewed this human intelligence? Daniel's countenance grew vague; his eye dimmed; his long, thin figure trembled.

"Fear thou not," he said, in a piercing whisper. "Jehovah hath not ordained the bereavement of the maiden from this cause."

Allit started, with a vivid blush. What necromancy had this young Jew, whose high and stern morality silently rebuked the practice of the court at which he was a captive? The captain of the king hastened to protest.

" By Ishtar, I covet not the maiden, either from her father or from herself.   I dare not."

" Behold," said Daniel, " such fear as thy fear containeth the highest courage of a man. Cultivate thou it in God's name and the maiden's. Go unto her, and bid her take courage in the name of Jehovah."

Something in the face of Daniel awed the captain of the guards. Involuntarily the two men clasped hands ; they were silent. Daniel seemed to warn and bless. With a religious gesture he turned and went his way.

Allit did not linger to ponder upon the perplexing scene between himself and the young Jew ; instead, he proceeded to obey him. Girding up his robes, he hastened to find Mutusa-ili at his house.

Allit had walked rapidly through the palace, and was on the point of emerging through the brazen gates into the Nana road, when he heard a puffing behind him, and a disagreeable voice called, —

" Allit ! Brave captain ! Good Allit, I bid thee stop ! "

It was the voice of Ashpenaz. The captain had halted, with an undisguised shrug of impatience, and would have left this revolting person in the lurch, had he not feared that the chief eunuch might be the bearer of a royal message.

"Thou art a plague, O mighty captain, and dost rejoice in the sweat of thy servant. Thou stridest like a camel. Who can overtake thee? Here is the summons of the queen. Here is her royal seal." The gorgeous and unpleasant dignitary fumbled for his order, which lay in a little clay tablet inclosed in a gold box.

Allit took the tablet impatiently, read it with a scowl, and crushing it in his hand, threw the ball far into the moat. The eunuch watched him curiously, but said nothing.

"Express my inconsolable regrets to the queen," said Allit, impulsively, "but I am departing for a space on inevitable business. In an hour I shall attend her, and delight myself with the radiance of her presence."

This was the first time that any subject had been known directly to disobey the queen, or even to neglect her orders.

Allit turned, made a profound mock salutation to the prince of eunuchs, and hastened across the bridge to the cottage of Mutusa-ili.

The eunuch hurried to tell the queen that Allit had refused her summons. Ashpenaz was as wily as his kind. He made the most of the defiance in Allit's answer, and the least of its deference.

"A pest upon Amytis!" thought Allit hotly. "This time the proud Median shall wait my will. Must I dance, a slave, to the nod of this shameful queen? Not I, and Raman shall be my guardian. I fear her not."

But almost with the words the courtier came to himself. The danger of his position occurred to him like a discovery. He felt as if he had been bewitched, and were recovering his equipoise. He thought of Daniel with displeasure. He dashed off the Jew's influence with the whole strength of his disdain. What could that pale-faced boy teach him? Was he to be awed by a pair of nebulous eyes and high-sounding words? Daniel might as well expect to rule the province of Babylonia. Save Mutusa-ili? Why had he, Allit, the favorite of the court, denied the queen? As for Lalitha, he had kissed a hundred girls fairer and prouder than she; and was he to be daunted by a coy trick? Of course Mutusa-ili must be saved at any reasonable cost. But if the worst came, a small bribe to Kisrinni, and Lalitha was his; and, by the groves of Ishtar, his she should be, if by fraud or force! But the maiden would not deny him. No woman had ever done that; not even the queen. Would Lalitha be the first to say him nay?

In such a mood, and with many maledictions on the interfering Jew, and on himself for yielding so tamely to the spell of Daniel's nature, Allit arrived at the barred door of Mutusa-ili's house and gave a thundering knock. He had no sooner done so than his heart failed within him. The imperious captain and intrepid reprobate collapsed, even at the sight of Kisrinni, into the timid lover. The young man had wit enough left to marvel at his own moodiness; the whole situation was wearing upon what in these days we call "the nervous system." But no Babylonian knew that he had nerves.

The slave woman received Allit trustfully. "The master has gone to the temple," she said, "and the poor maiden is alone. I will conduct you to her, mighty sir."

Kisrinni preceded the visitor to the apartments of her young mistress. Allit followed, with a throbbing heart. No shrine in the land seemed, to the man of pleasure, so sacred as that simple room.

Lalitha lay upon her couch. A short, stout stick beside the divan showed that she had attempted to walk. Her eyes were large with weeping, and her face pale with the portent of an immeasurable danger.

At the sight of Allit she impulsively stretched out both hands to him, and then drew them quickly back. This simple act, the sweet dependence and the instinctive modesty of it, had a powerful effect upon the courtier. Unknown delicacies in his nature seemed to rise before his own consciousness, like strange, shy creatures out of foreign depths. All that mad, rude, commonplace reasoning of a moment ago was gone, — who knew where, who knew why? When he looked into the pure eyes of Lalitha, Allit became a stranger to himself. He had not a thought that he could not have uttered to the world.

As for Kisrinni, she stood discreetly, close against the *portière*, a bent, gnarled figure, looking as if she had been cut from the trunk of an old oak.

Lalitha spoke first, with no more ceremony than a netted bird : —

"My father! You have come to save my poor father!"

"Would to all the gods of Chaldea that I had!" protested Allit; "but am I the king of Babylon?"

"Susa said you were the king behind the king," said Lalitha simply. She turned her wan little face toward him so confidingly that the tears sprang to the soldier's eyes. Unused to such emotion, he busied himself in checking it, and did not reply to the girl for the moment. "Ah," exclaimed Lalitha compassionately, "I am sorry I made you cry. I did not mean to."

"Thou art a lovely creature!" whispered Allit. "Thou art a little divinity! Thou hast wings, and fliest from me. I am not worthy to kneel in the dust beneath thy feet.”

“No one ever spoke to me like that,” said Lalitha. “I do not know how to answer you.”

She laid her head back, and looked at Allit through her half-closed eyes. She did not blush or tremble. The poor girl was too sad for coquetry.

“I forget,” she added, “that my trouble is not your trouble.”

“It *shall* be my trouble!” cried Allit hotly. “And, by Bel-Merodach and all his godlings, I will do for thee in the matter as if Mutusa-ili were father to myself.”

“I do not understand these things,” pleaded Lalitha, “for I am but a maiden; but tell me, sir captain, is not my father a wise man?”

“The wisest of the wise in Babylonia,” returned Allit promptly.

“Doth he not interpret the dreaming of dreams skillfully?”

“Like none other in the province.”

“Can he not tell the king this thing demanded of him? Will he not know what dream the king dreameth? Is that beyond the art of Mutusa-ili? Is not my father as wise as the mind of the king?”

“The mind of the king is as the mind of a madman!” blazed Allit imprudently. “Be comforted. Thy father is wiser than the son of Merodach. Weep no more."

"I cannot help it," sighed Lalitha. "I am very sad. I perceive that my father is sorely troubled in spirit. Tell me, honorable sir, can they put my father to his death if he read not the dream of the king?"

"May Beltis, Queen of the Land, brood over thee, poor bird!" said Allit; "but if thou puttest me on mine oath, I must tell thee that the deed can be done. Even in Babylon can such a deed be done."

"But *will* they?" persisted Lalitha, raising herself on one arm, and staring piteously in the soldier's face; the crimson and white coverlet of her couch quivered with the trembling of her delicate, sorrow-shaken body.

"By my soul, and by my faith, and by the honor of Babylon, they *shall* not, then!" cried Allit, starting to his feet. The dark color rushed over his swarthy face. His tall height rose before the girl like a fortified gate. "By my life, I will save unto thee thy father, if I die for him!"

A strange pang wrenched the heart of the girl. It was like a new disease. She did not know what it meant. She felt suddenly very faint, and thrust her hands out pleadingly. The gay Babylonian did not touch her. He bowed his head silently before her, crossed his arms in the attitude of religious reverence, and left her without another word.

As he departed from the house, a slave girl on the opposite side of the street veiled herself, and hastened away with the air of one who avoids recognition. The captain of the guards was too abstracted to notice, and if he had, would not have recognized the figure of Mariamnu, the Jewish captive, slave and forced spy of Amytis the queen.

Allit hastened at great speed back to the palace. He was absorbed in the idea of saving Mutusa-ili. Moreover, he felt the necessity of retrieving himself with the queen, though he revolted from her at this crisis with as much ardor as he had formerly expended in parrying the pursuit of his royal leopardess. On his arrival, he pushed his way as far as the entrance to the intoxicating gardens where we have already seen her. Expecting an immediate summons to her presence, as usual, for Allit never waited long in vain, he was stunned when a slave brought him word, with that indefinable lack of respect that is so quickly adopted toward fallen favorites,.that the queen could not receive him. She was occupied with affairs, and Ashpenaz attended her. The slave of the queen looked at the captain with veiled insolence, and abruptly turned away. Allit, in a storm of bewilderment, departed hastily from the court of the women. Perhaps it was only the coquette's caprice. But the break, if it must come, might as well come now. As he returned to his quarters at the gate, another slave, with undiminished deference, handed to him the king's orders. These were written on clay and stamped with the royal seal. The tablet was then enveloped with a thick coating of a coarser earth. Allit's name and title were on the outside cover, which he easily broke away, leaving the inner writing plain to the eye. He read, —

" *On receipt, do thou immediately arrest and imprison all the wise men in the city of the Gate of God. On thy head, do thou guard them, and let not one escape.*"

This was stamped with the royal lapis-lazuli seal, upon which Bel-Merodach, with uplifted hand and sword, attacked and put to flight the dragon of disorder, a monster half lion and half eagle. Such was the mandate and the crest of Nebuchadrezzar, king and builder of Babylon, son of Merodach, beloved of the gods.

CHAPTER IX.

The gates of the university were closed. The boys, headed by Susa, were in a state of patriotic rebellion. Mutusa-ili, their master, was under strict arrest, and the boys were fond of him. Even now, at trumpet-call, the venerable scholar was dragged (it is true, with great tenderness) to the audience chamber of the king. Nearly a thousand wise men were solemnly marched into the imposing hall, and were stationed in long ranks before the high and as yet empty throne of the king and queen.

Mutusa-ili, white-haired, bowed with the weight of a crushing responsibility, stood silently. Beside him, wearing an air of forced ease, Allit lifted his high bronze helmet to cool his forehead, or nervously toyed with the gilt rosettes that ornamented his linen breastplate. An attendant carried his shield and quiver. He held his own richly decorated bow. Allit watched his dignified but downcast captive apprehensively. He was revolving the problem of the sage's possible escape. The how and the when tormented him. Behind him were the

Rab-mag, high priest and chief conjurer of Bit-Sagila, the seven-staged temple of Bel, and the chief divines of Bit-Zida the temple of Nebo at Borsippa, which was now undergoing reconstruction.

" By the sun of Sippara, these fat, beflounced priests look glum enough. I fancy our king tosseth them as a wild ox doth a rabbit. I paid two maneh for a false sign, the other day. It serves the greedy dogs right," whispered an irreverent foreign subaltern to his mate, as they closed the rear of this woebegone procession.

The huge and stately audience hall was built in the form of a Greek cross, whose transverse arms were three times the breadth and twice the length of the other two. The pavement was of glazed red brick, but upon each block, before it was burned, writing was inscribed. The whole floor became thus a large and imperishable monument, describing, in characters that the world might read, the achievements of the king. The gates were of bronze and cedar. Two human-headed bulls, of sacred import, confronted the entrance. These were twice the height of the tallest warrior, and were carved of gray marble before they left the heart of the mountain to be sent down the sacred river.

Mutusa-ili stood before the throne. It was Nebuchadrezzar's throne of high justice. Seated upon this, the monarch rendered decisions that shook the land from the source of the "glittering arrow"[1] to its fortified outlet, from the Zagros mountains to the summits of Lebanon.

A nod from the ivory throne mulcted the swift Arabians of their fragrant fields. A glance hurled ten thousand chariots and one hundred and twenty thousand horsemen westward upon Jehoiakim and Necho, upon Tyre and Jerusalem. A scowl from the Chaldean monarch, and Zedekiah fell. A sign, and Uaphris lost Egypt and his life. A word, and twenty thousand captives breathed the deadly sirocco of the deserts, on their weary march to the city of the conqueror. Whenever this baleful throne was occupied, it meant misery: either new crowds of captives, Jews, Egyptians, Moabites, or Arabians, began to make burning bricks beneath the fiery sun; or native and unfaithful subjects lost their heads and were mutilated upon the city walls.

Truly, a fateful hall! Verily, a bloody throne! The wisdom of the Chaldeans appealed from it on this mournful day to their greatest of sages. The priests closely watched their chief and spokesman; all of them were curious, a few hopeful, but more undisguisedly despaired.

Mutusa-ili regarded none. His eyes mechani-

---

[1] The Tigris.

cally read the prowess of his master in the inscription at his feet. Then they sought the massive supports of the dazzling dais. Four golden lions upheld the fretted pedestals. Each clutched a victim in its claws. The first was a Nubian; the second, an Egyptian; the third, a Jew; and the fourth, an Armenian mountaineer. The ghastly group was life-size, and represented the conquest of the world. Each victim was carved of alabaster, and was painted his native hue. The artist, moreover, had depicted blood so naturally upon the wounds that, as one looked, it seemed to flow. The spectacle had a ghastly fascination.

The sage's eyes grew dark as they bent upon these emblems of tyranny; then they softened, in spite of himself, for Nebuchadrezzar, no matter what his hot and variant moods, was dear to Mutusa-ili.

But now tears of burning shame blinded him, for the seer had consulted the stars in vain. He had spent hours of the night in wasted prayer. The Babylonian gods, one and all, had veiled themselves, and granted not a sign, not an inspiration. And was this to be the end of a sacred life? Where was Nebo? Surely, Merodach, the god of justice, could not oppress his servant? Was Adar a-hunting? It could not be that the ears of mighty Nergal were heavy with the din of battle? Is it possible that Ishtar wantons in deadly sport with her aged devotee? Nay, teacher of mankind, hide not thy head when thy worshiper kneels for an understanding mind, to penetrate the secrets of the heart! Alas, Belus, King of Spirits, canst thou not leave Nipur but for the space of a single watch, to give an old man peace? Is Anu dead? If so, of what avail is Erech? Whither shall the shattered spirit depart, when the king commands to die?

Mutusa-ili dared not breathe these horrid heresies. " O, gods, — if ye be gods, — blast a stricken heart, sunken in despair! But are *all* the gods of Babylon but breath? And are my only hopes, the stars, decadent from their courses?"

Thus the trembling man despaired, not at the vision of death, but of faith. The religious belief that his intelligence had recently begun to question, but which his pride and habit openly accepted, was unveiled of its imbecility before this fierce crisis. Mutusa-ili knew perfectly well, as he stood awaiting the king's approach, that neither he nor any other priest, soothsayer, or diviner could tell the dream. He felt the dishonor of a false position. He saw a thousand lives hanging on a pretense to spurious wisdom. How soon would he, who had been revered above all the wise men of Babylon, be loathed as a pitiful pretender!   He cast his eyes about to see if Daniel were near.   An impulse of reverence for the young man's intrepid fidelity to a religion unpopular at court swept over Mutusa-ili.   At that moment he envied the young Jew his simple manliness.   He was adrift himself, as much as a solitary acorn swept upon the current of the Life of the World.[1]

Allit had been watching his charge narrowly. A great pity, strange enough to this careless soldier, almost overcame the captain.   It needed but a glance to see that Mutusa-ili could no more tell the king's dream and interpret it than one of the captives painted in the brilliant frieze above them.   A sullen despair now seized Allit. The scanty hope he had so assiduously petted flew away as suddenly as a scarlet flamingo startled by a wounded boar.   He looked sternly around; perhaps he might see one single face lighted with the glimmer of an inspiration.   He only encountered gloomy, stolid, self-restrained priests who were as ignorant of the great laws of mind as the bow he held.   Here and there were strange faces.   Many chief priests and their assistants from famous temples had journeyed hither for consultation and to feast themselves in the capital.   These also had been unceremoniously apprehended, and had not the look of men

<hr>

[1] **The Euphrates.**

who enjoyed this startling opportunity to test their professional skill.

At this moment the bow fell from Allit's hand, and clattered on the pavement. The captain turned deadly pale, beneath his painted cheeks, at this portentous omen. Emotions of vague terror became communicated, as such subtleties are, from man to man. Strong captives trembled in the sudden stillness, and coarse soldiers grasped their weapons the tighter. No one stepped forward to pick up the innocent bow. Allit stood haughtily erect, but not a slave sprang to his duty.

" How now, my brave brother! A captain of the king hath need of his weapons, this bloody day. Take thy bow and hold it."

A graceful boy, flying his brilliant mantle over his shoulders, stooped and mockingly held the weapon out.

" What! Susa? Thou here? Get thee gone, or the king condemn thee also."

" I'm afraid he has, Allit. A company led by Ashpenaz drove us boys like sheep in here, — and by our Lady Ishtar here I am. I begin already to see vultures and smell death."

Susa laughed merrily. His undaunted look encountered his brother's dark frown. He glanced, with the contemptuousness of a boy, over the rabble of lesser magicians cowering before their imminent doom. Softly Susa's gaze went back to his brother, and thence to his dear master, Mutusa-ili. Then the lad impetuously cast himself at the old man's feet, and put his forehead beneath the scholar's dry and trembling hand. Susa broke into something like a sob.

"O my master, my lord! May Nebo preserve thee! How can the king harm *thee?* If I were a king, I would fight him for it, and protect thee."

Allit was in torment. Was everything dear to him to be blotted out on this accursed day? He turned fiercely. For the moment he regarded the two with indecision: the venerable master and irreverent lad were clasping each other. The boy rose to his feet slowly, still bending his head under the old man's silent benediction. They moved apart, but spoke no words. Then Allit's heart burst aflame. The father of Lalitha, that white bird, — and Susa, whom his mother swore him to protect until the two-part earthen jar [1] closed over the elder or younger son!

"By the seven dark-browed thunders!" muttered Allit, "ye shall not die, or all the gods in Babylon avail not to protect the son of false Merodach from my vengeance" —

He stopped in the midst of the first trea-

---

[1] The coffin.

son that his hot blood had ever forced to his lips.

"Ah — ah?"

The low breathing of this disdainful interrogation brought the captain to his usual composure. He took his hand from his sword lightly, and with graceful energy motioned his captives back into line ; as he did so, he bowed superciliously to the wily eunuch. Ashpenaz darted a stinging look from his narrow eyes, but he added no private rebuke. When he spoke, it was loudly enough, so that every one could hear him : —

" The king, whom Merodach his father protects, approaches. Let his favorite captain attend him to his throne."

The faint music of stringed instruments was now heard droning its plaintive way through the corridors. The arrested soothsayers arranged themselves quickly in solemn and picturesque lines. Soldiers bearing spears surrounded the priests, and assumed a reverential posture. Allit hastened to the brazen doors. The stately procession advanced with measured tread. A band of eleven musicians preceded it. Seven struck the harp ; the rest played the flute and the lyre. Following them, a choir of nine boys and six women sang with uplifted hands and averted eyes, the praises of the king. Ashpenaz, the major-domo of the palace, stood opposite Allit at

the doors, and regarded his trained musicians
critically.   These played and sang with sad precision.   They were the most beautiful of all the
Jewish captives of a lower rank.   At a sign
from their leader, the hymn of praise burst forth.

> Thou king of lions,
> Conqueror of conquerors,
> Destroyer of nations,
> Shepherd of thy people,
> Destined of the gods!

As the full force of the clear, boyish chorus
fell, a single voice penetrated the obeisant silence of the audience room.   It was the voice
of a woman, young, and trained to her art.
A glance at her face, which bore a sensitive reluctance, and seemed to be pleading for a veil
denied it, revealed Mariamnu, favorite of the
queen, the Hebrew slave and singer, soprano of
the court.

Thus sang Mariamnu : —

> The world is at thy feet;
> There lie we.
> Strike the timbrel sweet,
> Let the sackbut ring.
> Fair the fetters be,
> Glad the captives sing,
> With the world beneath thy feet,
> Here lie we.

As the pathetic tones ceased, certain of the
captive Jews exchanged significant looks appre-

ciative of this adulatory sarcasm, which was too
fine for the royal perception.

Nebuchadrezzar walked in more than solemn
state, as befitted the dignity due to such a rare
decree. Before him, two attendants waved fans
of peacock's feathers, whose prismatic tints
looked like bronze rainbows high overhead. Beside him, in honor of this sinister event, the
queen was borne upon a purple palanquin.
Boys swung burning incense at her side. Behind the royal pair, two more attendants held
artfully embroidered umbrellas over them; these
were emblematic of absolute sovereignty. As
the king strode beneath the cedar lintel, he
paused, and cast a cruel look over the vast and
crowded audience hall. As moist and vigorous
wheat droops instantly beneath the sirocco, the
doomed priests dropped upon their knees and
touched their foreheads to the inscribed bricks.
The musicians had marched ahead, and had
taken their places behind the thrones. Their
harps were silent.

The king seemed to enjoy the fear which
he excited. The ranks of despairing devotees
stretched forth their hands, and lifted their
heads, and then dropped them to the pavement,
after their fashion, with painful regularity.
They uttered no cry for mercy. They were
dumb with terror. Of them all, one only bowed

low in a respectful posture, but did not abase himself.

The king observed the exception, and flung at the sage a look of mingled contempt and respect. Amytis, noting the king's expression, yawned a little; a sneer sat upon her handsome face. The train advanced. Ashpenaz hastened to assist the king to mount the throne. The captain stepped forward, with a profound military salute.

The musicians and the captives looked on drearily. When the queen descended from her litter and took her position on the smaller throne beside the king's, the buzzing of a bee could have been heard in that vast court. The sun glanced in cheerily from above, and seemed to have the only glad heart there. The king's scowl deepened. His eyes were wild and blood-shot. He looked like a soothsayer in a forced frenzy. The stricken men arose. As Nebuchadrezzar seated himself upon the throne, the musicians struck a resounding chord, and a low murmur of admiration arose and swelled from his assembled subjects.

In recognition of this prompt tribute, the monarch, whose morbid appetite such flattery often satisfied, brightened. A more hopeful atmosphere stole like an incantation into the audience room.

The king leaned back, and glanced again about him, whispered a word to Amytis, and smiled. As for her, she looked at Allit; displeasure and infatuation struggled in her eyes. The despot made a well-known sign to his favorite captain. Allit nodded towards the doors, and a large crowd of citizens rushed in and filled the suffocating hall. In all-important judgments the people had free access to the court. A few officials and favored citizens had reserved privileges, and moved to prominent seats with the leisure of position. Among these were Egibi the banker, and Ina, his daughter. Allit, when he saw her, was diverted for the moment from his gloom. He had the pleasing sensations of a man who is beloved by a belle to whom he is indifferent. He glanced gallantly at Ina. In this passing preoccupation, he failed to observe the entrance among the common crowd of two veiled women, one, it seemed, elderly, and one quite young, who attracted a certain attention because of their very effort to avoid it. Babylonian ladies were not so modest, as a rule, that a veiled face and figure and shrinking manner could wholly escape notice.

And now the trumpet commanded silence. It was obeyed; the mass of humanity in the great hall seemed to breathe like one agitated man. Mutusa-ili regarded no one. His eyes were on the claws of the throne. The king stirred, and slowly turned his dark glance abroad ; it moved over the swaying crowds like a cloud, rested upon the priests gloomily, then concentrated itself. Perhaps two thousand people were in the audience room. Of these, Nebuchadrezzar began to appear conscious of the existence of only one. He observed his favorite astrologer and master with an expression half of hope, half distrust, but wholly intense and terrible. Mutusa-ili drew a long breath, lifted his head with a greater than royal majesty, and their eyes met. Monarch and soothsayer studied each other.

CHAPTER X.

" Are all here?" Nebuchadrezzar turned his mace towards his captain, while his eyes still clung to the old man.

"O king, live forever! Yea, all are before thee, save a few young men of the captivity."

" They can be found?"

" Yea, my lord the king."

" Let them stay for one more watch. My mercy giveth them two hours' grace after Sin, the brilliant god, hath given up these carcasses to the wild beasts that wander without my city wall. Let this decree go forth."

" My lord the son of Merodach commands, and I obey."

Allit bowed his head to the pavement, while his breath within him stopped for joy that Balatsu-usur was still safe. But what could that young Jew do? Nay, what could he *not* do? Thus the heart of Allit consoled him, in this hour when love and life hung on a madman's dream.

" So! all are here? And for what? Did Ishtar mock me with a dream? Tell me, Allit, didst thou say that all are before me?"

"Verily, O king, thou didst hear thy servant say, Yea."

"Truly I have power. Hath Bel more? Nebuchadrezzar's planet hath come. Tell me, old astrologer, when shall that mighty star appear that flashed upon the zenith from north to south, whose tail spread like a reptile, and Elam was ravaged by the first Nebuchadrezzar, five hundred periods ago? It shall come. It shall come. Nebo shall protect my crown. I have power to raise on high and to kill. I am the son of Merodach. He that denies it dies in the dust before me, for I am a god."

The king rose, in a frenzy of excitement. His eyes seemed about to burst from his head. His high tiara trembled, his hands shook. He frothed at the mouth, and withal looked so terrible that soldiers, priests, and citizens hid their faces in their hands upon their knees, before this outburst of royal mania. At this moment Nebuchadrezzar seemed inspired, and many secretly repeated exorcisms to preserve them from his divinity. Allit was one of the few who had a suspicion that the dream, whatever it was, prolonged sleeplessness, and religious brooding had produced fever, and a consequent aberration of the intellect. But the multitude, having no such scientific explanation of the king's condition, swayed like stricken grain be-

fore the throne. This exhibition of power pacified the king; he rested grimly, as a lion does
before a fatal leap.

" Arise, my children. I am the shepherd of
my people. Behold the justice of the king."

Of course they all scrambled up as fast as
they could. Susa happened to be prostrate behind Ashpenaz, and was playing with the brilliant fringe of the eunuch's robe. · As the
corpulent major-domo had with much difficulty
almost regained his feet, Susa gave his robe a
quick jerk, and Ashpenaz fell backwards with
a loud crash, and rolled bellowing before the
throne. Here the eunuch lay upon his broad
back, and called upon half the gods of his acquaintance ; for he could no more turn over than
a turtle.

Susa laughed outright, and immediately Allit
turned his head away. Mutusa-ili, however,
took a quick step forward to help Ashpenaz to
his feet. Thereupon, for the first time that fateful day, Nebuchadrezzar was seen to smile. He
took no further notice of Mutusa-ili than to
order him back by a gesture with one hand,
while with the other he beckoned Susa.

" Hallo, thou young dog! Is it thus that
thou dost reverence the baldness of thy superior?
Fly, and raise thy fallen victim, or, by the city
of my hands, I give thee to the fiery furnace."

"I try, O king," said Susa, repressing a droll look and rushing up to Ashpenaz, "but do the gods decree that a stripling shall move a mountain?"

It was all the front rank could do to restrain their smiles as Susa began to wrestle (making as much as he might of the deed) with the master of ceremonies. The king stroked his beard to conceal his amusement.

"O my lord the king," wailed the eunuch, "he puncheth me; yea, between the ribs doth he punch me more than his duty requireth."

"My lord the king," protested Susa merrily, "he sprawleth; yea, he sprawleth in thy presence more than his case requireth."

Amid groans and curses Ashpenaz regained his equilibrium. His scarf of office was torn, his fringe mangled, and he looked generally so discomfited and disreputable that one might even have compassionated him but for the sour temper in which he received the lad's mischief.

"O king, hear thy servant." His shrill voice shook with rage and chagrin. "I demand his head, even the head of this cub do I demand."

Nebuchadrezzar turned his face, upon which anger was admirably feigned, toward Susa. The lad had always been one of his favorites.

"Take him out and away." Two soldiers sprang to obey.

" Whither? To the City of Death?" asked Susa, smiling saucily at the owner of a million lives. The lad stood undaunted. The contrast between the brave boy and the cringing priests was too evident to go unnoticed, and the king, who loved courage above all other virtues, hardened his heart against the soothsayers, and loved the brother of Allit, his captain.

" By my great Lord Merodach, no! That is too good for such as thou. I punish thee with worse, — with life. Begone! Now, Ashpenaz, good counsellor, art satisfied with my severity?"

In the little commotion which followed the removal of Susa from the hall, half the spectators failed to notice that the diviners were drawn into close rank before the throne, that the attention of the monarch had suddenly concentrated itself upon them, and that the by-play had changed in a moment to tragedy.

" Priests and soothsayers of Babylon, the Gate of God!" The voice of Nebuchadrezzar went clanging like bronze through the audience court. A thousand strong, the miserable men had crawled to their feet. Mutusa-ili, who had remained standing for some moments, now lost his conspicuousness among them, and seemed to melt into the common herd. There was something significant and sad in this; as if the choice nature given to the sage and devotee must sink into the clay of vulgar aims and names, science accept the fate of charlatanry, and all sacred illusions lap the dust beneath the feet of royal mania. Yes, but if *illusion*, let it go! There was something inspiring about the scene, after all. It seemed to be a challenge to divine truth, and the true heart sprang to it.

"*Interpret unto me my dream.*"

There was no answer to this preposterous command. The diviners bowed deprecatingly, but no one returned a word. Their wits were put to it. Who should risk the first attempt to soothe the alienated intellect of the tyrant?

"Diviners of Babylon! The king hath no leisure to wait your laggard skill. Interpret unto me my dream."

This time a voice answered firmly enough, —

"Tell us thy dream, O Nebuchadrezzar, that we may perchance interpret it to thee. Any priest of us will do the possible to serve the king. The impossible, that we may not do, for kings or gods."

It was Mutusa-ili who spoke. He was pale and had an agitated look, but it could not be called an expression of fear.

"I tell ye not!" thundered the monarch. "*Interpret unto me my dream.*"

Mutusa-ili made a striking motion with his hands; it was as full of dignity as of despondency; it needed no words, and was accompanied by none. The king understood it perfectly; so did the unhappy priests; they glanced at each other and trembled. Would their chief make no feint even of performing the miracle? For his life's sake and theirs, would he not pretend for a moment? Would he substitute inconceivable self‑respect for the natural effort to play with or delay the delusion of this madman?

The priests muttered together in strange tongues unknown to the common people. A diviner from the temple of Nebo at Borsippa, distinguished for his skill, gathered his breath, and stepped out from the rank and file.

" The son of Merodach is wiser than the children of men," he began, with a bravado which easily passed for assurance; " he dreameth as he pleaseth, and demandeth as he willeth. Behold I, even I, high priest of the temple of the Seven Spheres of Heaven and of Earth, do venture to interpret the dream of the king."

A murmur of excitement buzzed through the hall. Mutusa-ili did not raise his eyes; they had returned to the claws of the throne; he was watching the clutched and tortured Jew.

" The dream of the king," proceeded the priest, " was even as I say. Bel-Merodach hath revealed it unto me, even since I have been in the royal presence at this hour. Nebuchadrezzar hath dreamed " —

" Well ? " asked the king sardonically, for the priest halted.

" It is too terrible ! " groaned the priest, as if seized with sudden agony. " It tormenteth my soul. Behold, if I reveal it, a panic will snatch the people. Revolt will fire the land. So ghastly and so hideous to the heart of man is the dream of the king that Merodach commandeth me, and I obey. ' Speak it not,' commandeth Bel; ' tell thou not the direful thing in the presence of the king's people ' " —

" Thou art skillful," interrupted the king grimly. " Thy head will be a fair price for so shrewd a venture."

" Nay, does my lord the king command me to disobey the divine voice, even the will of his father Merodach ? "

This was regarded by most of the spectators as a poser on the part of the priest from Borsippa. The people were on the whole surprised, when the king reiterated, —

" Soothsayers of Babylon ! *Interpret unto Nebuchadrezzar his dream.*"

" I obey," faltered a magician known as the famous astrologer of the cupola of the temple of Zarpanit. " I can interpret the king's dream. Behold, my lord, thou hast dreamed " —

"Ye-es?" drawled Amytis pleasantly. The queen was becoming *ennuyée* with these priests, "It sounds easy. Pray proceed, sir priest. Hurry a little, to please a queen."

"That is precisely why I hesitate," answered the priest promptly. He blushed and stammered; he wore an air of superior delicacy. "Alas," he said, "it is even true. The dream and the interpretation thereof are no matter for the ear of the queen. Nay, they are not subjects for the hearing of ladies; and the audience hall aboundeth with ladies. I pray thee, my lord, have me excused from such an immodesty."

A slight laugh rippled through the hall at this piece of bravado; which, considering the state of morals and manners in Babylonia, was ingenious, to say the least of it. But Amytis frowned.

"Nay, then, my lord," she pouted, "if thou dreamest such things as may not be told thy queen, for my part I would that the king kept his dreams to himself and made them not public. I am indebted to the priest from the temple of Zarpanit, and I particularly request thy favor in consideration of his delicacy."

But the king was now so thoroughly angry that the queen's jest hit the wrong nerve. In terrible tones, he reiterated his demand: —

"Tell me my dream, and interpret it unto me, or ye die for it. Yea, even to the number of a thousand shall ye die."

Silence replied to this threat. Nebuchadrezzar leaned forward in his seat. Its arm was carved at the edge in the form of a sacred goose. The king's fingers closed over the ivory head and bill. The delicate handiwork could not stand the brutal strain. It snapped and broke. In ungovernable fury, the king tore off the arm and hurled the missile at the last speaker. It smote the unhappy priest straight on the temple, and he fell; and even where he fell, his false brains rushed forth, and there he died. This episode recalled the king to himself, but did not tend to soothe the anxiety of his subjects.

"And thou, Mutusa-ili, master of my youth, diviner of my manhood, and sage in whom I trusted, are the gods at the hunt? Are they asleep?" The king turned upon the old man with impetuous ferocity, tinged with a love and respect which he could not shake off, even in so mad a moment.

Mutusa-ili made no answer, but the tremulous motion of his robe revealed the convulsive agitation of his hands. After a pause, the king's voice raised itself sarcastically: —

"Awake thy words, old man. Recall thy wandering powers, or, by this dream, thou too liest like yonder corpse." He pointed at the body, which two slaves were bearing from the hall.

At the king's last words a terrible shriek tore the air. It seemed to proceed from the winged bull that guarded the entrance to the judgment hall. The sound fluttered wildly for a moment, and died away wailing.

"An omen!" cried the priests. Even the king seemed shaken by the weird and human cry. The bearded mouth of the majestic bull might have been thought to wear a sarcastic expression, but remained shut as tight as ever. At the cry, Mutusa-ili changed color, and, gathering his strength to his bosom, spoke to the monarch in severe tones : —

"O king, live forever! Be it known unto thee, by the tongue of a prophet of the gods, that there is not a man upon the earth that can show the king's matter. Therefore, O king, tell thy servants the dream, and I will show thee the interpretation."

"The thing is gone from me," said the king confusedly. "Even if I would, am I a magician, such as thou pretendest to be? Can I tell thee what is not? Tell me the dream, I say, — *the dream!*"

"But, O king, deign to remember. Hath great Sargon recorded the like? Hath Sippara or Cutha, yea, or Babylon, books that have

sealed upon the unperishable clay a like require-
ment? What king, since when Xisuthrus built
the bituminous ark, hath demanded such a rare
thing of any enchanter or Chaldean? I tell
thee, mighty king, that there is none other that
can show it before the king except the gods,
whose dwelling is not with flesh."

The old man's voice rang loud. These brave
words comforted the magicians with a short-
lived hope.

"Thou liest," said the king, scowling. "Ye
have all prepared lying and corrupt words to
gain a space of time. My will changeth not.
Ye have failed, and ye die. Thus do I purge
the land of rot. Here, bring me my tablet.
Write the decree. My judgment seal hath
struck the soft clay even as I shall strike the
heads from off this tribe of cursed impostors.
Yea, I say it, even I in my glory, ye shall be
cut to pieces; ye shall be fed to lions, to vultures, and to crocodiles; and your houses shall be
made a dunghill. Go, Allit. Lead them forth.
Pierce their tongues. Blind them with spears.
Let not the sun set upon a quiver of their carcasses, or thou too losest thy perfumed head.
Go, I say. By Merodach my father, that
which I have sworn, that will I perform."

Before the king ceased speaking, that wailing cry, which had seemed to proceed from

the human-headed bull, was repeated with such piercing insistence that every man looked at his neighbor, and even in the suffocating heat of the vast crowd grew cold to the heart with superstitious fear. From behind the paws of the stone monster a veiled figure shot; seemed to try to rise, as if it would fly above the heads of the people; and then fluttered down like a wounded or a netted bird. Men and women made way for the apparition; it bounded between them in lithe leaps, and, before a hand was raised to stay it, sank at the feet of the king. The veil fell in her flight, and the child-like face of Lalitha lifted itself like an exquisite, obeisant carving to the throne.

"Why, king, good king, dear king, you have made a mistake. You would not kill my *father?* You *could* not kill my *father?*" The girl's sweet voice, thrilling with unconsciousness of herself, uttered these naive words in a tone that could be heard to the ends of the hall. "He is a good man," pleaded Lalitha. "Everybody knows that we live alone together, with one slave woman yonder, who brought me hither. Great king! You have everything, — a queen, and all the people. I am a poor girl. I have nobody but my father. I have heard him say you are a good, wise king. You will not kill him, — you will not kill my *father!*"

" Ah, there," said Lalitha, suddenly dropping her voice, " there is the queen. I see her now. I was behind the stone god. The queen will save my father. She will beg the king for a poor girl . . . and an old man . . . my father's life, queen ! His life, king ! His old life . . . his precious, oh, his precious life ! "

" But I have set my seal," protested the king ; he was evidently much moved. He muttered to himself, " Beautiful ! beautiful ! " A relenting of the muscles softened all the lines of his dark face. Mutusa-ili held his breath. Lalitha had the wit not to add a word to her spontaneous plea. She drew closer to the throne. crawling upon her knees, and bent her head to the footstool of Nebuchadrezzar ; her lovely lips pressed his sandal.

Then Amytis, who had preserved an ominous silence, opened her petulant mouth and spoke distinctly : —

" I know the girl. She is a low creature. She should not touch thee, Nebuchadrezzar. Spurn her from thee."

The king drew a sharp breath, pressed his hand to his forehead perplexedly, and made a motion of dismissal to Lalitha.

" If I had not set my seal in the clay " — he began, with what seemed to be genuine softness and sadness. ".But the judgment seal hath stamped the condemnation in the legal clay. By the honor of the throne of Babylon, Mutusa-ili dieth. Trouble me not. Vex me no more!" cried the king wildly. "I am a-wearied of the matter. Take the girl away!"

In the confusion which followed this scene, only two persons in the hall noticed the captain of the guards. At the sight of Lalitha, Allit's face had become suffused, and as dark as his helmet. He motioned to an officer to take his place, and with bowed head rushed from the court. Two women observed his appearance and departure. They were Amytis the queen, who frowned, and Ina, the daughter of Egibi, who blushed. Lalitha neither frowned nor blushed. Lalitha did not think about Allit. She knelt, a prostrate, piteous figure, at the feet of the king, her being poured out in entreaty, as wine pours from a silver shell. Father love is older than lover's love; and in emergencies it measures deeper.

CHAPTER XI

Mutusa-ili felt that his humiliation was complete. Must a girl plead for his life? That it was his own girl did not seem to help the matter. The meanest slave was less pitiable than he. In a prominent place sat Egibi, his brother, the treasurer of the king. It could not be said that there was no affection in Egibi's face; but like most influential sympathy, it was more ornamental than useful. Mutusa-ili turned towards Allit for support, for his limbs trembled beneath him; but the captain had gone. At this moment was he preparing the death-warrant? It would have been something to the old teacher if he could have even seen the boy Susa. The circle of dependent priests about the disgraced sage had widened, and he stood severely apart and miserably alone. Death seemed less hard than this bitter moment, this huge and only failure of his life.

While Lalitha clasped the king's feet, Mutusa-ili would have prayed, if he had thought of any gods in whom he felt any particular confidence. He knew too well that her naive intercession was his last hope. When that failed his heart died within him.

But the queen's words stung the old man's disabled pride. It was the chief of the royal astrologers who raised his head from beneath that blow. When the decree of death had gone forth, Mutusa-ili, with a commanding gesture, approached the throne. He spoke with passionate but dignified emphasis: —

"Behold, I declare it unto gods and men, my daughter, this maiden, is as white as the wings of the morning. Let God deal with her accuser. She needeth a greater Judge than I. And thou, O king, hear me, thy master. The stars decree that neither I nor these die by thy impious hand. Before thou wast born, or Babylon was built, the gods were." The old man raised himself to a majestic height, and stretched out both hands; his long fingers beckoned the soothsayers to approach.

"Nebuchadrezzar, king of Babylon! I swear it by the seven planets, yea, by the hidden word of Il, I swear that thou diest, and thy kingdom become a piecemeal to many nations, if thou takest these anointed lives. Nay, hear me, son of Merodach, nor vex thyself at my inspired speech. Behold and see! Here we stand. I draw about this people the mystic circle of the skies. Fall back, ye slaves and soldiers. Step but a sandal within this awful ring, and Raman blasts ye in his wrath. Back, I say! or I hurl the curse of Anu, Il, and Hea at ye, and your first-born die!"

Now, Mutusa-ili was consciously perpetrating the last fraud of his life; it was for life's sake, and we may forgive him. He had small faith in his own incantation; but the people had,— that was the main thing. In vain the king commanded and threatened. Not a soldier would cross the magic line to arrest the diviner. Not a slave dared touch the hem of his garment. The priests fell on their faces before it. The spectators trembled with excitement. Only Lalitha turned toward him. The young girl, veiling herself, crept upon her knees from the feet of the throne toward the feet of her old father; but when she reached the sacred circle, she too paused thereat, and humbly, dutifully, beautifully, bowing her head, she kissed the invisible barrier, and passed it not.

This exquisite exhibition of trust in Mutusa-ili's sacred art created a momentary sensation, of which the soothsayer was not slow to take advantage.

We said that Mutusa-ili perpetrated the last fraud of his life. To do him justice, this scene was not entirely fraudulent. The wisdom of the East is a mystical wisdom, and Mutusa-ili had been trained not only in it, but by it. He could look back upon a novitiate of seven, yea, of fourteen years, in the most ancient, most powerful, and, so far as is yet revealed, the most honest brotherhood of seers known to the Orient. What he had seen, many a king would have given a conquered nation to witness. What he had performed, many a sage would have given his life to imitate. But these choice experiences were a law unto themselves. Their own masters might be entirely unable to control the force which they had evoked. Marvels which the diviner had wooed by fastings and scourges, and blood and tears and vigils, and sought for years and in vain, might flash upon him at the turn of a moment, blinding him with light and with glory. No one knew better than the sage of Babylon the caprice of mystery. Yet no one was as much moved as he, when the major-domo of the court, Ashpenaz, with haughty mien and defiant bearing, strode forward to re-trieve his awkwardness before the royal pair. Thus, with a bravado of obedience to the king's command, he boldly pushed the frightened sol-diers aside, and stepped to the magic line. Mu-tusa-ili stood towering. His gaunt eyes burned; they seemed to see nothing newer than the art and wisdom of ten thousand years. He muttered strange words in an untranslatable tongue. He

made with his long hands curious motions, unfamiliar to the popular necromancy and to the
common practice of his art.   Ashpenaz paused,
wavered; he put his hand to his heart; one
foot crossed the imaginary line; he gave a terrible cry, and fell, face down. The soldiers raised
him fearfully.   He was livid and senseless.

Mutusa-ili paid no attention to this incident.
He regarded the king solemnly.

"Thou art the greatest of the magicians," said
Nebuchadrezzar uneasily, "but canst thou interpret to me my dream?"

Alas for Mutusa-ili!   He made a pleading,
upward motion of the hands towards Nebuchadrezzar, but retained a piteous silence.   The
king leaned back on his ivory throne, and
laughed.

"Balatsu-usur! Oh, Balatsu-usur! Art thou
here?"

Susa stood panting before a wooden door set
in from the thick wall, and hidden in a dark and
narrow corridor of the state apartments adjoining the university of Bel, and set apart for distinguished students.   The lad threw his whole
weight upon the panels to force the barrier open.
But he could not; the wooden peg which held
the door was placed in sure position.

"Balatsu-usur, noble Jew, it is I, the brother

of Allit. He sendeth me in mortal haste. Answer, quick, in the name of thine own God!"

At the last invocation the peg was drawn, and the door swung back upon its bronze sockets. Susa drew back with awe. A figure, whose face was of the whiteness of an oleander, stood before him. Daniel's robe was refulgent; it harmonized with the tints of his countenance. It was as though the full moon had bathed him with a sheen which, like glaze on brick, refused to fade away. There was a tradition handed down from father to son, among the priestly class of Aaron, that Moses once, on the mountain of Sinai, caught the radiance of the one God, and that it abode for many days upon his countenance, to the destruction of those who dared to lift his veil and look. Daniel at this moment had such an appearance. Susa felt himself seized by a holy fear.

" At last thou hast come," said the Jew gently. " Hath Mutusa-ili shown the king his dream?" Daniel still stood in the narrow doorway, but Susa, he knew not why, continued to kneel outside.

" Quickly! quickly!" entreated the lad. " My lord, prince of Israel, stay not to question me, but fly to the judgment hall. My brother Allit, the captain, goeth out of his wits for grief. He bade me bring thee faster than the raven flieth, — for life's sake, he said, and for Lalitha's."

In his excitement, the boy leaned forward to pluck Daniel's robe that he might hasten him, but the seer drew it back with a strange reluctance.

"Nay, touch me not," he said solemnly, "lest the vision of the night go from me. Let me forth. Follow thou me."

"If a girl can kiss the incantation, I should fancy a soldier might cross it," observed Amytis scornfully. The challenge of a handsome woman always piques men, and dares them on in their own despite; and the queen, though none too much respected, was comely of countenance, and admired in Babylon. A guardsman responded impulsively to her taunt; and after a moment's hesitation, two or three others followed him. At the magic line they paused. Instinctive reverence, if not a genuine dread, withheld them a little. Lalitha's kneeling figure seemed to waver before their eyes like white fire offered to a goddess. She did not raise her head. She seemed as unconscious of their proximity as a spirit. Her lips touched the sacred circle; they moved in gentle prayer.

Mutusa-ili stood motionless in the centre of the circle. He had a majestic air. Something of scorn was in it. The terror of the people was his respite, if not his reprieve. He looked across the sweet protection of Lalitha; he could not trust himself to touch her, even to glance at her. He eyed the soldiers imperiously. Thus they stood, — superstition, womanhood, and force impressively arrayed against each other.

"Arrest the priest!" cried the king. "Arrest the soothsayer, or, by my own hand, your lives shall answer for it, and ye go forth like the corpse of him ye did behold!"

"Stay thy judgment, king of Babylonia!" The well-known voice of the king's captain rang manfully through the hall; his guardsmen recognized their superior officer, and, with military precision, turned about face and saluted him.

"Behold, I have found a man," cried Allit, "I have found a man of the children of the captivity of Judah, who will make known unto the king the interpretation of his dream." . . .

Daniel stood before the king and before the soothsayers. The young Jew shone like a god. A splendor clothed him as if it fell through a sun-shot cloud. Many spectators hid their faces. But Mutusa-ili regarded him steadfastly. The soothsayer said to himself, —

"This is the radiance of a pure heart and of an honest life."

Lalitha still knelt at the margin of the enchanted line, devoutly and devotedly. The first thing which the prince of Israel did was to lift the maiden to her feet; this he did with great gentleness and reverence. Kisrinni came forward from the crowd, and seemed to envelop the poor girl and to mother her out of sight. The next act of Daniel's was simple enough and tremendous enough. He crossed the circle of the incantation. He crossed it firmly and quietly, making no fuss about it in any way, and, respectfully moving Mutusa-ili to one side, took his place before the throne.

Cries from the priests, shouts from the crowd, protests from the soldiers, jangled through the air; but they sounded like the jeers of jackdaws at a sacred bell. Nothing happened, absolutely nothing. The Jew neither dropped dead, nor withered to a monkey, nor fell palsied, for his blasphemy. At the very moment when the young devotee saved the aged soothsayer, he ruined him. Mutusa-ili gave his reputation, his system, his faith in an art, his faith in himself, and the faith of a nation in him, for his aged life.

So Balatsu-usur told the king his dream. It is on record in an older Book than this that the young man did this deed; and the dream and the interpretation thereof will be found therein.

minutely related. It was, on the whole, rather a dull dream, like other dreams, of no particular interest except to the dreamer.

But wild rumors of the case had gone afloat. The audience in the judgment hall had grown to crushing proportions. Many fell, and were trampled on in their efforts to hear or to see. The crowd was so great that much which was said by the Jew was of necessity lost to the mass.

But when the young man had reported to the king the details of the dream — which was a much-mixed matter, worthy of the fantasy of a gifted maniac, — he raised his voice, and spoke loudly before the king and all the people ; and what he said was remembered in Babylon for many a year.

" Have I, Nebuchadrezzar, told unto thee thy dream ? "

And the king made answer gently :

" Thou tellest me the dream."

"Thou didst behold this great Image. Gold was its head. Brass was its belly. Iron were its feet ; but clay was in them. And behold, a stone, carved without hands, did smite the Image, and it fell. Tell I thee thy dream ? "

And the king repeated humbly :

" Thou hast told me my dream."

Then the young man answered solemnly, but his mien was modest, and in his eye could be seen no more human fear than in that of an eagle in mid-heaven :—

"Thou, O king, art king of kings, unto whom the God of Heaven hath given the kingdom, the power, the strength, and the glory . . . and after thee shall arise another kingdom . . . and another . . . and a fourth . . . but the God of Heaven shall set up a kingdom which shall never be destroyed ; but it shall break to pieces all these kingdoms, and it shall stand forever." . . .

It would have taken but the turn of a whim, when Balatsu-usur had said these words, to have torn him in pieces. Half a thousand soothsayers could have done it, though they took their lives from his white hand. Amytis would have done it; but she admired him too much. The king might have done it; but the king — where *was* the king ?

Prostrate upon his royal face, prostrate before the court, the queen, the people — down like a pleading conscience or a suppliant faith, Nebuchadrezzar the Great lay in the dust before his captive Jew, and worshiped him right royally.

"*Thou* art the Master of the Magicians ! " said the king. " For thou commandest the power of thy God, and thou controllest the spirit of man."

CHAPTER XII.

BEFORE nightfall, Babylon was astir with the facts and the rumors of the day's event. The captive Jew had become the hero of royal whim and of popular excitement. Plain moral purity and religious fervor had done for the young man what a lifetime of political scheming had failed to do for many a gray-headed, disappointed adventurer; then, as in all ages, intrigue regarded the success of sincerity with astonishment. On the whole, simple surprise overcame jealousy in the court. The deed was so confusing, it was so confounding, that it caused more intellectual embarrassment than ill-feeling. The Babylonians discussed it with hot attention, but for the most part genially enough. The truth was, it was hard not to *like* this extraordinary Jew. Something about him compelled the kinder feelings. The boisterous nature of that rude time did not know what to make of him. His motives were as inconceivable to them as the astronomy of twenty centuries to come. They discussed him as they would a discovery in science.

Daniel had hastened from the judgment hall

as soon and as fast as he was permitted. To the king's excessive adulations he had replied with much emotion : —

" Rise, Nebuchadrezzar. Worship me not, for I am but a man, and the servant of the Most High God. Worship Him who did reveal the matter unto me in the night-watches, and whose will alone I do. Behold, there is one God, and He is holy. Jehovah is his name. Worship thou *Him*."

" If thou art his representative," said Nebuchadrezzar, " verily I will consider the matter; for he appeareth to me to be an intelligent god, quite worthy of some attention."

Now, **as** Nebuchadrezzar was known to be pretty constant to one or two pet deities of the highest order, but was also agile in carrying on what might be called a kind of celestial flirtation with many minor gods, Daniel was not as much impressed with his proselyte as he might have been.

" Explain thou to him," said the king condescendingly, " that he may command the services of Nebuchadrezzar the Great, son of Bel-Merodach. It will probably be of some value to him to know the fact."

Half sick at heart in the very hour of his triumph, the Jew remained silent before the idolater, and glided from the court, that he might calm his soul in solitude.

"He goeth to pray," said the priest from Borsippa. "Jehovah keepeth him at it pretty constantly. He must be an exacting god."

But Amytis the queen watched the young man narrowly. She said to Mariamnu, —

"A very handsome fellow!"

Amytis was lightly attracted by success. She easily idealized prominent people. She leaned toward the king, and chatted about the favorite of the hour with unprecedented interest. It did not detract from her animation that Allit could observe this, if he would take the trouble.

Daniel was in his plain little room in the outer apartments of the university, at the hour of sunset: he stood, according to the custom of the captive people, with his face toward the west; his hands were outstretched for the evening prayer; his countenance was lifted away from the world of men and the affairs thereof. The captain of the guards, who had sought him upon an official errand, paused with a light foot and bowed head. Daniel remained at prayer for some time. Allit did not like to interrupt him. He could not understand this perplexing captive. The man of pleasure was thoroughly puzzled by the ascetic.

"No wine," thought Allit, "no banquets, no battles, no women. Not a woman! Not even a slave!   And, verily, I believe he is younger than I."

When Daniel came to the end of his prayer, he did not seem surprised to see the captain; Daniel, it was said, was seldom surprised. He gave Allit an extraordinarily beautiful smile, — warm, human, manly, tender; it made words of welcome unnecessary.   But Allit was used to talking; and, as quickly as possible, he made known to Balatsu-usur the startling announcement that the interpreter of the king's dream had been appointed governor of the province of Babylonia, and was expected henceforth to make his home at the court and near the person of the king.

Daniel received his incredible appointment with composure.

" A thousand pardoned men will see to-morrow's sun," said the Jew joyously; " and the maiden abideth with her father in her own place."

And so it was that Daniel, the courtier, was commanded by the king to attend his first hunt. Whatever political upheavals rent the court or the city, whatever the mood of the king or the season of the year, the hunt was not interrupted.   Once a month it fell due.   If very exciting, it was often prolonged for several days.

Perhaps the master of the chase led the court upon stocky Susanian horses, with arrow and with spear aimed against the wild boar, whose lair was along the banks of the great river; and the king was diverted when his mastiffs had brought one of these tusked brutes to bay; he enjoyed piercing it with a bronze-tipped shaft. Sometimes the leashed Lydian greyhounds coursed the wild ox or the shy stag upon the plain, and the stallion of the desert sprang to speed the royal hunter to the death.

But Nebuchadrezzar in his more violent moods was not satisfied to pursue either the boar, the wild ox, the hyena, or the bear. There is no more sovereign game than the lion, or the lioness with cub. Even the striped tiger is less dangerous than the dark-maned lions of the plain of Doura. It was fit that the king of men should meet the king of beasts on terms of equality.

As an additional effort to drive the cares of state from the mind of the king, this hunt was planned on the night of the full moon. It was to be held outside the southern walls of the city of Babylon. Here began the long extent of the plain of Doura. Canals intersected the land, and the fertility of the soil was famous in a country where wheat returned to a sower two hundred and often three hundred fold. Among mulberry and olive groves, many a private mansion, like a huge white cameo cut upon a brilliant green background, loomed impressively. Towers of temples rose from the low horizon, and before an elaborate shrine, set midway in the plain, the shadow of one of those numerous likenesses of himself, which Nebuchadrezzar scattered over the land, fell pompously.

The quick night had nearly come. The cavalcade of the hunting-party had ridden far and fast. Gates and bridges were open at their approach, and there had been no halt until they drew breath before this temple for refreshments. The party was a small one, but unusual, because the queen, with one female attendant in her chariot, accompanied the hunt. It was her freak, and the king denied her not. Daniel drove in one of the royal chariots, as befitted the governor of the richest province in the world. Allit rode his horse, and directed the attendants, mounted and on foot. By his side, a second horse was trained to keep perfect step. This insured another mount in case of danger. Nebuchadrezzar drove in his two-wheeled hunting-chariot, behind three eager Persian horses, specially reared for the chase. At his left, the bare-headed charioteer held the round reins. The hunting-chariot, with the exception of the double quiver attached to the outside, was unornamented, plain even to severity; but the equipment of the horses betrayed care, from their banged forelocks and tasseled breastplates to their long tails, tied in the middle with a yellow ribbon.

Nergal was the national deity of the chase, and his was the temple before which they stopped.

The king and his retinue halted at the outer gates of the walled inclosure. A hundred priests awaited him. Daniel and Allit, with a few others, alighted, while Nebuchadrezzar poured a libation before the god. Daniel would have remained behind, away from this idolatrous rite, but his rank compelled attendance.

It did not take long to spill the wines, to inspect the entrails, to consume the sacrifice, and to set all the pious flummery of the occasion in action.

The omens all proved favorable, and Nergal naturally gave his sanction and protection to his richest patron and to the moonlight hunt. That was the important point. The horses were exchanged. The party took their hasty lunch of roasted pheasants and rice, of fruits and wine. Daniel ate only dried dates and drank the tepid water of irrigation, to the disgust of the rest. The ram's horn rang, and they were away.

The entrance to the paradise of the king lay

not many rods from the temple of Nergal. This tract was at once a park and a hunting-preserve. It was a square of many miles, and was bounded on its four sides by deep and wide canals that cut each other at the corners, and thus formed an impassable moat. There was but one entrance to these grounds; it was given by a wide bridge supported on inflated skins. On the side of the park a heavy wooden gate forbade exit. This unapproachable territory was a natural jungle and an artificial grove. There were no houses in the inclosure; only a few huts, where the keepers of the captive beasts lived and guarded their dangerous game.

Near the centre of the grove were the cages; full fifty of these could be seen, gaunt in the moonlight. From many of them, fierce growls and the deep, unmistakable cry of the famished lions could be heard.

This was Daniel's first introduction to the king's private hunting-ground, and the new favorite asked his charioteer many questions as they drove rapidly towards the cages: Whence came the animals? From across the desert? Were not the most ferocious captured in the province? How long did it take to starve a lion? How many keepers a year perished, on the average? And how often a hunter? Slave? —yes. But courtier? Death by the jaws of a lion, — how was it considered, as death goes? Except for the horror, was it more than another?

When the huntsmen reined up before the barred inclosures, Nebuchadrezzar alighted, as he was wont, to inspect the game. He stepped from one cage to another, and jabbed the furious lions with a spear to test their temper. He uttered low chuckles of delight when a fierce snarl or a vicious slap of the paw made the strong cage shake.

The king taunted his antagonists. The onslaught, when it came, was the more desperate and deadly, for all animals respond to a taunt in proportion to their ferocity. Not one of these sportsmen, who shuddered before Mutusa-ili's false incantations, was afraid to meet a famished lion in single combat. Such hand-to-paw fights, where weapon and claw were matched, often made the issue exceedingly doubtful. Nebuchadrezzar had dispatched no less than nine hundred lions with his own hand. Judge if his fingers trembled on his bow-string, when the hot breath of the fiercest of its kind enveloped him.

By this time the hundred beaters had taken their positions on foot along the edges of the jungle, to frighten the game back into the open clearing when it came that way. There were three chariots in all ; these rolled up under thick shade at some distance from the cages, but near enough to see the direction the liberated lions should take. The king, the queen, and Daniel, with their respective foot attendants, formed one picturesque and eager group. Each was armed with a bow and two quivers full of arrows. At the left side of the hunter hung a double-edged short sword, and on the right hip a dagger. Every quiver held a sharp hatchet, provided for the last emergency, and at the back of the chariot a long spear rested in its socket. This was to ward off an attack from the rear. Amytis and Mariamnu, her slave, were armed like the rest, but they did not carry the sword. At their side a gigantic warrior held a high shield, and made ready to protect the women with his lance or his life. Allit was everywhere, stationing the men and giving loud commands. Amytis watched him out of her almond-shaped eyes. The order of this hunt was as follows: "If the lion come thy way, lift up thy voice. Yea, lift it till thou howlest, that thou frighten the game toward the royal party. Give the king the first attack."

The moon was full. The light on the long plain was intense. The jungle lay in the distance like a low cloud. Every object sharpened, stood out in relief, or took to itself a shadow black as bitumen from Hit.

" Dost thou tremble, Balatsu-usur ? " Amytis leaned over and touched his arm with the sharp point of an arrow. Her voice tinkled through the silence like a shallow bell. Daniel would have answered, but his horses suddenly shivered under their rattling harness. The door of the largest cage had been opened from above, and the captive had rushed forth to fatal freedom.

In the first pride of his recovered liberty, the royal beast stood with mane erect. His tufted tail lashed his sides with dull thuds. Which way would he turn ? The lion gave a disdainful look at the slave crouching in his cage built above the empty prison. It too often happened that the unfortunate man whose task it was to free the lions was burned next day in his earthen coffin, and sent to the City of the Dead. The perilous privilege of opening the cage was sometimes given to convicted robbers, as a chance to earn their lives.

This particular lion seemed a little puzzled by his freedom, and glared about him hesitatingly. Growls from the caged beasts greeted him far up and down the park. He threw back his head, and answered them by a roar that made the night start. In response to this came quickly the best thing that our poor race can offer in the shape of a human roar. The united lungs of the hunting-party raised the tremendous shout

which was intended to provoke the game. The
lion made a blind dart at he knew not what,
and espying a slave, who had been stationed as
a decoy beneath a palm-tree, rushed at him.

" Away! Away!" cried the king. His horses,
snorting with their sense of danger and love of
it, leaped to meet it. The governor of Babylonia followed fast enough; the queen was not
far behind. The lion had reached the palm-
tree; an arrow in his flank caused him to hesitate and turn. Nebuchadrezzar thundered down
upon him in his three-horse chariot. The animal seemed to reflect. There, like a self-pos-
sessed duelist, he awaited the shock. At the
distance of two hundred feet or more the king
sped a second arrow. It pierced the brute in
the shoulder. His nature awoke. With a roar
made terrible by pain, he sprang upon the royal
chariot. Not a muscle in the king's body quivered. Even the charioteer did not wince; he
trusted the king. Nebuchadrezzar's lips tightened. His brow contracted. The look of conscious power which he wore was cruel. He was
as fearful to look upon as the animal. Even as
the lion clutched the side of the chariot, it fell
shot through the heart. Nebuchadrezzar's aim
was as true and as leisurely as if he had been
target-shooting in his palace yard.

" Truly thou art king!" Allit rode up impetuously. *He* had trembled for his sovereign. The escape was narrower than the royal hunter was apt to make. The great lion with a muffled choke rolled back against the chariot wheel.

"Truly," said Daniel, "thou art king!" He had sprung down, dagger in hand, to help as soon as the courtesy or necessity of the chase permitted.

"Of course he is," said Amytis impatiently. "Now for the next! I had n't even a shot. Which one of you two can outhunt the king?" She looked from the soldier to the saint. If Allit would only retrieve himself by some great deed to-night, in spite of the low-born girl she would take him back. The vague nature of the queen dissolved and formed again like a cloud, at every puff of riotous incident.

But Daniel made no reply. He was pondering upon the king. Was this the same man who bowed at his feet but yesterday?

"In sooth, Nergal forgetteth not his suppliants. Can thy god do more?" The king turned lightly towards Daniel. In the flush of this splendid feat of courage, he estimated himself without even his usual standards. Being the favorite lord of creation, was he not doubtless a favorite of Daniel's god, too?

Daniel, in truth, felt some uninspired anxiety about his sovereign; which, being a devout man, he found it natural to explain religiously.

"May Jehovah guard thee!" he said gravely, "but this is a serious pastime."

"Away! Away!" cried the king impatiently. Allit's loud voice rang with the order promptly. Amytis followed the captain and the governor with a wavering look. The second cage yawned, and there bounded forth a lion captured in the Libyan desert for the king's amusement. He sniffed the air as if the scent of blood had reached his nostrils. He stopped but a moment to reconnoitre, and then, in the hubbub of shouts and halloos, started toward the jungle. Already the king was in hot pursuit. Daniel's horses were now racing by the monarch's side. Amytis caught the wild spirit, and dashed after them. The animal turned his tawny head and observed his pursuers. He seemed thoroughly frightened, and increased his pace to long leaps. Arrow after arrow overtook the fleeing creature, but he only shook his mane and leaped the faster. Allit was in despair. If the lion entered the jungle, it might take the rest of the night to find and slay him. There was poor sport in that. He gave order to the beaters far ahead to cut the lion off, divert him aside, catch him on their shields, and turn him back. It was some distance to the thick underbrush. The ground was level, the trees not too numerous, the sky favorable, and the pace tremendous.

"By Nergal, faster! Let him escape me not!" Nebuchadrezzar leaned forward and touched his horses' flanks impatiently.

"By the prophets, such a race is not in Judah!" Daniel's blood rose as it had not since he followed the chase in his native land. He turned to his driver. "Am I the governor of this province of Babylon?"

"Yea, my lord, thou knowest it."

"Then let not the king outstrip the governor by the length of a cubit!"

But Amytis, either in spirit or in body, was not to be outdone.

"Shall he who was yesterday a slave outride a queen? Let the prince of Judah lead by the breadth of a hand, and thou diest, charioteer of Amytis!"

Obedient to this practical hint, the third chariot began to gain upon the first two. Amytis grasped her bow as she urged the steaming horses. But Mariamnu stood behind, holding on as best she could. Even the captive Jewess had caught the fire of this mad chase. She wished she could dash through all her life like this. If only it could be without the queen! Allit easily kept the lead over all, by a few rods. Behind, a score of attendants on foot dashed on. They were trained to run like the gazelle.

The king of beasts approached the jungle.

The jungle was something which he understood. These arrows and spears raining upon him, these bewildering shouts, — how set the teeth or snap the claw at them? He stopped, and cautiously looked about him. He saw the chariots bearing down upon him in one stern rank. He was surrounded on all sides. But this brute was born a coward, and, in pursuance of his nature, he turned again and made for the underbrush. With a mighty spring he jumped upon the line of beaters. There was a terrible cry and the unmistakable sound of the crunching of bones, and the lion had passed over the body of one unfortunate and rushed on.

Allit had dismounted by the time the chariots were on the spot, — the three abreast. The creature had already done more execution through cowardice than he would probably have achieved had he bravely stood at bay.

"O king, it is a grievous shame! See, the beast hath sent one of our fellows to Ninkigal. Shall we let a third one out?"

The three chariots came to so sudden a halt beside Allit that the horses reared upon their haunches with angry neighs.

"Nay, save the rest. We will track this one for the blood he spilt until he die. Wilt thou follow me, noble Jew?" Nebuchadrezzar had leaped to the ground, with bow in hand.

" Verily, O king, thy servant goeth in the name of Jehovah."

" And I too, in the name of Ishtar." Amytis shot Daniel a sarcastic look. She had dismounted. Her body swayed with a lithe freedom peculiar to a cat or a panther. Allit admired her magnificent figure. But Daniel turned away, as if afraid of being seared.

" Nergal shall lead me," answered the king haughtily.

" And Amytis me ! " Allit bent low with his old sweet homage, as he softly whispered this word.

" Away, then ! " Allit spoke to the beaters as if they had been human dogs just unleashed ; and indeed they were. With shouts of defiance, the attendants spread into the steaming jungle. The king struck boldly into the black, luxuriant undergrowth, followed by the Jew, the captain, and the queen. Amytis, with all her Median spirit, was quite willing to allow the tall warrior with shield and spear to protect her. A woman values her courage chiefly that she may count it as naught before the valor of man. But Mariamnu was left behind, with the charioteer and the dead. She was forgotten ; nor did the captive maiden grieve at this.

. The small party had stopped for breath. A

slave had given them wine from a skin, and they were refreshed. Only Daniel fasted. The hunters had reached a little clearing, on which the moon lay like a high tide. Allit drew near to Nebuchadrezzar, and put a hand upon his arm.

" What? Where? What is the matter? " whispered the king.

The captain grimly pointed across the open space. Dead sugar-canes crackled about them, wild olive-trees shaded them, and the yellow-flowered acacia shot from beneath their feet like jets of fire from a burning world. Amytis had plucked a spray of scarlet mistletoe, as she brushed under a dead sycamore; this she had coquettishly twined about her hair and bosom. As the hunters stood to listen for the game, the flute notes of a nightingale cut the soft, moist air. In the rapture of this romantic spot, Amytis would fain have drawn nigh and hung upon the arm of Allit. But Daniel gave her a stern look, and her warm hand dropped at her side. The shrill cry of a bittern now arose like the voice of a herald in an amphitheatre.

" Look! Look! " whispered Allit. Not four hundred paces ahead of them, the lion cautiously stepped into the full moon, and looked about him. He seemed thoroughly aware of his danger. The lion approached the king, and the king boldly started alone to meet the lion. Every heart beat the faster; the king only was really calm. He had the unmistakable assurance of one of his own gods. His shadow seemed to fall like that of a mountain. The two monarchs of the earth examined each other. The lion shivered, and turned. As he did this, the king shot, and the arrow pierced through the mane into the neck. With a catlike motion of the paw, the creature swept the arrow from its wound, and turned upon its royal torturer.

Nebuchadrezzar did not swerve. He awaited the attack as calmly as he would receive a deputation in his audience chamber. His men sprang to divert the lion, but he waved them back. The lion did not leap upon the king, but approached him warily. This caution made the duel the more ominous. Nebuchadrezzar dropped upon his knee, and took a long, steady aim. He seemed carved from stone, and his bow stood out in white relief. No one dared to stir. As the lion bent for his fatal spring, the simultaneous whir of bowstring and arrow was heard. The beast leaped into the air. The king stepped aside, expecting to see his prey dead at his feet.

But the son of Merodach had missed his aim for the first time in many years, and before a heart could beat, the lion, with a stroke of his paw, had smitten the king's leg, and had felled him to the ground. The victorious creature now stood over the prostrate favorite of Nergal, and snarled at Allit and at Daniel. Who dared stir? The furious animal might mangle the king beneath him. The two men started forward together. The lion awaited them. The king had the wit not to make the slightest motion, well knowing that it were his death. Allit, with a mighty plunge, thrust his sword at the lion's breast. As he did so, he gave a great shout, hoping to disconcert the creature. But the Libyan was too quick at parrying. He caught the sword in its descent with his claws, and hurled it from the captain's hand. Allit, nothing daunted, grasped his dagger, and gave a brave leap towards the lion's jaw. As he did this, he slipped in the marsh, and fell short across the head of the king. The dagger struck a stump, and lay there useless. The lion's hot breath fanned the two men. He tossed his head, and growled confident summons to a sure death.

Daniel was left. His slight figure looked ridiculously disproportionate to such a mad venture. His nervous hand tightened upon his short blade, and he took a step, fastening his wonderful eyes upon the hungry creature. The lion did not cower before the governor of Babylon or the seer of Judah, but his motions became less restless. He eyed the Jew with respect and interest; he seemed for the moment to forget his victims in some new sensation powerful enough to divert vengeance. Daniel had the appearance of one who hesitates for an instant between two courses of action. Would he trust too far to magic or mysticism, setting Heaven knew what incomprehensible power against a wounded lion?

Suddenly he tore off his outer cape, and flaunted the woollen cloth in the reflecting, almost calmed face of the animal. This taunt was too much. The lion jumped for the Jew. No trained gladiator could have anticipated that leap more surely. The young man left the cloth in the clutch of the claws, and, bending low and to one side, plunged the dagger up to its chased hilt into the lion's heart.

"There is no sorcery in *that* blow. He is a king among hunters. Allit is a child beside him." Thus spoke Amytis to herself. She ran forward lightly, and perched herself upon the quivering carcass.

"Nergal is great. He hath preserved his servant," groaned the king when Daniel sought to lift him up.

"Nay, my lord, it was Balatsu-usur." Allit spoke with the deference a man of power feels towards his physical superior.

"Nay," said Daniel solemnly, "it was Jehovah."

"Not a single shot to-night!" Amytis still sat upon the warm beast, and spoke with pert petulance. She did not concern herself about the king's wound.

"Another!" The king's voice rang with its usual imperiousness. "Let the third beast out!" He tried to rise again, but fell, groaning.

"Get me to my chariot," admitted Nebuchadrezzar, "and let us to the palace. Haste, or I bleed to death."

CHAPTER XIII.

Relief from mortal emergency either strengthens the enduring power or perceptibly decreases it. Little troubles become so paltry by contrast that one disregards them; or else they fret us more than ever, because the greater misery has left no strength to bear the less. In the house of Mutusa-ili there dwelt the dregs of sadness fallen from the first foam of joy which had bubbled about the escape of the sage.

Several things contributed to the despondency which Lalitha could not help sharing, while her whole strong, joyous youth protested against it. It might be natural to an aged man, — she supposed it was to be expected that old people should be gloomy; but for a well girl with a live father, what was the use in moping? And the captain of the guards had been to see them twice, thrice, and another time, since that dreadful day in the court of judgment. Lalitha ran about the house singing. Life was delightful!

But when she looked upon her father's face, Lalitha stopped singing. Mutusa-ili had aged fifteen years in as many days. His professional humiliation, his wasted skill, his ruined reputation, the quiver of an awakening sense of neglected honor, the outcries of an abandoned faith, the pressure of beliefs that he found it equally hard to choose or refuse, — all were heavy upon the old man's spirits. His strength broke; he had been a vigorous man, but physical weakness, like a new acquaintance, took hard hold of him, and puzzled him. He wondered whether the darkened life which the Jew and the Babylonian had saved were worth the cost at which it had been bought.

He spoke gratefully and decorously to Allit and to Daniel; neither of the two young men neglected the disgraced scholar; but when they had left the house, he turned wearily to Lalitha and murmured, —

" Are our guests departed? Leave me, my daughter, for I would commune with mine own heart."

Now, another calamity had befallen the shadowed home. Lalitha thought it a pretty piece of good fortune, and Kisrinni chuckled about it like an ape. Only the old father understood it. Lalitha had received a summons to court.

The lion-hunt was over. The moon had waned. The king was fretted by his wound, which did not heal as it should; a certain virulence, new even to the morose nature of Nebuchadrezzar, began to creep into the royal moods. The king needed incessant excitement. He demanded every day some new thing under the sun. Novelty, in all ages the most difficult pleasure to provide for caprice, evaded the skill of Ashpenaz and the captain of the guards. Nothing happened. The city was without event. The court was dull. The lion was killed, and the king was torn, and the war was over, and the dream was interpreted, — and what now?

One day the king took to his fancy a thought, which (Allit had blessed all the gods of Babylon) had escaped the royal reflection up to this unlucky moment.

"Behold," said Nebuchadrezzar, "I would have before me the maiden. She was a comely maiden, and pleaded bravely for the soothsayer her father. Verily, it was a pretty beggar! Now, I bethink me, she did kiss the latchet of my sandal. Bring her hither to me."

Now Allit, who was the official bearer of the command, received it with a heavy heart. Like other men of his sort, he was ready enough himself to play with the down on the wing of his white bird; but the aim of another hunter startled him with strangling rage. Up to this time, be the truth told, it had never occurred to the captain that he might not, whenever the time came — why hasten? she was so young, so fair, so pure — " make love " to the daughter of Mutusa-ili in any fashion that should best please him, and to any end, or no end, as his mood might dictate.   He regarded Lalitha as, in a sense, his own ; these new impulses of his higher nature, these strange movements of an emotion as different from passion as the maiden herself was different from, say, the queen of Babylonia, puzzled the captain of the guards. He treated them as fine, fresh flavors in the wine of love, not to be drunken too quickly or too rudely ; for even the Babylonian found himself refined by the delicate atmosphere of an experience not usual to his nation or his class.

But when the king —   Ah, that was another matter !

Lalitha at court ?   *Lalitha* ordered to the harem of Nebuchadrezzar ? The captain clutched his sword and set his teeth.   Too terrible !

" Bear thou my command," said the king moodily.   " Why standest thou there hesitating before me ? Bring unto me the maiden, and that forthwith."

Instead of obeying this mandate immediately, the captain of the guards took his life in his hands, and delayed on the way at the gorgeous apartments of the new governor of Babylonia, in the outer palace. In hot words he poured forth his story, and entreated the assistance of

the Jew who kept no women, and who had, for
the time, — Allit dully wondered what, frater-
nal, unearthly, divine tenderness and protecting
care for the daughter of Mutusa-ili.

Daniel heard him to the end without remark;
then said composedly, —

"But, pray, sir captain, why is thy soul
troubled? Why may not one fate as well as
another befall the maiden? In Babylon these
things are the fashion. The king's favor is
grateful unto women. Why should not the
damsel go before the king?"

"Thou ravest!" blazed Allit. "Thy preferment hath turned thy head and poisoned thy
spirit. I did think thee a god, unspotted, — not
like other men. Thou art worse than other men,
for thou hast the power to free the netted bird,
and thou refrainest. I will have none of thee,
thou spoiled captive!"

"Nay, softly, my good friend," said Daniel,
with a strong smile. "Listen to me. Answer
me the question of my soul to thine, before thou
judgest of me. . . . What wouldst *thou* with
Lalitha? Tell me, captain of the guards! Is
the favor of the monarch less honorable to the
maiden than the secret thoughts of thine own
heart?"

"I have never wronged the girl!" protested
Allit. But his eyes fell before the stern gaze of
the ascetic.

"Nay," replied Daniel quietly, "nay, thou takest thy leisure. . . . Go from me, Allit. Ponder my words. As for the maiden, leave her case to me."

"Must she *come* to court?" groaned Allit. "Is there no way of preventing — of interfering" —

"She must appear within the gates," said the governor of Babylon. "The king will be obeyed."

Allit, who perforce bore the royal mandate to the house of Mutusa-ili, was closeted with the weakened sage for a long and painful consultation; but to Lalitha he did not explain the situation. The two men understood its full gravity. The girl comprehended it no more than she did the secrets of the worship of Ishtar. She regarded a visit to the court as a gala occasion, and innocently prepared herself for it with girlish delight. It was very perplexing to Lalitha that when Kisrinni had robed her in a gay costume of crimson silk heavily wrought with golden beads, and had clasped her soft arms with her mother's jewels, — bracelets of cornelian and gold, and curious agates bound with golden chains, — Mutusa-ili should frown darkly at the slave.

"Knowest thou no better than *that?*" he demanded, with something of his old force. "Remove these baubles, Kisrinni! Robe thy mistress in her white garment, even such as she weareth at her daily tasks; and see thou to it that she is veiled exceedingly, for I cannot accompany the maiden to the palace, as I would."

Alas for Mutusa-ili! The disgraced soothsayer would not be welcomed, probably not received, within the palace. The debilitated old man had not the pluck to force an entrance into the gay world which had abandoned him.

"I cannot protect the maiden," he had said to Allit, with a despondency all but abject. "She goeth more safely in the shelter of her own innocence than within my palsied arm. Mutusa-ili hath become naught, and less than naught, at the court of Nebuchadrezzar. I will entreat Balatsu-usur that he may exercise his mercy for the damsel, if danger befall her. To the Jew, and to the God of the Jew, do I commend her."

Thus it was that Lalitha with the old slave made her way to the palace unattended. Having seen the king before, the girl did not find herself overawed by him. She thought him quite agreeable, and answered his inquiries naively. But the palace absorbed her. Her wide, innocent eyes wandered over it like a child's.

"It is very pretty," she said, with a long

breath. "I have been counting the fountains in the court. There are twenty-seven. I would my dear father had one. He complains of the drouth, since he has been sick."

"Is Mutusa-ili ill?" asked the monarch, melting between a smile and a frown.

"Oh, yes, king, did you not know that?" replied Lalitha, sighing. "I must go back to him now. I must not linger. He will miss me."

"Thou hast a fair face," said the king dreamily. "Thou art like a flower. Stay awhile with me, for I too am not well."

He looked at the trembling girl gloomily. Nebuchadrezzar's weakness was not for women. In his present dark mood, he regarded Lalitha almost coldly. But her exquisite beauty, her artlessness, her innocence, seemed to spring to him like budding blossoms. As he watched her, a curious tenderness, half paternal, half devout, overcame him.

"I am not well," he repeated complainingly. "I suffer. Comfort thou me."

"I will come another day," replied Lalitha, fluttering. "My dear father must not be left alone too long. I pray you, good king, to let me say farewell now, and go my way. The palace is very pretty, but I have seen enough. I would go home now. Come, Kisrinni!"

"Verily," muttered the king, "she hath no

more fear than a dove in mid-heaven. She is a choice creature for a man not overborne with affairs, or who desireth to rest himself therefrom. Methinks at another time I might not feel so ill. I might arouse myself, and appreciate the maiden."

He made a sign of dismissal, which Lalitha joyfully obeyed. She could not have told why, but she began to be very anxious to be at home. In the outer court, she fancied that she heard the voice of Allit, and was comforted to believe that he protected her. She hastened to pull Kisrinni after her, that they might depart swiftly.

But at this moment Ashpenaz, followed by a slave girl, sauntered across the mosaic floor, and brushed by Lalitha, so near that she winced and shrank away from him, and in so doing slipped upon the marble. In the effort to regain her balance, she lost sight of Kisrinni, for whom she called loudly.

"Hush thee!" whispered the slave girl. "I will show thee the way. Follow me."

Before sunset, Allit, raging in the outer court, where he stood on duty and on watch, understood perfectly that Lalitha had been decoyed into the harem of the king.

Once again the captain of the guards made

hot haste to the governor of Babylonia; this time he was ready to tear him in pieces.

"Thou boastest that thou wouldst save the maiden! And there thou standest — at thy prating prayers — like a slave about to be cast into a den of lions; while Lalitha — By Bel-Merodach, and Jehovah" —

"Nay, nay," interrupted Daniel serenely, "take not the name of Jehovah upon thine idolatrous lips."

"Verily, I would take Jehovah for my god," cried Allit furiously, "if that would help the maiden!"

"The spirit which Jehovah respecteth is not thy spirit," said Daniel. "Thou knowest not of what thou ravest. As for the maiden" —

Allit interrupted the governor by a terrible groan. He hid his handsome face in his fashionably ringed hands. Daniel had never seen such emotion in the man of pleasure.

"What wouldst *thou*," repeated the Jew sternly, — "what wouldst *thou* with the daughter of Mutusa-ili?"

"Worship her!" cried the captain. His face came up from his hands. He had not known until that moment that he did worship Lalitha. But now there seemed to be no doubt about it.

"And wed her?" asked the Jew.

"*Wed* her!" —

Allit changed color. His heart felt as if it overturned in his body. His large eyes opened widely in genuine astonishment.

" I had not thought of — *marrying*," replied the courtier frankly.

" Go thou," said Daniel sternly. " Go from me. Leave the damsel as she is. Verily, she is safer in the harem of Nebuchadrezzar than in the peril of thy false heart. . . . She loveth *thee*," said the Jew. " She *loveth* thee," he repeated, one could not say how mournfully. " Love is the net. Yea, love is the danger."

" I believe," returned the agitated captain, " that thou thyself " —

But he faltered before the Jew's deep glance.

" I myself do honor her," said Daniel, in a low, awed voice ; " thou hast said it. I do honor the damsel, and thou shalt do her no dishonor, neither now nor at any time to come. As Jehovah is my witness, Allit, thou shouldst take shame upon thyself that thou lookest upon the face of the maiden, for thine eyes do work sorrow upon her, and thou regardest it not ! "

" I do but go the way of my people," protested Allit, " and the way of my times. It is not demanded of a man that he *wed* the woman whom his choice prefers."

" The way of thy people is the way of abomination ! " answered the Jew energetically.

" Babylon is the whore of the world.   Behold, there is yet another kind of manhood from the manhood of Babylonia.   The living God taketh pleasure in it, and the heart of a modest maiden turneth safely to it.   Be thou, Allit Arioch, be thou that man."

" Thou demandest of me a miracle ! " said Allit, in a low voice.

" If the purity of a man be a miracle, then do I," answered Daniel. " But more than this do I demand of thee : yea, verily, that thou shalt plunge thyself in the waters of the soul and lave thyself, and cleanse thy heart, and abhor thyself, until thou becomest fit to touch the hem of the garment of this maiden, than whom is none so white of soul in all Babylon ; and that thou pray the living God to have mercy upon thee, if so be thou mayst become worthy to take the damsel from his hand, and abide with her, and her only, and cherish her, and protect her, and endear thyself to her, as a man endeareth himself to his wife in the sight of God and men."

Allit made no reply.   His brain whirled.   He felt as confused as if the Jew had commanded him to take a throne beside Jehovah ; which, to the fancy of the aristocratic idolater, was not an incredible proposition.   He looked at Daniel perplexedly.   Then his eyes dropped like a little boy's.   The seer's gaze transfixed him.

That indescribable radiance which sometimes surrounded the Jew began to scintillate, and a throbbing, like a pulse, beat through it; it seemed to overflow and to flood the Babylonian.

The moral force of the young devotee overwhelmed the captain of the guards. He felt that he was becoming conquered by an incomprehensible superiority. Curiously enough, he put his hand to his sword. The military instinct came first; of his soul he knew next to nothing. What was this impalpable power? Could not the truest blade in the battalion stab it? Allit tried to recover himself, but the Jew stood sternly. Moved by he knew not what that was irresistible, the soldier bowed his head; he took the attitude of devotion before Balatsu-usur; his large lips moved silently.

" Thou art a god," he whispered. " After all, thou must be a god."

" Nay," said Daniel gently, " I am but a man who serveth a God."

" Preserve thou the maiden," entreated Allit humbly. " Snatch her from the trap that hath set its teeth upon her. Then shalt thou command the commander of the king's guards. Lo, I would be the officer of thy heart, for it is not like the heart of other men."

But Daniel made no answer. He had become again absorbed in prayer.

CHAPTER XIV.

It was the dead of the hot night. Babylon was gay that night. There was a carousal at the gate of the king, and the streets were sympathetically merry. The larger palace was awake and athrob. Everybody of importance was there. The women of the harem bestirred themselves languorously, and looked out of their cage with soft, long, narrow eyes. It had been the royal pleasure that the news of the banquet should reach them at a late hour. When it came, the girls chattered among themselves like peacock chicks. What an event, to have something to say! During the first long hours that Lalitha had shared their perfumed prison, these women had uttered but two or three remarks. An Egyptian said, —

" I have been trying to count the flies. I miss the count. I think there are a thousand."

A Babylonian danseuse had yawned, and murmured, —

" I am very sleepy."

The liveliest girl in the harem played at tossing an ivory ball from a silver cup. When she caught the ball, she laughed excessively, and said, —

"See! See!"

But now that the announcement of the carousal had been allowed to penetrate their flowery dungeon, the girls found their mute tongues; their dull minds stirred; their light natures puffed about like down. The king, the queen, the feast, the dance, the chief eunuch, formed exciting topics of what they called conversation. To Lalitha it was a great relief that the women had at last found something to speak of. They had stared at her, and examined her robe, and mocked at her tears, till she could have crushed them all, like poisonous gnats. When the Egyptian said, " Oh, you will get used to it ; " and the danseuse said, " I, too, cried — I cried as much as an hour," Lalitha shrank from them, as near the entrance to the guarded rooms as she could get, and put her veil before her face, as if they had been rude men. Now, at least, the harem had forgotten its new inmate, and she could weep in peace. Lalitha listened, in hope and terror, for every sound. She expected her release each moment. She considered that the slave had made a mistake, and that she would be immediately freed and taken home. She scarcely gave a thought to the details of the harem. She had a vague sense of sumptuous draperies, rugs, and skins; of half-robed women prone upon them; of a stifling atmosphere, in which it seemed the air of heaven never blew; of musk and attar of roses; of incense and old tapestries; of fountains playing idly; of peacock's fans, and cups of wine half drained; of pillars and apartments opening, dim and gorgeous, beyond the closed court; of tinkling music, frail and foolish, trickling from unseen instruments; of the voice of an unseen singer, languorously singing : —

> Fold the wing, — fold the wing,
>   Soft-eyed bird.
> Sleep and sing, — sleep and sing.
> Do not weep, — do not weep,
>   Pretty thing !
> Love and sleep, — love and sleep.
> Pluck the flower of the hour.
>   Joy is deep.
> Red the flower, rich the hour.
>   Sweet is sleep.

Lalitha had listened to this song with her face hidden in her veil; her hot tears scorched her own sweet flesh, and she lifted her arm and kissed them off, as if she had been consoling a child. When she looked up the harem was empty. The last of the girls had been called to her place at the feast, and she was, or seemed to be, quite alone. This terrified her, and she began to sob afresh. At this moment the fringe of the long curtain of cloth-of-silver, near which she was crouching, swept inward and brushed against her arm ; the little gust which came with it puffed into her face like a warm breath. A low voice, sadder and sweeter than any she had heard in the harem of the king, said apathetically, "Thou art to follow me."

Lalitha bounded to her feet, and dried her tears with the quickness of youth and hope. She looked into the delicate, despondent face of Mariamnu.

"Thou art come to take me home !" cried Lalitha joyfully. She followed Mariamnu without a word of protest. The captive singer made no reply to the girl's artless outcry. She walked in advance of her, with bowed head. Once she extended her hand backward, and touched the white robe of Lalitha; then gently let it drop. Lalitha looked at her inquiringly. The two girls traversed the court and the corridor in perfect silence.

"But we are going *into* the palace, not *out !*" cried Lalitha suddenly. She stopped short. "This is not the way we came. This is not the way out. This is not the way home. Take me home ! I must go home !"

But Mariamnu shook her head. "Thou must follow me," she said hopelessly. "The queen commandeth audience of thee."

The night, as we said, was hot. The heavy air gave no breath to the revelers, and they dropped out in groups, or by twos, to rest in the great gardens. Here, at least, one could steal a march upon whatever breeze there might arise, and, languidly sunken upon the cool grass, or a leathern couch, or thin rug of fine silk, rest, and rise, and play again. Flowers, oh, flowers! What a world of them! The Babylonians were the great flower lovers of the world. The palaces were tapestried with them; the revelers were festooned with them, even as people of a more sparing taste decorate pillars or shrines; the gardens seemed not by a blossom depleted of them.

The queen, tired of the carousal, and, if the truth were told, annoyed that the captain of the guards had not chosen to approach her, willed to rest herself without the palace. She had chosen a mat of golden tissue flung upon a bank of red oleanders. Her women stood at a little distance, her deaf-mutes behind her; Ashpenaz looked on decorously. But the queen was, to all practical conversational purposes, alone when Mariamnu brought Lalitha into her presence. Lalitha made no pretense of any manners, but was crying now, right heartily. She remembered the queen only too well.

Amytis regarded her in cold, critical silence.

"It is a blubbering creature," she said at length. "Stop that boo-hooing, or I'll have thy fool of a head from thy bundled shoulders. Pull off her robe, Mariamnu. Teach her how the slaves dress at the court of Babylon."

To these royal words Lalitha answered by sinking on her knees, and begging for her freedom, with all the fervor of fright and ignorance.

Amytis laughed lightly.

"We consider *that*," she said with significance, "when thou hast shown some courtesy to thy queen. Answer me such questions as I shall ask, and then we will consult upon thy freedom."

"Gladly will I!" cried Lalitha happily. "Anything thou desirest, so that thou send me home to my poor father. I fear me he will die of terror by this time."

"Knowest thou," asked the queen abruptly, "the captain of the guards?"

"Yea, verily," said Lalitha promptly. It did not occur to her that there was any reason why the queen's eminently proper question should not be answered.

"His name is" — began the queen idly.

"Allit. I call him Allit. I think the soldiers call him Arioch, also."

"Ah, yes. I remember. He cometh to the house of thy father?"

"Yes, indeed, surely he cometh. He is a great friend of my father."

"Ah, yes.   Cometh he often?"

"Not so often, once. Very often, lately," said Lalitha artlessly.

"Yes?   As often as " —

"Every few days, it may be ; or a day longer. He is very kind."

"Hum — yes — I see. Thou say'st it.   And to thee ?   Is he kind to thee, my girl ? "

"Oh, yes, indeed ! " cried Lalitha.   "He saved my poor life, to begin with. He caught me from under the chariot, thou knowest. The captain has been always kind to *me*. I am grateful to him. We are very fond of him."

The openness of the girl's tone was no more to be mistaken than its joyousness. The queen's face grew dark.   In this dialogue the good and the evil were almost equally candid. Amytis had too unchastened and unchecked a nature to play the politician, either in love or hate. Simple as Lalitha was, she could not fail to perceive the expression of rage which mounted slowly to ferocity upon the handsome countenance of the Median.

"You see this captain — let me say — how often ? " demanded the queen. "Your father is shrewd enough to wink at the intrigue, I make no doubt. Tell me ! How many days in the seven ? "

There is a turn in such moral duels when artlessness becomes discretion itself. Lalitha suddenly grew as mute as the deaf-and-dumb slave who fanned the queen. Her ingenuousness rose upon its guard, like the ruffling fur of a tame doe that is abused. She put her pretty lips together, and received the questions of the queen in soft and obstinate silence.

What might she not have done? Could any poor word of *hers* hurt her captain? It did not occur to Lalitha whether her *naïveté* could hurt herself.

"Answer me!" commanded the queen.

Lalitha burst into tears.

"I was never moved by the tears of a slave," said Amytis scornfully. "Yours and you are not worth the leisure of the daughter of Astyages. You cease to be amusing to me, you toy of the king's captain! And now — and now" — repeated the queen, with a rising voice — "you last new whim of a half-mad king — come hither!"

Lalitha hesitated, advanced, and drew back.

"Come to me!" cried Amytis shrilly.

Lalitha trembled, but obeyed, drawing quite near to the reclining figure of the queen. Amytis raised herself on one elbow, and, putting out her small, dark hand with a catlike motion, drew the girl's arm within her reach. Suddenly bending her head, she laid her lips to the soft curve of the inner forearm, as if the sardonic fancy had seized her to feign a kiss upon it.

Lalitha drew back, with a loud cry of pain. The small teeth of the Median had closed and met upon her flesh.

There was something so vicious, so unqueen-like, in this act of vulgar jealousy and brutality that even Ashpenaz uttered an expression of surprise or protest. This recalled the queen to herself. She pushed the bleeding girl away violently, and summoned the eunuch to her side. A whispered order shot into his dull ear. The eunuch seemed to reply, or to be about to reply earnestly. But Amytis waved him away, and, gathering herself like a pantheress from the oleander bed, with a light bound moved up the garden toward the palace. Her women followed her, swaying like paper lanterns — bright trifles — in a shadowy scene. Ashpenaz laid his hand upon the robe of Lalitha.

"Your way," he said, "is with me."

"I will shriek!" cried Lalitha. She raised her young voice. "I will call on the whole world! *Some* of these people will save me! There must be *one* who would take a poor girl out of this awful place!"

"If you utter a sound," replied the eunuch, "she will have the head of your captain for it."

Lalitha and the eunuch came to a sudden halt at the extreme limit of the royal pleasure-grounds looking toward the Nana road. She had followed him pathetically, a quelled creature. The name of her lover had conquered the girl. She could only die, at the most. But oh, not a hair of *his* perfumed head should come to harm because of her. Lalitha set her teeth upon her terrors, and gave no alarm. She had stumbled through the shrubbery blindly, half dragged, half supported, by the eunuch, who cursed the queen, but obeyed her, as his nature was. In the distance, in a solitary spot, Lalitha saw two tall guards. They had spears; the light from the gardens behind caught the tips of the spears. She began to sob, like a little frightened girl; but she did not attempt to cry out.

When Ashpenaz came to so abrupt a stop, she looked about her wildly. No one was to be seen. The guards were still at a distance, and had not observed her. What ailed the eunuch? He staggered, and put his hand to his head. He drew his breath with difficulty. He acted like an asphyxiated person. Suddenly he thrust out both hands before his suffused face, as if in protest against an invisible power. Then they dropped at his side. He had thus released the girl, apparently quite unconscious that he did so, and now sank slowly, like a man overcome by sleep or wine. As Lalitha, sick with repulsion and terror, watched him, he rolled upon the grass at her feet, and fell into a deep swoon, or slumber.

Lalitha was too frightened to dare run, nor did she know where to run. She made a little start out into the street, and stood panting. By this movement, she came out from behind the shadow of the shrubbery, and thus brought herself face to face with Balatsu-usur. He was standing quite still. He looked as tall and white as a marble pillar.

"Veil thyself," said the Jew, "and come unto thy father."

He spoke strangely, almost dully. He had the distrait appearance of a mystic or of a hypnotizer; of a man interrupted either in communion with his God or in an experiment upon a fellow-man, it was not easy to say which. It might have been both. Daniel had an extraordinary duality of nature. If ever there was a spiritual man of the world, he was the man. He did not glance in the direction of the eunuch.

"Thou savest me!" cried Lalitha softly. She was still afraid of the soldiers. She crept around the other side of her preserver, so that he should be between her and the spears.

"Jehovah saveth thee," said the young man solemnly.

"That fat man in the bushes has tumbled down," said Lalitha, with the irreverence and irrelevance of girlishness and pity. "I think he has a fit."

Her protector made no reply.

"I am afraid of the soldiers," proceeded Lalitha. "The man was fain to give me to them. Would they put out my eyes with their spears, do you think? And pierce my tongue with a red-hot iron?"

Lalitha's imagination dwelt upon one of the prevailing punishments of her time, with the high colors of terror and inexperience. A slight tremor passed through the body of her calm companion; he drew her hand upon his arm, as they passed the guardsmen in silence. The two spears were lowered instantaneously. The officers saluted the governor of Babylon. When he had passed them, he gently dropped the hand of his charge, and turned the corner of the street. He seemed to be reflecting, that he might use the highest words to the maiden; that he might take from the rarest opportunity the richest treasure.

"God love thee, Lalitha," he said at last.

But might not a man do as much? Oh, but he was young, and a man, after all! She was so lovely, she was so lovable, she was so soft. She clung to his robe so prettily, and leaned toward him so confidingly; she was so wan with her fright, with her wound, with the blood upon her arm, and her tears; she was so pitiful and adorable; she was so weak and so mighty; she was so harmless and so dangerous! Is a man a god, that he shall neither see, nor know, nor feel?

As Daniel walked beside Lalitha through the streets of Babylon, his holy heart held, who knew what human tumult? The devotee had never before, in all the years that he had known the girl, passed as much time as this alone in her sweet presence. A perfectly new experience awaited the saint. He moved down the streets beside her, in a silence which awed Lalitha, as if he had been a deity. His lips stirred. Did he pray? At the threshold of her father's house, the young man turned, and gently raised Lalitha's bleeding arm and examined it. His lip quivered. Then he lifted her face by the tip of one finger beneath her delicate chin, as he would touch a child, and looked upon her longer than he had ever looked in his life. His countenance was blinding beautiful.

"May God watch between thee and me," he said gently. "And now go in, my child. Arouse thy father with thine own voice. Dearer than the voice of angels will it be to his ear. And, verily, I wonder not thereat."

CHAPTER XV.

LALITHA's girlish voice, pealing joyously at
her father's door, brought no response. She repeated the call, but without effect.

"Try the door," said the Jew quickly. It
was not barred. The latch yielded to her light,
obedient hand ; and the two stepped into the
house. It was perfectly still, and very dark.

"He is asleep," said Lalitha uneasily, "or he
sitteth in his tower to calculate. I will run and
call him."

"I attend thee," said Daniel gravely, "and
by thy permission, I precede thee."

He pushed on before toward the apartments
of the sage. The dumb and darkened house
echoed to their footsteps. Lalitha ran, calling,

"Father, father, father!"

The sickening sensation which possesses one
who utters a beloved name vainly is never without a premonition of the hour when it shall have
been uttered for the last time. Lalitha, too
young to know what she feared, but fearing the
the more for that, began to sob. They had
reached the lower story of the tower in which

the sage worked. The apartment was dimly lighted by one small oil-lamp that had well-nigh spent itself. Heavy shadows crouched in the corners, as if they had flung themselves there headlong. In one of these, a figure prone upon an ottoman, and covered with a rug, could be imperfectly distinguished.

"Maiden, stand back!" said the voice of the governor of Babylon, with the full note of authority. He held out his devout, athletic arm to bar her way. Deftly as the motion of a light leaf before a great wind, the girl dived, — her sinuous body dipped below the Jew's hand, — she swayed to her balance, and flung herself upon the ottoman with a loud cry, which waked — Kisrinni ; soundly sleeping, and perfectly comfortable in spite of her excessive anxiety. This she hastened, in the full flower of Oriental speech, to make known, with such facts as she had to add to it ; they were few enough.

When she had returned from the palace without her mistress, Mutusa-ili stared her in the face, " like a man gone five days dead," and demanded his daughter.

"Thou must demand her of the king," said the slave woman. It did not seem to have occurred to her that she was not bearing agreeable intelligence. Mutusa-ili, at these words, bowed his head, " as if he had been a slave," said Kisrinni, and had said no word to the woman, but departed from her, and ascended to the tower where he was accustomed to wed solitude to study, and bitterness to age. He had walked so feebly, and he trembled so in climbing the projecting bricks that led to the conical tower, that Kisrinni, for very anxiety, had remained on watch in the room below. She could not understand why it was not an honor that Lalitha should enter the harem of the king; but an old man who tottered on a brick twenty feet above ground, — this was comprehensible. Kisrinni's fidelity was proportionate to her nature. At all events, since he ascended the tower, nothing had been heard of Mutusa-ili. Kisrinni could not climb the bricks, and that was the end of the matter.

Lalitha was quite used to the tower, and she flew up the narrow steps with wings in her feet. The governor of Babylon followed her more slowly, as best he might. When they came out together upon the top, the girl, by a pretty instinct, for very girlish fright, drew back and clung to him.

The young ascetic trembled.

"I protect thee," he whispered, — "I protect thee."

In the open space beneath the stars, Mutusa-ili sat upright. His gray head was bare to the

now rising wind. The dew had touched it. At
his feet lay his diagram of the planets and their
prophecies; the shallow Persian glass of water
used by astrologers to prescribe a fate stood beside the diagram; dark scrolls and rare tablets
of ancient clay, familiar to magicians and famous
among them, lay scattered in unusual, it seemed
to be perhaps intentional, disorder around him.
He sat stiffly. His face was turned toward the
palace. The music of the revel came faintly,
like the language of another planet, to the
tower. His eyes stared before him. An open
scroll lay upon his lap; the edge made a little
crackling noise in the wind. His hands were
clasped upon the scroll. When the two came
up behind him, the old man did not stir.

"He slumbereth," whispered Lalitha fearfully. "Shall I waken him?"

"Remain thou," said the Jew, in some agitation. "I will awaken him."

He stepped up and laid his hand upon the old
man's shoulder. He called him, Honored sage,
Dear master, Father of Lalitha; and each name
came in a louder voice, and seemed more imperious and more precious than the last. But
Mutusa-ili made answer to none of them. Daniel gently stooped, and tried to unlock the old
man's cold, clenched hands. As he did so, the
dim light revealed to these devout eyes, so fami-

liar with the sacred writings of his faith, the contents of the scroll which the despairing captive soothsayer of Babylon had substituted for the mysteries and mockeries of the Chaldean magic.

Mutusa-ili held beneath his stiffened clasp the holy writings of his unacknowledged ancestors, — the hymns of David, prophet, poet, and king of Israel. His finger rested upon the words:

"*My soul longeth, yea, even fainteth, for the courts of the Lord.*"

"He sleepeth," said Lalitha decidedly. But she shrank, and did not touch the silent figure. She had come around in front of it now, so that she stood between the old man's fixed eyes and the palace which he had watched, — who shall say how long, or how piteously? With what unrecorded prayers had the disgraced and helpless father sought to avert the dishonor of his house and the anguish of his child! Had he exhausted the craft of the idolater, or discarded it? Had he come at the last, driven by a deceived intellect or drawn by a broken heart, to the God of his abandoned people? Did Bel-Merodach deny? Would Jehovah reply? Poor old disappointed eyes, turn but once. Give but a glance. Is there not a gleam of recognition in your steady look? Look at Lalitha! Oh, look but once at Lalitha!

" He sleepeth," repeated Lalitha uneasily.

" If it be the will of God that I do tell thee," said the Jew in a deep voice, " his will be done. For thy father sleepeth not, save as they sleep who wake no more."

" But thou saidst thou wouldst waken him ! " cried Lalitha. She had begun to tremble, but not to understand.

" I may not," replied Daniel solemnly, — " I may not do that deed."

" But thou art the master of the masters," pleaded the girl. " Thou *art* the Master of the Magicians. All Babylon knoweth this. Since the king dreamed, thou canst not deceive us of thy art. Waken my father ! Thou wiser than the Chaldeans of Chaldea, waken my father ! Thou greater than Mutusa-ili, waken him ! "

But the Master of the Magicians bowed his head before the girl.

" Behold," he whispered, " there is a greater than I. The magic of the living God hath been wrought upon Mutusa-ili. If he waken or no, at some other time, God knoweth. It is not revealed to me. . . . Come thou ! This is no place for thee, my child. Go thou below, to the slave woman. I will attend thee. . . . Perhaps," added Daniel, in genuine masculine desperation, " Kisrinni can explain the matter to thee."

Lalitha walked a few steps obediently, like a child. At the top of the brick ladder which led from the tower, she turned and looked back. The Jew had fallen upon his knees, and, with his face toward the west, prayed silently. His hand lay upon the hands of her father, and the three hands upon the old scroll that crackled in the wind. Now Daniel seemed to be making an effort to turn the old man's body, or the low, movable seat upon which he sat, so that Mutusaili's fixed eyes, too, should seek the Holy City, while the captive prayed.

Lalitha did not go down the brick stairs. She stood perfectly still.

"My father dieth," she said distinctly. "My father is dead."

She did not say anything more, or cry out. She thrust forth both her hands confusedly, tottered, and sank. He caught her on the brink of the stairway, down which, otherwise, she must have dashed headlong.

"Run thou!" called Daniel to the slave woman. "Run quickly to the nearest guard at the corner of the Street of the Tamarisks, and make known to him that the governor of Babylon desireth the attendance of the captain of the guards."

It was almost dawn when Allit came into the

presence of Lalitha. The two young men, without other help than the old slave's, had done all that was needful upon the top of the tower. The dead astrologer lay in the lower room, among his parchments and his diagrams, his tablets and his calculations. Even in his death he looked more solitary than most men, and more comfortless. Beneath his clasped hands, the songs of David, prince of Israel, remained undisturbed.

Balatsu-usur gathered the soothsayer's manuscripts and planisphere into a corner of the room, where he covered them from sight with a woolen cloth, as if the eyes of the dead might see them, and find some disturbance in the sight.

"Let them lie there," he said authoritatively.

"Come thou. Be witness unto me while I read what I did observe."

Beneath the Psalm of David, upon the dead man's knee, a second writing had been found. This was a small tablet, inscribed with a stylus. Upon the words of clay the clay hand rested heavily; there had been some difficulty in removing it. When Daniel had brought the tablet close to the little oil-lamp, and had examined it, he laid it down reverently. It was the will of Mutusa-ili. It bore date of but a week ago. Thus it ran : —

Methuselah, Jew, worshiper of Jehovah, inhabitant of Babylon, known to men as Mutusa-ili, invoker of idols, interpreter of the stars and diviner of dreams.

My fields, my house, and my goods shall be for my daughter, Lalitha. I appoint Daniel, Governor of Babylon, Prince of Israel, worshiper of Jehovah, guardian to Lalitha. Let her be subject unto him. May the great God, whose name is recorded on this tablet, curse her with irrevocable malediction, and scatter her race even to the last days, if she cleave not to the God of Abraham, Isaac, Jacob, and Daniel, whose servant I am, alas, too late.

Witnesses : —

> EGIBI, royal treasurer and banker,
> son of Adamu.
> HANANIAH, son of David.
> MISHAEL, son of Elzaphan.
> AZARIAH, son of Jezaniah.

BABYLON, month Ululu, day 25th, in the fifteenth year of the accession of Nebuchadrezzar, king of Babylon.

The two young men, when they had read the will, exchanged glances. The eye of Allit was feverish and half-closed with emotion; it was more nearly wary than the captain's boy-like gaze had ever been before in his life. But Daniel's expression had the steadfast illumination of a man to whom duty is as dear as it is clear.

After all, both were men, and both were young. This will threw Lalitha absolutely under the control of the Jew. The governor of Babylon could do as he would with his ward, and there would be neither law nor sentiment to ask a question of him. Power more precious to Allit than the throne of Babylon lay in the hands of this promoted captive, this saintly courtier, the captain's official and moral superior, his friend — and his rival?

Had he a rival in this sacred youth? Was the Master of the Magicians the master of the last and finest magic of human life? Would he will away or woo away the inclination of the fatherless girl? Nay, had he already wrought upon the spell?

The captain was not an imaginative man; but as he laid the tablet back in the hand of Balat-su-usur, his fancy took an unprecedented flight. He felt to the full of his nature the possibilities of the situation. Daniel's invaluable presence at the crisis of the girl's bereavement, his endearing tenderness, his dangerous ability to be of use to her, the glamour of the dead father's confidence and evident preference, the supreme personal beauty of the prince of Israel, — what would these mean, what would they *do*, to Lalitha?

The man of a hundred successful intrigues,

he who had held the fairest women of Babylon at the feet of his light fancy, felt before these facts something like the surprise of a child at its first hurt. It seemed to Allit as if he had received a sabre thrust contrary to the tactics. He looked at Daniel almost stupidly. The moral force of the Jew, which had already begun to lift the "soul sodden with pleasure," found a tremendous aid in the plain human complication. To spiritual momentum there was now added the push of commonplace jealousy. Thus, the lower motive, like the higher, found, as it often does in our strangely economic scheme of things, its unexpected and important value.

Allit opened his full lips to speak — some hot-hearted words. But he glanced at the dead astrologer, and bowed his head silently. Daniel followed the look. A strange, bright smile curved his delicate mouth.

"Go thou," he said gently, — "go thou and comfort the maiden because of her father. She awaiteth thee. Perchance she hath need of thee, for her sorrow constraineth her sorely."

"Thou art not as other men!" said Allit reverentially. But he went. And thus at the hour of dawn he came to her. He thought of that other debt he owed the Jew; by whose power — whether of magic, or of man, or of the gods, the Babylonian knew not — the girl had been spared from deadlier than death. He did not know, at that moment, whether he most honored the man or most loved the woman. What purity had Daniel preserved! A delicacy and embarrassment, new to his experience, overtook the captain of the guards. He scarcely dared to raise his eyes to her. When he did so, an instant taught him that the girl was as unaware of what she had escaped as she was of the eternal fate of the dead man in the next room. Lalitha knew no more of moral disease than she did of physical dissolution. Allit approached her with awe. He had not seen her since her escape from the harem ; and his emotion at the rush of events was great.

Lalitha was in the ante-room to her father's apartments. Further than this no one had been able to persuade her. She was walking up and down and across the little room. Her fluttering movements reminded Allit of the fancy conscious to him the first time that he saw her, — more than ever she had the look of a bird. She was not sobbing, or moaning, but yet it seemed to him as if she would beat her heart out. The room was still very dark. At the eastern door, but a little ajar, day struggled to enter. Babylon was quiet, uncommonly so, after the night's carousal. In the streets, the early water-carriers had begun to stir sluggishly, but the citizens slept.

Upon the date-palm that grew between the house and the street, a swallow had found itself awakened, and suddenly swung upon the lintel, and pecked thereat. Lalitha stopped her tempestuous pacing, and watched the swallow.

"It is the spirit!" cried Lalitha. "It is the spirit of my father! Let him in! Let him do as he willeth, Kisrinni!"

But Kisrinni had stepped into the adjoining room; the Jew had summoned her; some last service to the dead needed, or was made to need, her presence. Allit stepped forward quietly, and opened the door wide, thus bringing himself into the full sight of Lalitha.

"Ah," she sighed, "*thou!*"

The swallow flew in. The captain closed the door. The bird beat wildly about the heads of the two. Lalitha watched it fearfully. She was full of the superstitions of the people to whose faith her father had apostatized, and among whom she had been reared. The swallow settled slowly toward the girl. She held her breath, and lifted her beautiful, wounded arm, raising her forefinger tip. The bird descended gently, regarding her with the mingling of caution, suspicion, and trust, seen only in its kind, and then delicately dropped and poised upon her outstretched finger.

" He blesseth me," whispered Lalitha.   Allit did not speak. What could he say? It was but a swallow, — and a girl.   Yet the soldier was as dumb as any mute slave in Babylon.   Purity, delicacy, exquisite girlhood, devoutness, imagination, — these were matters hard to be understood.   Add the sorrow of one of the sorest of human bereavements, and the Babylonian bowed before the mystery.   Lalitha, unconscious and sweet, was the unconquerable fact of his experience.   As she stood, rapt, with the bird upon her hand, the captain of the guards instinctively took the attitude of devotion before the girl; then deliberately retained it.

The bird rose slowly ; fluttered above her upturned face, and made a long, fine circle overhead ; then darted into the room of death. Lalitha watched, but did not follow it.   The astrologer lay in the state which age and scholarship and high repute give to human clay; the sensitiveness of defeat and cruel anxiety added pathos to his features.   Here, if ever, lay a man dead of a broken heart.   Daniel and Kisrinni were praying beside the corpse; the one addressed Jehovah, the other muttered a charm, well known to have been revealed to the mother of the king by Bel-Merodach.   The swallow circled over the body of Mutusa-ili : then, mounting slowly, sought the tower of the sage, and

escaped through the exit of the brick stairway. As the bird broke free, day burst upon
Babylon.

"He is gone!" moaned Lalitha.

When she turned, the dark room was flooded
with the sunbreak from above. The bird could
be heard singing without. The captain of the
guards still stood in the attitude of devotion;
Daniel communed with Jehovah. The slave woman whispered snatches from a familiar hymn
to "The House of the Land of Death:" —

"To the land of no return he hath departed;
  To the afar off, to regions of corruption,
  Where light is never seen, where the dead exceed the living;
  Where ghosts, like birds, whirl round and round the vaults
    of dust."

But Allit prayed to Lalitha. She wavered
toward him, with a little appealing motion.
Her chin began to quiver, like a child's. Her
eyes filled, and overflowed. But she was pathetically quiet.

"I comfort thee," said Allit impetuously. In
an instant the worshipper had become the lover.
He sprang toward her, and held out his arms.
"Thou shalt not weep, for thou art precious
to me," whispered the Babylonian. "Only love
me, and I will comfort thee. Try to love me!"
pleaded the captain humbly.

Lalitha's wan little face changed color delicately. She made a motion, as if perhaps she nodded; but she did not speak.

"Love me, Lalitha, love me!" entreated Allit. "Make me worthy, for I am unworthy. Make thou me fit to take thee to wife."

"My father is dead," said Lalitha.

At this moment the Jew entered the room. An unearthly radiance illuminated his face. He held in his hand the tablet of clay. She tried to read it, laid it down and sighed, and tried again. Her eyes wandered from it to him, to Allit, drearily.

"By the authority of death, I ask thee," said Daniel tenderly. "Wouldst thou wed this man? Lieth thy happiness in his keeping?"

"My father is dead!" repeated Lalitha.

"Verily, I have chosen an untimely hour to woo the maiden," whispered Allit between his teeth. "Better is she, it seemeth, in thy holy company. I am only a man like other men!"

Devoutly raising her cold little hand to his forehead, the captain of the guards made obeisance to the girl, and, suddenly wheeling, like a phalanx in retreat, left her with the Jew.

CHAPTER XVI.

O HOT Babylon! The Gate of God had become the mouth of hell. This was the time of the year when rivers, dashing from their mountain sources, were devoured by the sun before they reached the Euphrates. A lizard, leaving its shady nook in the crumbling wall, was roasted to death as it touched the pavement. Birds sank in their stifling flight, and fell broiling upon the bricks. Not a breath shook the most delicate leaves; pistachio and olive branches drooped pitifully; melons and rare grapevines shrank to skeletons. Without and within the city, householders buried themselves deep beneath thick walls of unburnt brick, and vagabonds dug into the hot earth like worms, hoping for an air to breathe that was not aflame.

Upon the ramparts the captains of tens and of hundreds wrapped themselves in thick woolens and hid in massive chambers, awaiting with impatience the evening eastern breeze. But the luckless private often fell upon his sentry beat; and frequently he lay where he dropped, for the exertion of lifting him might bring a sunstroke upon several still valuable soldiers.

But who pitied the slaves within the walls? Babylon was but a royal citadel built for kingly pleasure. The ruthless builder, under whose lash a thousand frequently perished in one day, was not likely to spare himself the least of his luxuries in this deadly weather. Twice ten thousand laborers had not rested during the long night, that the last caprice of the monarch might be finished upon the day appointed. The Hanging Gardens were built.

Amytis was beside herself with joy, like a child with a new bauble. She had arisen early, that she might personally inspect the finishing touches given to the great work.

After the queen had sent her chief henchman to conduct Lalitha, who knows where? she had gone to such rest as satisfied vengeance gives, and had dropped the matter. Her commands were always scrupulously obeyed. Why refer to them, especially if they carry an unpleasant tang in the mouth? But when morning came, it pleased her to mention the subject to her eunuch. Ashpenaz stammered in confusion, when, after a few casual remarks, Amytis asked him sarcastically whether the girl objected to her escort and her fate. His hesitation aroused her quick suspicion.

"Is the deed done? Answer, on thy head!"

The silver parasol held above her trembled in the suffocating air, for the queen had stamped her foot with a concussion worthy of a market-woman in a quarrel.

" Yes — yes " — stuttered Ashpenaz, — " that is " —

" Thou liest ! " said the queen succinctly. Then the eunuch fell flat upon his fuming face, and kissed her embossed sandal, and implored mercy, and told her all he knew. The demon of the southwest wind smote him with a sunstroke. He swooned. He had a fit. When he came to himself, the girl had escaped him. A god must have snatched her. She must be dead. He was sure of that. She was probably turned into a vampire. It was hot enough for any transformation. The omens he had consulted did not deny this supposition. And so forth, and so on.

" It is a great disappointment," said Amytis thoughtfully. But she did not have the head of Ashpenaz for it. Her garden was finished, and that was occupation enough. After a round feminine scolding, she forgave the chief eunuch. She found herself amused. Her loves and her jealousies were light. When she had anything else to do, it was quite possible to forget the daughter of Mutusa-ili. Lalitha was the plaything of the queen's *ennui*. Amytis tossed off the subject for the nonce, and turned merrily to the Garden of Ascents, one of the seven wonders of the civilized world, the regal gift of Nebuchadrezzar, her lord and king.

Nothing was impossible to this king. No potentate known to history has ever displayed such constructive faculty. He converted it into temples and palaces, fortifications and gigantic reservoirs, as easily as a woman converts fancy into embroidery. Nebuchadrezzar was the Augustus of Babylon. His most ambitious designs were achieved with such painstaking elaboration, with such conscientious workmanship, and with such marvelous celerity that his contemporaries whispered of occult enchantment, as explanatory of his success. It was he who rebuilt the wonderful seven-towered pyramid to the god Bel-Merodach. Nebuchadrezzar found eight other temples in Babylon dismantled and sunken in ruins, besides scores of neglected shrines throughout Babylonia; among them the marvelous temple of the Seven Spheres at Borsippa. All these he restored to greater than their original proportions, and furnished them with gold and silver and brass; with the richest stones and woods and stuffs that the world could produce. By way of pastime he had excavated the Nahar Malcha, the royal canal, whose broad and deep waters connected the Tigris with the Euphrates. But the indefatigable builder rested his fame chiefly upon the double walls that inclosed and protected his holy city. These he raised, and without he ditched them, and thus he strengthened the city. The skeptical may think this no great work. Let it be remembered that this outer wall was fifty cubits wide and two hundred cubits high, and inclosed over one hundred square miles. Four Parises or two Londons could encamp therein; and the number of the largest Babylonian bricks required to rear the outer wall, or Imgur-Bel, would be eighteen thousand seven hundred and sixty-five millions, or twice the amount of masonry used in building the great Chinese wall.

One is therefore not disposed to wonder that this king (as we have already noticed) built his new palace on the other side of the river, over against Kadimerra, the old palace of the kings of Babylon, in the incredible space of fifteen days. Nebuchadrezzar at his best energy could annihilate time; and slaves, to whom the Egyptian captivity of the Jews would have been Elysian ease, wrought the marvels at which the world wonders.

The palaces, the pleasure-grounds, the bastions that formed the royal fastness, on the eastern bank of the river, were four miles in compass, and were protected by three frowning walls surrounded by deep moats. These fortifications formed the impregnable citadel of the city. Their outline took the shape of an oval. On the west, the Euphrates bent like a bow about it. At the north, a few hundred yards above the new palace, the Shebil canal drained the river, and carried its waters into a huge rectangular reservoir. This was also dug by the king, and called the Yapur Shapu, great basin. This body of water formed the eastern protection of the citadel. From the southern end of this reservoir, the Shebil canal flowed, turned, and again joined the river at the distance of a few thousand cubits. It was on the southern extremity of this reservoir, opposite the ancient royal palace, that the king had built his latest freak and most daring design. Here Amytis, embowered in moist trees and unwithered flowers, could defy the fearful heat under which the builders of the mound had dropped dead. From this towering height a breeze was possible. From all sides the water cooled the air, and the vast basin rippled below. From the side of the reservoir the garden rose to a perpendicular height of two hundred and fifty feet. Arches supported each tier on this side. Those in the Coliseum give some idea of the architecture. From the three other sides, the structure rose in five pyramidal stages, each fifty feet in height, and upborne by pillars of brick and stone over twenty feet in circumference. The second stage was supported on six hundred and twenty-five pillars, and the fifth on one hundred and sixty-nine. Imagine the grandeur of these ascents, when the total number of columns reached fifteen hundred and twenty-four, of the same height and circumference. Each of these platforms, as well as the top, was finished flat: first in reeds mixed with bitumen; over this a solid brick masonry; next covered by a coating of lead from across the desert; the whole surmounted by a layer of earth thick enough for the roots of the largest trees. A winding, decorated staircase led from within to the top. Fountains flashed everywhere. Groves grew, — who knew how? Seen from a distance, the forest seemed to have leaped into mid-air. Flowers ran over the mathematical accuracy of the design like freshets of color. Every plant known to Babylonia, or imported by her florists from Persia, Judea, Syria, or Media, was fostered here. While soldiers dropped of sunstroke and slaves died for water, these royal flowers were shaded and cherished day and night. Should a vine droop, chosen by Nebuchadrezzar to please a fickle queen, or a bud die that had been honored by the royal selection? A line of slaves carried the water, which they dared not taste, in skins, to freshen this dream of delight. Garden houses and exquisite apartments looked from between cool leaves. The sumptuous fancy, which was highly cultivated by the race and by the age, gave itself every possible trick to make the mountain garden agreeable to the mountain queen. What if the treasury were depleted? Let the people groan beneath the most capricious and exorbitant taxes of the civilized world. The queen must be happy. What if the slaves sank by the score? The queen must be cool.

It was now a lunar month since the omens had proved favorable, and the work had been undertaken. This day the stupendous fancy must be finished. Obedient to the decree and prompt to the hour, overseers were withdrawing their men, and squads here and there along the terrace were planting the last shrubs, or straightening the last full-grown tree, or giving an artistic and natural pose to some jagged boulder, wrenched from mountainous cliffs, and brought down the river for many a mile on huge rafts of inflated skins or pitched reeds.

The king was particularly morose and cross. Nothing went to suit him. Allit trembled lest the task should not be done. The captain was very uncomfortable this morning. He had hurried from the house of Mutusa-ili to the royal presence, more concerned with his private distress than with public affairs. No woman had

ever before delayed to drop into the arms of
the king's captain, if she had the opportunity.
Allit was confounded by Lalitha. He could
not explain her. Was it possible that she did
not love him? The captain could think of no
other reason for her extraordinary hesitation in
responding to his suit. What then? Had the
pious Jew allured her fancy? Yet Allit could
not cultivate anger with Daniel. Here was
the second mystery. The finer side of his nature revolted from a low jealousy of this high
soul. That seemed to Allit like making a spear-
thrust at a marble god. He had the military
temperament, with its accompanying sense of
honor. When he had said to Balatsu-usur, " I
am the officer of thy heart," the captain spoke
with prosaic seriousness. He had surrendered
to the Jew. He felt like a man on parole. How
could he seek a vulgar vengeance? That were
out of the question, for that were dishonor.

It was therefore with a cordial manner, though
with some constraint, that Allit went forth to
meet Balatsu-usur, who had followed him to the
hanging gardens by some half hour's delay.
Both young men looked pale and worn; but the
Jew had the air of a tired spirit; the Babylonian of a worried man.

" The king hath the temper of a demon this
morning," said Allit at once. " Thou must

make the news to him. I have no mind for the venture. He would have tossed two slaves from the topmost terrace of the garden, because the flower-bed thereon was not completed and trimmed to his mind; but I constrained him. Deal thou with Nebuchadrezzar touching what we have witnessed."

"Hast thou broken the matter to the queen?" asked Daniel briefly.

The captain shrugged his fine shoulders. "Does a man turn from the dove to the vampire?" he cried, in a tone of hot disgust so unmistakable that it was well for his curly head Amytis was two hundred paces above him, winding her way to the top of the gardens, through bloom, and blush, and scent, and height, and breeze, and moisture that wrought upon the senses and the fancy like a diviner's spell. Amytis was hard to please; but she was pleased. Nebuchadrezzar had wrought a miracle for his young and petulant queen, and it was agreeable to her. Some historians have held that he feared her fickleness, and would spare himself her infidelity; and the result was the mountain garden. At all events, Amytis was busy, and had for the time being no interest in her flirtations or her intrigues.

While the two young men stood apart together, a slave brought imperious summons to the captain of the guards, of whom the king had immediate need.

Daniel passed on at once, and up the winding stair. He overtook the queen upon the fourth tier of the garden. She was bathing in a perfumed brook that trickled the full length of the cool, green, alluring arcade. Mariamnu held her outer robe. Daniel started back. Amytis laughed, and beckoned him to approach. Mariamnu deftly threw the golden tissue over the brown, bare neck of the queen. The Jew obeyed the royal mandate sternly enough. He thought of that white girl —

" Why so grim a face, governor of Babylon ? " cried Amytis, with an imperious motion of her forefinger. " Have you no smile for your queen's gala day ? At the least, I supposed you had come to wish me joy of my mountain garden."

" And thus I have," returned Daniel politely enough. " Truly the king, thy lord, hath wrought a marvel in thy behalf " — Here the courtier stopped ; the dreamer in him seemed to float up like a mist, and drown his beautiful face ; his eyes closed ; his lips moved ; he stretched his hands out with a blind motion.

" *Between heaven and earth,*" murmured the seer, — " *a doom between heaven and earth* " —

" What say you ? " demanded the queen sharply. She stepped from the brook, and held out her small bare foot for Mariamnu to dry with silken towels. She was absorbed in the brook and the bath. She was not paying much attention to the Jew. His evident distress and embarrassment scarcely appealed to her. He had thus time to recover himself from his short trance, and to realize his position, before harm came of it.

" Your pardon, my queen," said the governor of Babylon contritely. " I am not well. I stumble in my words. I have watched all night, and for that came I to have speech with you. Mutusa-ili, the master, lieth dead in his house."

" Ah ! " said Amytis, putting her wet foot down hard, and crushing a cluster of red Judean lilies. " So the old man is dead, is he ? And the daughter ? "

" God hath preserved her out of the snare of the fowler," said the Jew gravely. " She weepeth beside her dead in her father's house."

" She escaped from the harem," observed Amytis, without raising her narrow eyes. " The king will be in a rage. He is so cross, lately, one cannot abide him."

Now the king had forgotten Lalitha in an hour, as Amytis knew, and Daniel suspected.

" If the maiden hath no foe more dangerous than Nebuchadrezzar, she will fare well," observed Daniel, in a lower tone. " Nor is it my

intention that she shall.   By the will of Mutusa-
ili I am become the guardian of the maiden and
of her property."

"Is it possible?" interrupted the queen, in
unqueenly curiosity.   "Has she property?"

"I protect it," replied Daniel firmly; "and I
protect her.   Thus runneth the law of Babylon,
which I both serve and represent."

The queen made a petulant gesture.   She was
too happy that morning to fly into a fury; but
still she was ill pleased.   She flung the tissue
higher over one shoulder, and lower on the
other; moving her long neck from side to side
impatiently.

"Come yonder, Mariamnu.   Let us away
from this glum fellow.   I am tired of the matter, sir!   Everywhere, it is that girl — that girl
— that girl!   And now *you*." . . .

Amytis glided away in the shrubbery like a
beautiful snake.   She seemed to hiss a little as
she moved.   Yet she admired the governor of
Babylon immensely.

The Jew went up to the topmost tier of the
mountain garden, alone, and anxiously.   He
dreaded to break the news to the king, whose
irritability was of late becoming dangerous to
his lower subjects, and serious to the higher.
But it was necessary to make some arrangements for the public funeral of Mutusa-ili.

CHAPTER XVII.

Surgery was not an accomplished science at the court of Babylon; and even the king, who scorned the baser superstitions of his subjects, was impatient over the mummeries performed upon his lacerated leg.

"The star Marbuda hath passed into an eclipse," said one enterprising and comforting physician, "and the son of Marduk is involved in the tempest of the elements. Surely thou art joyful that thy grievous wound doth balance the portents of the heavens?"

"Not a bit of it!" roared the king, with a grimace of pain. "Out with this false astrologer into the ditch beyond the wall!"

"Let the sacred python be twined around his majestic leg, and the evil spirit will slink away," suggested another rash practitioner, after an uncomfortable diagnosis. But the sacred snake exhibited an unheard-of friskiness of temper united with marked disinclination to twine; so the unlucky prescriber was forced to spend several days soothing (if he could) the sacred reptile.

Every spirit in heaven and earth was implored to ward off the attack of the seven evil spirits from the stricken monarch,

> " Seven are they, seven are they.
> In the abyss of the deep, seven are they.
> Disturbers of thy peace are they.
> Evil are they, baleful are they."

Thus chanted magicians in vain exorcisms, burning Arabian spices and muttering strange incantations to appease the torments of the king. Amulets were of no avail, for the wound gaped, and would not heal.

But worse was the wound upon the mind of the royal patient. Nebuchadrezzar owed his life to a power which was represented by an unfathomable quantity, the governor of Babylon. And what a life it had become! Nebuchadrezzar was an ardent devotee to the gods of his peculiar choice. As the shepherd of his people, he had made himself the religious primate and example of the land. He had manufactured gods of every description, and worshiped them promiscuously. But it had occurred to him that jealousy might be aroused among the divinities if he coquetted with too many at the same time. Therefore, advising his subjects to do the same, he gradually confined most of his attention to the pet deities of the city of his restoration. Who worshiped Bel-Merodach and Nebo more devoutly than the king? Who was more loyal to the traditions of his country than he? His father had recreated the ancient kingdom of Babylon; and he had consolidated it, and extended it by the power of one policy, — the ecclesiastical. He united the nation by humoring its whole intricate system of worship. Did statesmanship or a religious conscience govern his life? Now the king was not dull, and he had noticed that whenever he had invaded Judea, and had deported thousands of captives to Babylon, he had encountered an invisible power which force of arms could not subdue.

Captives from Carchemish or from far Cilicia might accept the deities of the bewitching and luxurious capital; but the Jews, as a race, demanded and maintained the worship of a God who shamed the voluptuous votaries of Ishtar, and mocked the curling frankincense of the Ziggurat of Bel. The one God Jehovah, whom the king, with his usual spirit of liberality, at first patronized, and then tolerated, had become the object of his personal respect. What was at first an incident in politics was now a controlling factor that demanded recognition. More than once he had come up against this Jewish Jehovah, as if a man dashed against the wall of Imgur-Bel; each time his pride received a wound.

There was that dream which mocked his memory till it maddened him. Then it mocked the priests whose temples he had built. It ruined his chief soothsayer, the president of his university. What magic had the fates evoked, when Daniel read like a scroll what the king's mind had clean lost? What sorcery saved the priests, and compelled the monarch to humble himself before the slave?

These thoughts preyed upon the king, until he grew unbearable to gods and men. At moments, his brain became clotted with revenge against a force which he could neither comprehend nor classify, but only bitterly admire. Daniel had inflicted a blow upon Nebuchadrezzar's ecclesiastical pride which the building of a thousand temples could not efface. Time and again, the despot would have given his captain the order to strangle the governor of Babylonia, but he dared not arouse the only divinity that had ever awed him.

But this, though enough, was not all that ailed the king. Not only Merodach, but Nergal, had forsaken him. For the first time in his life he had missed his aim at the hunt, and the victim had become the victor. Was that accursed lion sent by Balatsu-usur's god? If so, to what political end? Nebuchadrezzar's vaunted prowess had become the sport of the whole province.

His sacred life had been at the mercy of a beast — and a Jew. The disgrace haunted him, and unnerved him. He was, in short, a sick man. Was poison from the lion's claws stealing into his vitals? Unconsciously, his head swayed monotonously, like a wild beast's in captivity.

His natural moodiness became chronic moroseness. He sought solitude, and yet thirsted for society. His personal cruelties multiplied; his subjects lived in terror and perplexity. His officers held aloof from him. His women shrank from him. His queen grew cold to him. Only Daniel and Allit remained in faithful, voluntary attendance upon him. Threats of their young lives flew over their heads fifty times a day; but the governor and the captain served him with a persevering and courageous quiet which the sick monarch respected, as madness always respects serene·courage, and feebleness strength.

The condition of the king had, unfortunately, been emphasized by the events which followed the death of Mutusa-ili. The circumstances of the sage's death and burial had created an unlucky complication. Babylon rocked with excitement when it was made known that the chief diviner of the province, the most distinguished of living Chaldean soothsayers, had died abjuring the art which had made him famous, and the religion of the land which had educated and honored him. Mutusa-ili had not lain four hours dead, before every intelligent man in the city knew that the master of her great university had acknowledged the faith of the captive race; willing his family forever to the faith of the Jew, and his eminent name to the worship of Jehovah, — an uncultivated god, favored by a poor lot, who amounted to so little that they could have but one.

With the fickleness and forgetfulness usual to the people of a restless nation, Mutusa-ili's recent downfall at court seemed to slip out of mind. No one said, "He failed to interpret the king's dream. We disgraced him and deserted him;" but only, "This was a great man. He was an honor to Babylon. He was a Chaldee of the Chaldeans." Half of Babylon stopped there, and waived his religious abjuration as the fantasy of a stricken, old, unhappy, dying man; these called for a great public funeral. The other half cried out upon them and upon him. The seer had apostatized. The royal favorite had descended to the captive creed. Dishonor to his memory, and to every Babylonian who honored it!

In the university of Bel the excitement culminated. The students, headed by Susa, were in a ferment. A riot in the classes threatened to become a rebellion. The boys demanded the ashes of their great master, and would take no less. An imposing ceremony, an incineration in the court of the university, a tremendous occasion, — nothing else was to be thought of.

Susa, followed by his committee of arrangements, marched boldly to the palace, and requested as much of the king. Now this young gentleman, since his last unlucky appearance in public life, had remained in an obscurity which he felt to be unnatural to his career. A dull life, led at one's scrolls, and over one's dusty tablets of science, philology, and religion; tyrannized by masters, and never once summoned to court, — this had lasted long enough.

A brother in authority had his disadvantages as well as his uses. Allit had of late confined Susa so strictly to the unimportant sphere of the university that this young person did not feel called upon to take the captain of the guards into his confidence in the matter of the master's funeral. He explained to the boys that this was unnecessary; he himself being a favorite of the king, and quite competent to attend to the business.

Now, in truth, this was so nearly the fact of the situation that Susa met with a better chance than he deserved. He did, indeed, make his way, with his confident air, to the presence of the sullen king; to whom he presented the petition of the students with a bright assurance that would have cost him his curling head, if it had not gained him his case.

The king's frown blurred into the first smile seen upon his haggard face for many a dark day.

"Thou art young," he said, "and demandest of the king as the young lion roareth for its food. . . . Thine eye is bright, and wandereth to and fro. Thou hast not care. Thou knowest not sorrow. Thou fearest naught. Nebuchadrezzar doth not affright thee. . . . Would that I were young!"

"Our master was old, and we honor age," said Susa, with the adroitness of extreme candor. "Give us our way in behalf of our dead. I told the boys," added Susa, "that the king was always kind to me. They would think I lied if we could not have the funeral."

The king looked with emotion deeper than the case called for, upon the lad. He repeated the word, "Kind? Kind!" He could not remember when any one had called Nebuchadrezzar kind. He rose suddenly, to conceal the signs of tremulousness upon his face.

"Bury thy master as thou wilt," he said. "It shall not be said that Nebuchadrezzar faileth to honor his dead seer, or the petition of his high-born students. Go from me, and see thou to it."

Thus it befell that the sage received the last courtesy from the university over which he had presided. The body of Mutusa-ili was burned to ashes in the court of the schools, with all the mortuary pomp of the times. It had been embalmed in honey, as the custom went, and laid in the earthen jar, preparatory to its last dreary journey, a hundred miles through the hot country to Erech, the common cemetery of Babylon. The remains were detained by order of the king. A public funeral of the largest proportions resulted. The thousand priests who had failed to tell the dream came from their thousand altars to do honor to that other failure, their dead chief. The priest from Borsippa said, "After all, he was but one of us," and the successor of the priest from Zarpanit shook his head, and asked, "Can you tell me the genealogy of this Jehovah, to whom our late brother apostatized?"

At that moment, Ina, the daughter of Egibi the banker, was saying to her father, "He must be a *very common* god." For Egibi was at the funeral. All the world was at the funeral. Court and people, throne and university, did honor to the dead sage. The hired mourners lost their usual importance. Egibi's large face was of a dull pallor. But he did not arise before the people, and join the wailing friends.

The treasurer of Babylon did not say, " I am his brother." Lalitha and Kisriuni wept apart together — a forlorn little family to lament a man — until the governor of Babylon, being by law the guardian of the girl, stepped out with torn garments and placed himself, as a mourner, at her side.

So Mutusa-ili came to his last rest in the university which he had cherished with the passionate devotion of a scholarly and unworldly man. While the body, swathed in honey and spices and sacred oils, was burning, the students chanted in an ancient tongue an unfamiliar dirge. When the urn which received the ashes was lifted upon the bier, to be taken before the altar in the temple of Bel, and thence borne back to the library of the university, where it should be honored for time and times and a day, Susa's clear young voice rose above the chorus of the students : —

> Unto his rest,
> Hands on his breast,
> Bear him apart.
> Flame hath his heart,
> The worm and the rust
> Touch not his dust.
> We hold his name ;
> Earth hath his fame.

It was at the moment when the chorus repeated, —

> Keep we his name ;
> Give earth his fame !

and the boys had bent to the bier to carry it within the courts of the temple for the final ceremonial, that the interruption came which convulsed Babylon, and would have turned the burial into a riot, had it come from any other source than the governor of the province. For Daniel did no less nor more than step forward, and authoritatively forbid the students to carry the body into the temple of Bel.

"These ashes go not within the idolatrous gates of Bit Sagila, the Ziggurat of Merodach," he said. "Bury the Jew Methuselah in the faith of Jehovah, the living God."

The effect of this interference was intense. The crowd swayed and murmured. The thousand priests muttered together. The students protested in decorous undertones. The seven colored stages of the insulted temple seemed to glitter malignantly, then to frown and reel a little. By virtue of the law and for decency's sake, the will of the dead man's executor was, perforce, respected. The burial procession turned about, and reluctantly deposited the urn in the library of the university, without the sanction of Bel-Merodach. It was a tremendous event.

The students, with the superior tolerance of education, made the best of it, but the people made the worst. Before night, the city was in an uproar, — these defending, those berating, the whole affair. The interment, the governor, the king, the dead man, all came in for their share of popular blame or approval. Mutusa-ili, who of all people had loved and required peace, became in death the cause of a popular disturbance which would have sorely troubled his quiet spirit. The excitement subsided too slowly, too fiercely. Nothing could have happened which would have presented such tests to the unassailable position of the captive governor in Babylon. But the sick king was worried by the matter, and brooded over it to his own hurt.

It was not until the afternoon of the next day that the governor and the captain found leisure to discuss the events which were shaking the city. They met in the pleasure-grounds of the king's outer garden — the garden bounded by the Shebil canal. The sun had passed far into its third quarter; the shadows were long; the air stirred with the ghost of a breath; it was not yet night.

Allit was much moved by the interment of Mutusa-ili; he had been allowed to pass some moments with Lalitha that morning; he experienced the new, sweet sensation of grieving in the grief of her in whose life he wished to live. He felt a filial tenderness toward the dead man

which astonished the soldier. But this delicate
sympathy was all he dared offer to Lalitha then.
It was not an hour for love-making. The girl
looked at him through a wall of glass. It was
the wall of sorrow. The lover could not pass it,
and must not shatter it. He had to content
himself with tears when he perished for kisses.
Allit had never been denied joy before, by the
pain of life. It seemed to him very unnatural.
He was quite puzzled. Like other men of his
sort, he turned readily from the private perplexity to public affairs. These, at least, were comprehensible. Conversation diverted his discomfort, — he was not accustomed to being uncomfortable.

He watched the Jew with an obviously new
expression, in which respect for executive ability
was added to spiritual deference.

"Verily, thou art the master," he said heartily; "there is no magician in Babylon who could
do thy deed. Thou defiedst the religion of the
nation as if thou gavedst an order to a guardsman.
I looked for a riot; nay, a revolution would
not astonish me. Behold, the people growl
at thee like little dogs; but they kiss the hand
and obey thee. Bel-Merodach hath received an
insult from thee; but thy head is as firm upon
thy shoulders as the Ziggurat upon its base.
Thou art not like other men!"

" My God is not like other gods," replied Daniel quietly. " That is the explanation of the matter."

" Do all the worshipers of thy god deeds like thine?" inquired the Babylonian shrewdly. " I have known many a Jew. I know but one Balatsu-usur."

Daniel was silent. The two men paced the length of the path, — they were at the open end, known as the "green end," of the gardens, where the grass was most abundant, — and returned again to their starting-point, before the careless and boisterous soldier put to the saintly politician the abrupt question, —

" Where, O prince of Israel, did Mutusa-ili go ? "

" To the bosom of Abraham," replied Daniel promptly.

This answer seemed to give but vague theological light to the Babylonian, who knitted his bronze brows like a boy in the university over his first translation. " Tell me," he insisted, " is there one place for a dead Babylonian, and another for a dead Jew? Where will *thy* breath [1] go, — to the west [2] or to the east ? "

" As there is but one God, who createth and governeth all things, so is there but one Heaven and one Sheol," answered Daniel readily, after

[1] Soul.   [2] The Babylonian Hades lay in the west.

the manner of the law of his people. "Whosoever forsaketh idolatry and worshipeth the living God shall abide with Him in the latter day; but whither he who cleaveth to his sins shall go, whether to the west or to the east, none knoweth but the iniquitous dead, nor shall know until the end of the world. The will of Jehovah shall be done."

"From all accounts, I feel an interest in this Jehovah," admitted the captain. "He seems to me to be a well-meaning god. I think, myself, a god shows to better advantage, not to go hunting, or to meddle with wine and women. I have no objection to Jehovah. Teach thou me more of his worship. I understand it not, but I find it very respectable."

Allit was thinking of Lalitha, though he did not say so. By the will of her father, Lalitha was now an acknowledged Jewess; and must remain so.

The Jewish seer looked at the idolater helplessly. He had the tact not to say how impossible he felt it to explain Almighty God to a Babylonian soldier. He proceeded to skirt the outlines of the subject with the aptness of his race for religious polemics. The Jews were the greatest theologians of the world.

"We are the children of Adam," began Daniel, "who was created of God in Eden "—

" Ah, yes," interrupted Allit, " I know that story. It is very like our own. There are books in our library whose antiquity no man knoweth. Susa showed me one last week, — the lad is better educated than I ; I was put to the horse too early to study. But it is known, even to men no more cultivated than I, that our Lady Tiamat brought forth the first deep, when the clouds were not, and in the earth was no seed ; then had none of the gods come forth. Is thy scroll more ancient than ours ? "

Allit struck the hilt of his sword with the palm of his left hand, repeatedly, as if he had made a great point.

" Go on," said the Jew composedly.

" We had a flood," continued Allit, " in our religion. It was a mighty flood. It overspread the world. Xisuthros was saved by Bel, and his house with him, upon the mountain of Nizir. Even upon the mountain of Nizir was Xisuthros snatched from the deep, and his seed after him. I have been told that thy religion relateth a similar freshet. Now how can there be two freshets of this kind ?   Tell me, learned Jew."

" Say on," said Daniel quietly.

" Our Lady Tiamat," proceeded Allit, " hath been called in some of our tablets the ' Great Serpent.' She was a most remarkable goddess. Merodach, the brilliant god, did battle against her. She, it is well known, was the temptress of mankind. She sat behind the Tree of Life. On one side of her was the man. The woman stood upon the other. Thus were the man and the woman tempted, in the beginning of time. Every Babylonian knoweth as much as this. Yet I understand that the worshiper of Jehovah worshipeth a tree, a man and a woman, and the serpent, who did tempt both the woman and the man."

"What else?" asked Daniel.

"I understand not how these things can be," urged the captain. "There are many other difficulties, but I am not a scholar. These are all I can think of at this moment. What makest thou of them, Balatsu-usur?"

"I make the will of God of them," replied the Jew, without embarrassment, "and the will of God no man may understand."

"Perhaps not," said Allit, with a troubled air. "But I play not with the matter. I desire to understand. Is intelligent man a foolish fellow, that Jehovah should not respect his intellect? Is thy scroll more ancient than our scroll? I have been taught that our religion was before the first Jew was born into the world."

"If thou art indeed of an earnest mind toward these matters," said Daniel more gravely, "then will the living God meet thee earnestly.

Religion is the most difficult study of all the world, O favorite of Nebuchadrezzar. It is not to be struck at, as thou fleckest the horse with thy whip. Know thou this, and respect the knowledge: In the childhood of the world did Jehovah reveal precious truths to many men. These have the wanderings of men scattered, and their sins corrupted. The living God did breathe into the clay, and the first man was begotten of the spirit. Pass me thine amulet; nay, do not blush. I know that thou wearest the spell against thy heart, beneath thy breast-plate. Behold the tree. It is the Tree of Life. Behold the woman. She is the Eve of the Jew. Behold the man, for he is our Adam. Look upon the serpent. Thou callest her Lady Tiamat. We call her the Devil, for God hath named her."

"I begin to see," said Allit, brightening a little over the theological dilemma. "You call the Lady Tiamat the Devil. Then there is our Xisuthros. You call him " —

" Noah," interrupted the Jew.

" And we have the mountain Nizir. You call it " —

" Ararat," said Daniel promptly. " It *is* Ararat," he added, with perfect assurance.

Allit looked puzzled. " Perhaps so," he sighed.

" Know thou," proceeded Daniel in a different

tone, " that the living God gave truth to man, and man corrupted the truth. Unto many nations are many marvels given and many words related. Even as the relating of a tale goeth, captain of the guards, within the battalion, many mouths make many versions thereof. But the tale is the same tale."

" There is some sense in that," observed Allit.

" Jehovah is the living God," urged the Jew. " He is but one, and the nations have dealt with him even as they have with the writings of his people. The living God is cut apart among many men, even as these tales are distributed and cut to pieces.

" I deny not, nay, I urge, that it be remembered that our father Abraham came out of Chaldea, in the times before the times. I am an instructed man, learned in the lore of Chaldea, as I am in the law of my people, and know I not that it was given to our father Abraham to know the religion of Chaldea? Yea, verily. But it was given unto him to know the will of the living God, that he should discern between the false religion and the true. Thy people have *lost* Jehovah Our people have *kept* Him. The idolater knoweth not the truth when he seeth it, but the Jew hath what he did choose, for God is with him." Daniel paused, but proceeded impressively : " There is but *one* God.

He existeth. He remaineth. And He dwelleth in the judgments of men. Worship thou *Him.* He is holy. Be *thou* holy. He is pure. Purify thyself, son of Babylon, that thou mayst become fit for the service of Jehovah. For He is a jealous God, and he scorneth the worship of an evil heart."

" If the maiden will look upon me," interrupted Allit ingenuously, " it is my purpose to wed her."

Daniel smiled gravely at this practical application of his theology. It might be worse, indeed! Perhaps his proselyte was as promising as the circumstances permitted. He had opened his lips to reply to the Babylonian, when Allit touched him on the arm, and pointed across the garden. The king was coming toward them, and was unattended.

Daniel was a little sorry that their conversation was interrupted. He had much that he would have said, — more, perhaps, than the attention of the soldier would have borne. The Jew wished to explain plainly to the idolater that the writings of the chosen people were preserved with more ecclesiastical fidelity than those of any other nation known to history ; that his had been the devout people of history, and had therefore saved the correct records with supreme success. He wished to make the captain understand something of the superior morality, the enthusiastic piety, and the sacred patriotism which had wrought out of the Jewish heart the finest proof of monotheism possible to that age of the world.   He wished to say . . . But the king was coming.

CHAPTER XVIII.

Nebuchadrezzar approached slowly. He moved with his head bent and body bowed a little forward. He walked with difficulty, limping perceptibly. His brow was dark. He opened and closed his lips, and moistened them like a child or an animal. As he came near, it could be seen that he muttered. He did not raise his eyes.

The two officers awaited the king with an evident discomfort. The civilian was the more at ease. Neither spoke until the king had well-nigh stumbled over them. It was not etiquette to turn the face from royalty ; and the governor and the captain were already backed up against the wall of the pleasure-ground as close as they could get. When Nebuchadrezzar was within a few inches of them, Daniel begged his pardon in a firm voice, but must needs call his attention to the presence of his servants. The king started, and stared upon his favorites. He had a lowering look. His muttering ceased ; but no articulate words succeeded it. A slight wheezing sound came from his throat. He seemed to make an effort to smile, but to have lost the power to do so. His lips moved grotesquely. The upper one turned back above the teeth. He watched the two men narrowly. He had a suspicious and alarmed air.

"My lord the king hath an illness upon him," ventured the captain sympathetically. "Suffer thy servant to lead thee within the palace, or to summon the physicians to thy relief."

The king turned slowly upon his heel, and limped away. As he walked, his hands hung down straight in front of him. This, with the increased bowing of his body, gave him an unpleasant appearance. His figure swayed from side to side; it looked like that of a young animal learning to walk, or of a man who had forgotten how. The two officers followed him at a respectful and perplexed distance. The path down which the three were moving was a narrow one, and edged with broad spaces, upon which the artificially cultivated and irrigated grass of the royal garden grew richly.

Grass was a treasure fit for a king in Babylon. It had been one of the whims of Nebuchadrezzar that his private garden should make the most of it. Give Amytis her mountain, her trees, her brooks, her blossoms, and her out-of-door boudoirs, but to the king a severer style of landscape gardening. He had constructed plain and serious expanses touched with moss and imported rock; he liked wild flowers and tangles of shrubbery, and little mock fields of grain. The corner of the garden on which the king was walking was popularly known as " the pasture." The narrow path of which we have spoken shrank to a foothold; then sank into short, thick grass, beaten only by the royal tread. A space of some nine hundred feet square — it has been estimated, indeed, at twice that — spread unbroken beyond, bounded by the fortified walls on three sides, sloping into a hedge of young forest trees upon the fourth. This hedge was solidly protected behind the shrubbery with an invisible grating of iron and of brass; it was impossible to cross it, unless one were a superior climber, and willing to drop into the canal below, for the sake of the venture. Upon this field the grass grew abundantly. It was irrigated six times a day. One or two fawns, and a lamb favored by the king in a gentle moment, cropped the grass sparingly, pains being taken that they should be too well fed to spoil it; they were there only for the pastoral effect.

Nebuchadrezzar walked down the pasture path tottering. His officers followed him, stricken with inexplicable alarm.

" It is a sick man," whispered Allit. " He must be taken care of. I try again, if so be, I may withstand him."

He pushed by Daniel, and lightly touched the robe of the king; as he did this, he raised his voice, and distinctly, respectfully, begged the sovereign to make known to him the nature of his physical distress.

"I would relieve thee," urged Allit with real fondness. "I would not witness the suffering of my king."

Nebuchadrezzar turned and looked upon his captain. The young man saw that look in his dreams for many a year to come; for the like of it he never witnessed before or after; nor is it often given to any man to do as much. Physicians attending one of the most violent of incurable diseases sometimes meet with an appearance akin to it, but as much less terrible than this as mockery is less than reality. Nebuchadrezzar's eyes narrowed. His upper lip curled again from off his long teeth. He made a darting motion toward the captain with one of his hanging hands. He did not speak, but he did worse. He set his teeth, and snarled upon Allit like a beast.

"It is a madman!" whispered Daniel. "Go thou. Go quickly. Call the queen unto him. I remain. I fear him not. Get thou the queen hither, and delay not, for his life — or ours!"

Allit saluted and departed. The royal maniac and the intrepid Jew remained together.

No person was in sight. Not a guard was within hearing. Daniel realized the peril of his position imperfectly, perhaps; but duty always seemed to him the safest thing to do. He stepped forward quietly, and took the arm of the king. Nebuchadrezzar did not resent this familiarity, but appeared the rather to be calmed by it. The two paced together for a few turns up and down the green path, and over the grass of the mimic field. The lamb was quietly nibbling at a little distance ; the fawns started, ran into the shrubbery, and peeped out with the pretty coyness of half-tame creatures. The king watched them wistfully.

"So cool," he muttered, "and so gentle. *They* have not black thoughts. Their hearts are soft. They go not bowed with cares of state. Religion teaseth them not. Pleasant things! Call me hither the one that eats. I like the one that eats ; for his food is gentle ; peace must be in his blood."

The Jew gave no answer. He had made a dreadful discovery. Alone there, with the maniac, unprotected and unprotecting, he experienced the sudden vertigo which preceded his own strange physical conditions. His trance, call it what we will, whether of divine interference or of human disability, whether prophetic or hypnotic, — his trance was coming upon him. He made a mighty effort to wrestle with it; but it closed about him solemnly. He was conscious that the king drew back and regarded him with displeasure; that the maniac's voice broke into a storm of wild words; that he glorified himself, Babylonia, the city, the province, the throne, the temples of the idols, the triumphs of war and religion; that he deified himself blasphemously. Then strange power overshadowed the Jew, and strange words fell in his own despite from his quivering lips. Whence came they? Who sent them? For his own will gave them not.

"Thou, Nebuchadrezzar, king of Babylon, to thee it is spoken: the kingdom is departed from thee. And thou shalt be driven from men, and thy dwelling shall be with the beasts of the field; thou shalt be made to eat grass as oxen, and seven times shall pass over thee; until thou know that the Most High ruleth in the kingdom of men, and giveth it to whomsoever he will."

As the seer uttered these words, the king gave a piercing cry. His tall form shrank together. He sank to the ground, as if the hand of God or man had smitten him, and lay there groveling.

Daniel, who came as suddenly out of his abnormal conditions as into them, called loudly for help, and stooped to raise the king to his feet.

But Nebuchadrezzar resisted the effort with a savage growl. To his horror, the Jew saw his sovereign drop upon his hands and knees, and crawl out into the field.

When Amytis and Allit came to the spot, the king of Babylon was huddled beside the lamb; he was breaking the short grass with his teeth, as the animal did. The lamb observed him with pleasure. The fawns came out of their hiding-places and approached him. Amytis gave one glance at the hideous sight; then fled, shrieking.

There is a disease but imperfectly understood even by the medical science of our own day, and unnamed by the crude skill of that remote age. It is one of the most terrible known to pathology. The physician who has met with one case of it is fain to pray, " whatever gods there be," that his first may be his last. It imposes peculiar and dreadful strain upon the healer. The sympathy is tortured by it. The nurse sickens of it. Friends fail before it. The dearest and nearest of soul to the patient find it almost impossible to separate the suffering from the sufferer. The husband loathes the wife. The mother shrinks from her child. The father becomes horrible to the son. Even the brave heart of a truly tender woman falters before this trial, and the bride, who would have died of torture for her lord, pronounces life worse than death because of him. She extends with repulsion the barest necessities of humanity, where once she flung her being away in the rapture of womanly service. Love endureth all things. We know that it may even intensify under almost every form of human misery, self-denial, and bodily disillusion. Before this disease — shall we say that it must be doomed? According not only to its nature, but to its experience, let love reply.

Lycanthropy is a form of madness — whether of the blood or of the brain, or both, let wiser than these narrators of an ancient love-tale testify — wherein the patient believes himself to have become an animal. This belief gradually grows from hallucination to a fixed consciousness. The periodic mood becomes the permanent conviction. The victim, who at first put his delusion on and off, now wears it as a body wears a coffin. The sweetest, the dearest quality goes out before this hideous fate. The purest instinct, the most delicate habit, the most tender emotion of the spirit, is crushed by the inevitable march of the disease. The animal nature sets itself upon the human nature, like the teeth of a beast in flesh, and wrestles therewith till humanity is overcome. Too slowly for the palliation of the victim's torment, the low life kills the high. The last fine impulses of a godlike race yield hard. The man fights, he knows not why, before he becomes a brute. His struggle is piteous to witness. His defeat is worse, because it makes of him a thing which murders pity. Recovery is possible, but it is rare. Healing may exist, but it is without science and without hope. This disease differs from the more familiar form of rabies, in which the virus of animal anger, being introduced into healthy blood, causes violent and fatal conditions. In the worse fate of lycanthropy, the miserable man may not hope for death. Life holds him under her claws. In a state worse than that of the brute whose fate he assumes rather than simulates, he endures his doom until its laggard end.

Upon Nebuchadrezzar, the great king of the greatest nation in the world, this horrible lot had fallen. The royal autocrat had become the bestial maniac. Smitten of God by the cruelest of human diseases, he went out from the natural conditions of human life. All that was wholesome, sweet, and holy in character succumbed to the brute nature that had been — shall we say, evolved from, or superimposed upon, the royal one? His desolate fate obeyed its own law. Whence did it come? Did tooth or claw do the deadly mischief? Did the spirit of the wild beast demand this price for his defeat and his life? Or did the wound, working on a sickened soul, shock some sensitive ganglion, blur the brain, and blot the man? Who shall say?

In the kingdom of Babylonia, the affliction of the king was regarded with ignorant, almost brutal horror. He was the condemned of heaven. He was the sport of the gods. The deity of the Jew had been offended with him. Jehovah had spoken unto him; he had cursed him with audible curses. Nebuchadrezzar was his victim and plaything. The country was threatened. The throne was vacant. The people shook. It was impossible to keep the hideous secret. The fable of a fever having befallen the king, which pacified the popular curiosity for a week or two, soon gave place to a glimmer, then to the knowledge, of the truth. Their king, overcome by a fate too horrible to discuss, was driven from the daily life of men. In an incredibly short time, every soul in Babylon knew that Nebuchadrezzar was closely guarded and confined in " the pasture " of the royal gardens; where he lived, protected, loathed, and dreaded, like the brute he had become.

In spite of his tyrannies and cruelties, Nebuchadrezzar was admired by his people; in a sense, he was even beloved. Above all sovereigns who ever filled the throne of Babylonia, he fed the pride of the province; between pride and a certain sort of affection, the line is too vague for most men to define. His misfortune was a profound grief to the nation. All little matters were forgotten in the great public calamity. Private gossip became too unimportant to cultivate. The death and apostasy of the distinguished soothsayer, the fate of his family, even the slight displeasure with the governor himself, which had muttered upon the lips of the people, gave way to the emergency.

The nation was very uncomfortable. Not the least of the catastrophe was the fact that the king's disability threw the regency into the hands of the Median queen. There was one son; but he was a lad still in the hands of his tutors, not yet available as a sovereign. His mother had never cared for the child, and any attempt at that time to make use of him as a royal figurehead would have resulted, probably, in civil war. Not a soul in the kingdom loved Amytis; few trusted her; all feared her. In their calamity, the heart of the people turned by instinct to one man. Before the king's affliction was a week old, Balatsu-usur was visited by a deputation of Babylonian princes, with the formal request that he use his authority, as governor of the province, in sacred trust to steer the people through their emergency, to the full extent of the law. Egibi, the banker and treasurer of the kingdom, headed the deputation.

"We do in particular feel the need of some trustworthy intelligence which shall have a desirable influence upon — the regent," observed the state treasurer, with a significant glance. "It has occurred to us that thou art the man."

"Ah, yes," echoed the deputation, "thou art the man."

The Jew accepted the trust, as he did all other political honors, with a serenity which had almost the aspect of indifference. But, in his effort to fulfill it with the simple loyalty of good morals and good sense, he was, of course, exceptionally overborne with care. In his occupation with public affairs, his private interests necessarily yielded a little. At the house of Lalitha, her guardian became perforce, for the time being, a less frequent visitor.

Daniel had made every arrangement for the safety and decorum of the girl's manner of life. Desiring another inmate of her family beside the fond but feeble slave woman, he had made some especial effort to purchase Mariamnu, the favorite of the queen, that she might become companion or maid to Lalitha. But Mariamnu had too good a soprano to be spared from court. Amytis would not listen to it. At the time of which we speak, Lalitha was still living alone with Kisrinni in her father's house; her guardian had not as yet found the right third person to instate there, and he would run no risk with the wrong. He himself visited the house as often as he could; but continual oversight of the girl became temporarily impossible. Lalitha received him dutifully, and dreamed of him enthusiastically. But she found it possible to live — even to grieve and to take comfort — without him. The captain of the guards did not fail to perceive, and was not slow to take advantage of, this fact. In proportion as the holy man became less necessary, the human lover made himself more so, to the unobservant girl. Lalitha did not reflect; she felt. She did not argue with fate; she received it. Daniel was adorable, but Allit adored. The governor was busy; the captain was there. Allit had never undertaken an expedition as seriously or as shrewdly as he organized his wooing. Love developed tact in the soldier, as well as refinement. He pursued Lalitha without frightening her. He taught her to confide in him; she began to need him. It did indeed occur to Allit that the overworked governor trusted him; but it did not once occur to him that Daniel did so as much of deliberate purpose as of necessity. The only important stipulation which the guardian of the girl had made, in regulating the little affairs of her life, required that she receive no visitor without the presence of Kisrinni. He made no exception of the captain in the enforcement of this rule.

"I may not talk with thee — by ourselves," said Lalitha prettily; "my lord Balatsu-usur forbids me."

"Art thou sorry for that?" asked Allit, in a low voice. Lalitha dropped her eyes.

"It is in thy power to deal with me always — by ourselves," urged the captain.

"What aileth thee? Why what aileth thee?" he cried. For Lalitha's delicate frame trembled so that it was as much as the man of many battles could do to command his own great feeling. It moved upon him like an army. Oh, to snatch her to his heart and hold her there, until for very helpless joy she ceased to fear the power she loved!

"I will revere thy faith," whispered Allit tempestuously. "The will of Mutusa-ili will I respect."

"I may not wed to abandon the faith of my ancestors," pleaded Lalitha; "my father hath said it. That makes it quite impossible, as thou seest, for thee — for me — for us — we may not — thou must not" —

"We may, and I must!" insisted Allit, with his military air. He drew himself to his full, great height. Lalitha looked up at him shyly.

It seemed as if she would efface herself in her own sweet fear.   It would have been hard to say which of them was more enraptured.

" I will follow thy gods," said the captain gravely, " if *that* be all."

Now it was impossible for a Babylonian to concede more than this to a Jew, or a man to a woman.   Lalitha blushed divinely.   She tried to whisper a few words.   He bent to understand them.   She said, —

" I will mention the matter — to my guardian."

CHAPTER XIX.

Night was coming on quickly; a dark one for Babylon. For three or four days the khamsin had blown balefully. This is the wind known as the fiery sirocco, called in some parts of Assyria the sherghis, — a dreaded and deadly wind. It came from the south, and came viciously enough, laden with particles of scorching sand, that burnt the flesh, and smothered the breath, and blinded the eyes. Travelers in the open country fell beneath it, from sheer exhaustion. Animals panted and dropped. Vegetation withered. The citizens of the towns shrank within their doors; he who had a home made the most of it. Slaves, forced to continue the daily routine, died at their tasks. The hot sand drove through the hotter air in such masses as to obscure the light of midday. It was expected to be a very dark night.

Lalitha came to her door to see how dark it was growing. She was tired of the house. Everybody was. Neither she nor the slave woman had put foot in the street for four days. Kisrinni complained that they were out of barley, and she must needs go forth to renew their supply from the market, which opened in the evening on the Street of the Tamarisks.

When Lalitha came to the portico to examine the weather, she found that the khamsin was subsiding.

"See, Kisrinni!" she cried, with the quick spirits of youth. "Let us be happy! The khamsin abateth. I see three persons in the street. Thou canst venture to go for the barley."

"The khamsin rageth in the sky after it abateth on the earth," said Kisrinni learnedly. "It will be a dark night, little mistress. I go, but I hasten back again. Guard thyself till my return."

Lalitha nodded happily.

"I watch for thee," she said affectionately. "Thou art dear to me. Thou art all I have."

She poured her young tenderness upon the aged creature,—a precious overflow; it must go somewhere.

She felt a little lonely that night. Nobody could come in. Balatsu-usur was detained by official business, and there was a banquet at court. This meant that the queen, who made the most of the arbitrary power of the regency, required the presence of Allit. It was necessary to be very fond of Kisrinni in default of any other person.

So Lalitha stood on the portico, a lovely shape, wrapped in cool tissues that tossed in the subsiding khamsin like little clouds about her. Her robe was white, confined with a crimson scarf. Her black hair was braided closely to her small head, and fastened with a silver dagger, whose hilt was delicately chased and set with garnets. She wore one amulet set in ancient silver, bound high upon her round arm close to the shoulder; it was a Jewish ornament that her father liked. Lalitha opened the door, and stood on the threshold to snatch the first breath of relative coolness from the disturbed air. She did not feel at all uneasy at being alone. One was safe at home, and Kisrinni was never gone long enough for one to wonder where she was.

While Lalitha stood at the door, a slave, wearing the royal livery, approached the house, and courteously inquired for the daughter of Mutusa-ili, for whom he bore, he said, an urgent message. The fellow was an inferior eunuch, a mere detective or messenger. Lalitha had never seen him. She listened to him with no more than the vague, general objection which any association with the court excited in her.

"Comest thou from Ashpenaz?" she inquired suspiciously.

"Nay, I come from the governor of Babylonia," replied the eunuch. "I am but the messenger of thy guardian. He requireth thy presence on important affairs, in the lesser palace beyond the river. I bear his command in the writing in my hand. Behold it."

"I never knew my lord Balatsu-usur to ask me to come to *him*," hesitated Lalitha, examining the clay tablet, "but this is indeed his command. Why cometh not my lord to visit his ward, according to his custom?"

"He aileth," replied the messenger. "He is sickened of the khamsin, and may not leave the palace. He desireth thy presence as speedily as possible."

"Oh, *sick!*" cried Lalitha tenderly. "Is Balatsu-usur *sick?* I come at once! Kisrinni will attend me in a moment."

"I was to fetch Kisrinni," answered the slave readily, "so my lord commanded. But if the slave woman were not at hand, the governor bade me to make no delay for her coming. The matter is an urgent one."

Lalitha looked troubled, but she closed the house door, and stepped into the street. It seemed impossible to disobey her guardian, and since it was not Ashpenaz, why fret or fear?

"Let me see the seal," she said abruptly. "The governor sealeth his commands to me with the seal of state. I am acquainted with it."

In the dim light, in the puffs of the dying

wind, and with the blasts of sand driving into her face, she examined the seal that stamped the edge of the tablet.

"It is broken," she objected.

"Unhappily, I fell on my way hither," protested the eunuch, "and the clay bruised in my hand. I was blinded by the khamsin and I fell. . . . But thou beholdest; it is the great seal of the province of Babylonia."

"Yes," admitted Lalitha, "it is the seal. It is the seal of my guardian. How sorry I am that he is sick. I will hasten to him! But I go not without Kisrinni. She hath but gone to buy the barley. To save the time we will go to meet Kisrinni; her errand lieth straight upon our way."

Lalitha veiled herself carefully from the khamsin, and stepped out into the darkening street. But they did not meet Kisrinni. Whether the old woman had taken another way, or had not left the bazaar, or whether, in the driving of the sand and descending of the dark, her young mistress actually passed without recognizing her, Lalitha never knew. She hurried along, excited and oppressed at heart, in the whirling twilight. It darkened rapidly, fearfully. A sudden vicious gust of the perishing wind, what one might call a convulsion, or hysterical rattle in its throat, tore at the delicate draperies of the girl, and wrapped them about and about her. Her veil swathed her like a mummy. She could neither see where she was, nor breathe what air she had. She swayed upon her light feet like a falling top.

"I stifle!" she cried. "It is not fit weather for a girl to be out. I thought the khamsin was quite over. I do not meet Kisrinni. . . . I shall go home. Take me home at once!"

"As you say," replied the eunuch, with an air of deferential disappointment. "The noble governor is sorely indisposed, but I obey you; we will return at once."

"I *must* go home!" insisted Lalitha. "I will explain it to my guardian. I *must* find Kisrinni to attend me."

"As you say," repeated the eunuch. They turned, and walked for some time; the eunuch preceding, to mark the way for her as the gloom increased; the girl following in uncomfortable silence. Lalitha felt ashamed of herself for her timidity, and reproached herself for her venture. She was torn between two irreconcilable views of her situation. Unused to acting or deciding for herself, she wavered from this opinion to that, with the distressing ease of quick, undisciplined minds. Suddenly she stopped short, and cried to the eunuch, —

"But you are not taking me home!"

"Nay," said the discordant voice of a third person, who had stepped out from the now fast-darkening night and had grasped the girl by the arm. "When the governor commands, a Babylonian obeys. I will relieve my messenger, and myself conduct you to Balatsu-usur."

When Lalitha recognized the voice and grasp of Ashpenaz — it was too dark for her to see his face — she did not shriek nor struggle. She was far too terrified. A dumb horror settled upon her. She lifted her face piteously to the chief eunuch. Her large eyes widened, and grew filmy, like a dying bird's. She managed to articulate a few thick words : —

"I came — to — meet — Kisrinni. It was — it was his seal " —

A fierce blast from the sirocco tore up from the far south, and beat upon her cruelly. The night seemed to grow hotter. The darkness rose high against the blurred sky. The sand grated between her teeth and burned her throat. Her ears rang with it, — they were filled with fire. Agony struck her eyes, — their lids closed upon flame. She felt herself tossed to and fro wildly. Gasping, and beating out her hands for breath, she fell, half the victim of the khamsin, half of fright, but wholly helpless, and as unconscious as any slave lying dead of the sandstorm without Imgur-Bel.

" The deed will be easy enough now," said the messenger coolly to the chief eunuch. " She will know nothing more about it. . . . Verily, a hard job had I, to pacify her with thy clumsy seal. She must needs examine the forgery like a little politician."

They lifted the girl in silence. Ashpenaz half hated the errand. But the queen had become absolute monarch of the empire, and she had trusted him with her vengeance for the second time. One of the first uses which Amytis made of public power was this dark deed in gratification of her private jealousy. Ashpenaz was not the person to hesitate between killing or dying.

The river Euphrates was to Babylon the " soul of the land " in the same vital sense that breath is the " soul of life." This river divided the capital of Nebuchadrezzar into two triangles. Broad, and deep, and swift, the stream shot through the city as through an open sluice. Quays were built of burnt bricks cemented with bitumen ; these rose to the height of fifty feet on each side of the river bank, thus protecting the city from the terrible rise of the waters at the annual inundation. At Hit, an eight days' journey above Babylon, as the crow flies, the average width of the Euphrates is about one fourth of a mile, and this natural engine discharges seventy-three thousand cubic feet of water a second. From this point, the overflow begins. Nebuchadrezzar, realizing that the soil of Babylonia could never support its enormous population unless drenched in moisture, persistently, one might say passionately, renewed old levees, canals, and water-courses, and dug new ones. He built one canal for the benefit of his merchantmen alone, that was seven hundred miles long.

The surest way to collect unpaid taxes was to cut off the water from a rebellious locality. A soil teeming with food thus became a desert in less than six months' time. Starvation stared at the people whose streams were confiscated. Water was more sacred than Nebo, and its channels were in a better state of repair than the temples of the popular god Merodach. From Sippara to Babylon large reservoirs were excavated to catch the annual overflow. The Nahar Malcha, the royal canal, interlocked the Euphrates with the Tigris. As we have seen, great Babylon herself was encased in a moat that surrounded Imgur-Bel, the outer wall. This was large and deep enough to anchor a fleet. Canals intersected the city like streets. Babylon was the Venice of antiquity.

Now, besides the brick quays which guarded the Euphrates, two walls skirted the river, affording additional protection from an invasion therefrom, and following the stream closely until it left the southern ramparts of the city to water the plain of Doura. The tremendous engineering feat of deflecting the course of the river had been accomplished, and while the captive current filled the reservoir at Sippara, its city bed had been paved with bricks laid in pitch. This helped the easy flow of the stream, and prevented the natural erosion of its bed and a consequent escape from the embankments.

Where the Euphrates entered the double city walls, gratings like the teeth of a crocodile were let down at nightfall. These iron incisors replied to any strategic movement on the part of an ignorant enemy. After sunset, no boat could enter the city. Neither could any depart, for at the river's exit southward another grating snapped its jaws, and the city slept in safety. Imgur-Bel and Nevitti-Bel were pierced by a hundred gates of brass, twenty-five on each side of the square. These corresponded to the number of streets which ran parallel and gave upon the river. As each street approached the water, it passed through the two walls that protected the quays, and then dipped to a sloping landing-place, where steps descended to the margin. There were the ferries; boats being kept ready to convey such passengers from side to side as preferred the row to the long and hot walk over the bridge. But here also, at sunset, a brazen portcullis dropped. At none of the twenty-five landing-places was entrance or egress possible after legal hours. The gates opened only to the king or to the governor of the province of Babylonia, or to order of their official seals. Such precautions will not seem excessive when one remembers the bands of robbers, organized within the very city, and restless for prey. A sleepy watchman on a tower gave chance for any amount of mischief threatening from the other side.

The river had a swift, powerful current. One of the worst accidents possible to a Babylonian was a fall into the stream after the gates were shut. The strongest soldier could not cling like a bat to perpendicular brick. If he was not drawn down by watchful crocodiles, he was impaled on the sharp teeth of the lowered portcullis, where the current leaped from its confinement to a lazier, broader, freer life.

On the night of our story, the keeper of the river gate guarding the Street of the Setting Sun performed the most treasonable act of his life. When the trumpet sounded at sunset, the order to release the gates that they might fall to their locks, this man stood irresolute, peering from the top of the stairway down the dark street. He seemed to be in a tremor of indecision.

"By Nebo, if he come not in the sixtieth part of a period, I close the gate, and there is no opening until the morrow!"

He slowly crept down the steps, growled a curse at the long, black snout of a crocodile that rested on the lowest step, now covered with water, and took his place in a recess of the wall, with his hands on the rude wheel. A round boat, built of reeds and pitch, bobbed near him in the water. It was tied by a rope to a bronze ring; there seemed to be no paddle in the boat. The gate-keeper gave a vicious look at the clumsy craft. He muttered, ill-naturedly, —

"Ten silver shekels will be a fair price for it. It is a good boat, especially when it is bailed out. I think it fully worth twelve shekels, if he come not on the moment."

He took a half loaf of bread from a brick in the recess, and cast it into the water. "Catch," he said sardonically, "and haunt me no more."

The aim was true. The bread bounded from the mailed head of the saurian into the black current. The monster slipped back, and noiselessly disappeared in the darkness.

"Hallo, thou keeper of the gate! Light thy torch, lest we stumble into the river!"

The imperative voice of the chief eunuch roused the guardsman of the gate from his gloomy hesitation. He hurried up the slimy steps, cringing.

"I dare not light, my lord. There be those who might discern that no gate is down. For that, the law tosseth the gate-keeper over his lock. What have we here? Another? Verily, the crocodile hath more than his share of Babylon's pretty girls."

The fellow bent over Lalitha, and touched her rudely. The girl shrank with an instinctive sigh of horror, but showed no other sign of consciousness. Ashpenaz uttered an uncomfortable exclamation.

"Do you want three bricks and a bag?" asked the guardsman stolidly. Ashpenaz did not reply.

"It is the usual way," urged the gate-keeper. "They stay down best."

The chief eunuch was trembling visibly. He was not man enough to refuse to do the queen's deed, or to perform it. He beckoned his subordinate with shaking finger.

"Go thou," he whispered hoarsely; "hasten to Amytis. Report to her that the deed is done, upon honor of this ring she put upon my finger. Return it unto her with the obeisance of her servant. Thou beholdest the girl. I toss her to her death. Go thou, and report that thine eyes have seen it."

When the messenger had departed, Ashpenaz lifted Lalitha from the wet step. His arms shook so that her lifeless body fell from them. The guardian of the gate caught her, and the two men staggered, with chattering teeth, bearing their burden to the water's edge. Deeds like this were common enough in Babylon. The gate-keeper had seen his share in his time. But the agitation of the eunuch was infectious.

Ashpenaz stooped at the water's edge, and peered around. He saw the rude boat. He kicked it with one foot; bent over, and felt of it; his hand touched water in its bottom. While he stood examining the boat, something snapped at his foot. He felt the slight grazing of teeth. A long, black outline turned viciously in the water. With a cry of horror, the eunuch rushed up the step. He said, " No, no, no! " He repeated, " Horrible! Not in there! Too horrible! "

A blast from the sirocco struck the river at that moment, and the two men covered their heads with their garments. The hot sand smote upon Lalitha's unveiled face. It was so hot that it blistered the flesh.

" Raman is offended with me," groaned Ashpenaz. " He flayeth me because of the deed. I dare not! I dare not! . . . Is the boat thine? "

The gate-keeper nodded sourly. He was tired

of the business, which went off less easily than usual.

"How much?"

"Fifteen shekels."

"Help me put her in."

The other silently obeyed. Lalitha's body fell over helplessly against the side of the crazy craft.

"She will upset it!" cried the eunuch. "Straighten the boat!"

"It is only a question of time," replied the accomplice grimly, but he balanced the boat. "Shall I cast off the rope from the ring?"

Ashpenaz nodded. He could not speak. He turned away his eyes.

"I give her a chance!" he muttered.

The keeper of the gate threw back his coarse head, and laughed.

He unfastened the rope from the bronze ring, and threw the end off. It fell short of the boat, and splashed into the water. The man pulled an old boat-hook from a niche in the dripping wall, and gave the boat a shove. It tipped, and took in water, recovered itself, and whirled into mid-stream.

Silently, the long nose of the crocodile slipped into the water. As silently, the bronze gate dropped into its socket.

CHAPTER XX.

THE first realization of a horrible situation is like the awakening from any common dream. One regards the facts for the moment with a kind of shuddering curiosity; divided between wondering how long the delusion will last and the anguish of having been deluded. When Lalitha came to herself, she looked about her at first, with no more than the agitation which she felt at finding herself in her own little room at home after some unusually unpleasant nightmare. She raised herself on one elbow, and gently called, —

" Kisrinni ! "

The slight motion tipped the round boat. It took in water, and righted sullenly. Then the girl sat upright, and stared at her hideous surroundings.

She sat in several inches of water, in what was probably the maddest craft afloat on the Euphrates, — and that was saying a good deal. The boat had swirled into the middle of the stream, and was now driving madly down. There was no paddle. There was no rudder.

Lalitha was tossing like a chip, or more correctly speaking, like a ball, upon the river. She was in the power of the current. Below her the black torrent made a sucking sound. Far above, she could see one or two stars; these pierced through the veil of dust left by the khamsin. It was very dark; the wind was still abroad, and puffed upon the boat irregularly, like the snarls of an animal. There was no other boat in sight. No human creature was visible. On either hand, a shadow, black as death and solid as the tomb, towered above her. Fifty feet of sheer brick wall shut her in. She was pitching along at the rate of three or four miles an hour. Even to her inexperienced eyes the boat leaked visibly. Every motion threatened to capsize it. Her very cries made the frail thing throb. When she shrieked, it seemed as if the reeds would start apart, as if the tremor of her voice would plunge her into the abyss.

But the river rang and rang with her terrible cries. The opposite walls caught her young voice, and tossed it back and forth from side to side. The brazen gates made a snatch at it, as if they would hold it for sport; then let it go, with a piteous echo. She called upon Bel-Merodach and Jehovah, Balatsu-usur and Allit, Kisrinni and the chief eunuch, the spirit of her father and the mercy of the queen, — the guards, the gatemen, and the citizens. Fifty feet above her, in the blast of the sirocco, on deserted walls, and after river hours, who should reply? She shrieked, until she stopped for very horror at the sound of her own solitary and agonized voice. Then she fell back in the boat, and looked about her in a kind of stupor. A wave within a wave moved behind her relentlessly in the sinuous current.

"It is a fish," thought Lalitha, with a faint sense of relief. She did not feel so drearily alone. It occurred to her to put her hand out and touch the fish, if she could; but the boat tipped to the edge, and she shrank back. Suddenly she remembered the gates. In her ignorance of the outer world, she had the vaguest idea of the river fortifications. But once her father had taken her through one of these brazen gates and across the river in the ferry.

"How foolish I must be!" said the girl aloud. "Of course I can get off at the next gate. There were steps and a man."

She strained her eyes for a sight of the gate. She peered into the darkness; she tried to push the boat up against the bricks. But with what? At every motion the mad craft shook. She noticed the rope which dragged behind her. She pulled at it with all her strength. It seemed to have caught in something. As she tugged, the hold upon the rope yielded, and she swirled out of the current. A long, dim shape rose from the water angrily, dived, and disappeared. When Lalitha saw what it was, she uttered a cry that might have pierced to the top of the Ziggurat, or to the throne of Heaven.

At that moment, the boat shot by the first gate. The poor girl had wit enough left to perceive that it was dropped for the night. Unguarded and deserted, the brazen surface presented an impassable front to the current. The boat dashed up against it, and whirled away.

In an age when the simplest incident of sheltered life suffices for a tale, the perils of ruder times have a certain shock, which grates upon the ear like the thunder or powder of a noisy play. It is well to remember that brutal revenge or mortal danger in its grossest form was to the people with whom our narrative deals no more than the daily episode of the street or of the fireside to a happier civilization.

Lalitha's fate, almost too ghastly for our fastidious sympathy, was, in fact, perhaps a little more ingenious, but no more dreadful or deadly, than the lot of hundreds like her in lands and under laws where womanhood was accepted prey, and helplessness and ignorance stood small chance at the hands of social or civil power. We feel it to be our privilege to shrink from following what thousands of obscure girls endured. A life like Lalitha's might go out like the wick of a little candle, any night in Babylon, and who the wiser? It might be quenched in tortures indescribable, and who the sadder?

The intelligence reached the poor child's friends in an unexpected way, — the last against which the queen was likely to provide, even had she cared to take the trouble. And why should she? No power gainsaid or checked the regent.

There was a banquet, as we said, at court. Amytis was unusually gay. At the moment when Lalitha was tossing to her death, the queen raised a cup of wine high in the hot air, and pledged the captain in it, laughing lightly. She had beckoned him to her side from the lower table, where he sat at supper.

"I give thee the health of her thy heart preferreth," lisped Amytis languorously.

Allit put the goblet to his lips in silence. Into that mad, bad scene a sacred moment entered. He shut himself in it reverentially. He did not look at Amytis. She was half drunken and half draped. She had never been so revolting to him. How had he ever played the game of light love, and with *her?*

He set the goblet slowly down, gravely saluted the queen, and, excusing himself as soon as he could without discourtesy, returned to his own table. It was the custom of the place and time, at banquets like this, to seat but four at a table, according to rank, age, and other affinities. But etiquette went easily at court since Amytis came into power. A mad carousal suited her better than a decorous entertainment. Her guests were not thoughtfully seated, and Allit had shared with Ina, the daughter of Egibi, a table occupied by two courtiers, a man and a woman of high position, both so far under the influence of wine that Ina had already withdrawn from the table in unbearable discomfort.

She had been absent from the banquet-hall for perhaps ten minutes, when Allit, returning to his seat, observed her reënter. The expression of her face arrested his attention immediately, and it quickly became evident that she desired to attract it.

It was a matter of plain politeness for the captain to respond to the summons of a lady whom he had attended at the feast, and his crossing the hall to do so aroused little notice. Amytis watched his mighty ·figure with dull eyes; she was too sodden with the carousal to feel displeasure or express curiosity.

When Allit reached the side of Ina, he was

shocked at her appearance. She trembled violently, and her handsome face was quite pale. She put her delicate hand upon his arm, and whispered close to his ear: —

"I have horrible news. Come!"

Allit followed her instantly. Ina was very much in love with him, but she did not pursue him. He obeyed her with the trust a man feels in any woman whom, despite a little coquetry, he can respect. They threaded their way quickly through the lower end of the banquet-room, and came into the outer hall. The curtains swayed and fell. The great blaze of the banquet darkened behind them. The rude laughter, the ruder songs, the shrill voices, were suddenly muffled. A cooler breath replaced the stifling air. In the outer hall, a few of the young nobility and titled students, who had supped by themselves, were playing at dice. Some servants passed in and out. Allit looked at Ina confusedly. Then he perceived that Mariamnu stood there, shrinking against the long Persian curtain.

"Tell him!" said Ina authoritatively. She shook the captive to arouse her. Mariamnu seemed half dead with horror or with terror, one could not say which; perhaps both.

"She has risked her life to tell me," said Ina contemptuously, "and now she is as dumb as any fool in Babylon. She hath overheard a dreadful plot. How can I tell thee? Oh, what shall I do?" cried Ina, greatly disturbed. "I wish to tell thee, and I tell thee not."

"In Jehovah's name!" whispered Mariamnu, "make no delay, for the girl is in the river by this hour."

Allit uttered a startled oath. As yet he comprehended nothing, but feared the more for that.

"Out with it, women!" he commanded, with masculine brutality.

"Lalitha drowneth," said Mariamnu, in her apathetic way. "By the order of Amytis, she" —

But the women stood looking at each other blindly. The captain, without word or sound, teeth set, head bent, hand on hilt, had dashed from the palace.

A laughing boy, who had just tossed a high number, threw down his dice, left the group of students, and followed Allit. Susa never lost a chance to share in any promising excitement.

Mariamnu shrank into the curtain and hid herself. Ina, greatly agitated, returned to the banquet-hall to seek her father. She dared not tell him. She had done the only thing she could think of for her cousin Lalitha. She hoped Allit would like her for it. It had not been wholly easy to do.

For a woman madly in love, voluntarily to save her rival for her lover's sake, was not a common deed in Babylon. There was the fine blood of a nobler stock in the daughter of Egibi. She had acted with impetuous humanity, which had a certain reaction. When she went back, alone, to the blinding banquet-hall, — darker now to her than any desolate black spot on earth wherein she might have heard *his* kindly, friendly, indifferent voice, — the Babylonianized Jewess had one moment of something like regret for her generosity. But it passed into the higher mood which found itself at home in the nature of Ina. Besides — besides — she would not have been a woman, had she not remembered that Lalitha was probably dead by this time. And then —

Allit bounded into the night. His brain, stupefied with wine and horror, had scarcely the power to command his feet to run. With a vacant instinct, the captain made for the high quay of the river. Mechanically he plucked intoxicating flowers from his head and heart, and cast them as he would vipers into the dust. Then he freed himself of his brilliant outer robe and sash. These he threw away, and they struck Susa in the face, behind him.

The boy, being the prize runner in the gymnasium of the university, had easily overtaken his clumsier brother. Susa had concluded that Allit was wild with wine; he followed him conscientiously. The two had now come to the embankment that frowned above the river. Its long line extended like the black curve of a serpent's back; the watch-towers broke the outline; the gates below them dropped within the masonry of the walls, piercing the quay to the water's edge.

Allit stopped, and peered stupidly into the water fifty feet below him. The hot breath of the expiring sirocco stung him; the physical pain where the sand-blast hit his face gave him a sense of relief; the captain knew so little of mental anguish that he experienced surprise at this fact. Susa, fearing lest Allit were about to jump into the whirlpool, clung to his arm, entreating some explanation of the situation with boyish persistence, half anger, half fright. Allit looked wildly about him. He managed to articulate a few sentences. Susa caught the words: —

"Lalitha — drowned."

All the fashionable oaths of the university of Bel burst from the lips of the lad. He had come out for a frolic. He found a tragedy.

"Why, follow the stream!" cried Susa.

Allit obeyed him dully. In a moment the lad

had become the leader. The wretched lover followed, plunging on, past gate after gate; now bending his head to one side to listen, now running too sharply on the edge of the walls, leaning too far over the turbid river, scanning it with his trained, keen, military eyes. Gradually his furious pace slackened. The hopelessness of the situation began to make itself evident to his cooling brain. What fool's play was this? Would glaring at the Euphrates restore the dead? The courage that the rush inspired had died away from his heart, as the soul dies out of the body, and left nothing but a dizzy, despairing mass of moving clay.

Allit stopped short. He was above the gate of the Setting Sun. He leaned against the closed guard-house. The soldier's legs trembled beneath him like a deserter's. Allit was indeed in a pitiable state. Hot tears burned furrows in his dusty cheeks. He dashed them away from his eyes, and groaned, —

"Lalitha! Lalitha!"

It occurred to him to plunge into the water after her. He had never before understood why people do such things. He had led such a happy life. How strange was misery!

"Hear! Hush! Hark!" Susa ran up to him. "Don't you hear a cry below us?"

Allit held his breath. At that moment it was

supremely still. Then came the shriek. Twice
—thrice repeated, the sound curdled the blood
in the hearts of the listeners. It was a woman's
cry of mortal agony.

"It is her spirit. It howleth in the night,"
whispered Susa superstitiously. But Allit answered, with a mighty cry, —

"If it be her spirit, or her body, or aught of
Lalitha, I follow her!"

He dashed into the darkness and disappeared.
Above one gate, past two gates, making a perilous pace upon the narrow wall, he pushed cra-
zily. What was the speck eddying yonder in the
water? A counter-current brought it backward;
it approached the wall; it swept within eyeshot.
He distinguished a round, rude boat making the
sullen motions that are peculiar to water-logged
crafts. Was it empty?

"Lalitha! Lalitha!" The walls and the
river rang to the musical word. Vaguely, a
shadow within a shadow stirred below. As it
did so, the boat tipped and struck the wall with
a crackling whir.

"*Lalitha! Lalitha! Lalitha!*"

The boat made a vicious plunge, and whirled
away. Fifty feet above it, Allit looked down
the perpendicular wall. Oh, to reach the gate,
— to leap, to cling, to clamber, to snatch at
something, to get within sight of her, touch of

her, life with her, death with her! But the gate, piercing the quay, was inaccessible. Was he a lizard that he could crawl down a straight, smooth wall, cemented with the dreadful skill of Nebuchadrezzar? The boat spun madly, and dashed against the wall again. This time it struck one of the brazen gates that guarded the river streets.

" Lalitha?" cried Susa for the first time, in his unmistakable treble. " Catch the gate, if you can, and hold it!"

A voice came back, like the note of a broken flute; but what words it spoke, if any, it was impossible to tell.

" Ye gods! Ye gods!" groaned Allit. " She dieth. I cannot open the gate. I cannot reach the maiden. I plunge. I die with her."

He had thrown himself flat upon the bricks; his head hung far over the escarpment. He implored her to tie the boat — not to speak — to save her strength — to do something — anything — he knew not what. He would save her — alas, he knew not how.

Lalitha, exhausted beyond further endurance, tried bravely to obey. She grasped the hot grating, as the boat shot past. What could her weak arms do? Against a boat heavy with water, and a current mighty as death, what was the muscle of a girl? She clutched for a mo-

ment, hoped, and held. Then the skiff twirled
about and dashed on. Her despairing cry, as
she swept down stream, was enough to break a
man's heart.

"Balatsu-usur!" cried Allit, giving Susa a
push which almost thrust him from the wall.
"Haste to Balatsu-usur! Bring him hither
upon his fleetest horse! Bid him to the lower
gate, with the keys thereof!"

"It will take me half an hour," groaned Susa.
"Oh, I shall be too late!" But he obeyed the
hopeless command, bounding through the darkness with a fine, fleet, sure step.

"The teeth of the river's mouth will gnaw her
to pieces before we are done with our Balatsu-
usuring," moaned Susa.

But if it gave Allit comfort to think that he
was doing something — The lad was very fond
of Lalitha, and he sobbed as he ran along.

Allit, alone upon the quay, followed the motions of the boat as well as he could. He called
her persistently : —

"Lalitha! Lalitha!"

It seemed to be all there was to say. His
voice gave her a certain courage; there was love
enough in it for a girl to die by gladly. In that
supreme moment, Lalitha felt almost as much
joy as horror.

When the boat came within sight of the next

gate, half a mile beyond the last, Lalitha prepared herself for her last chance with more composure. She came whirling up to it madly enough. She flung herself against the bars of bronze. Each hand grasped a thick rod. Oh, wonder! The gate trembled. It fluttered beneath her. It rose. Allit's tongue clave to the roof of his mouth. He could not articulate; he dared not move. Whence came this miracle? Susa was not half-way to the palace by this time. It was impossible to have reached the governor, to whose order alone (excepting the royal seal) the gate unlocked. The great gate moved silently through its grooves. Lalitha's white form rose slowly from the boat. Her garments clung to her limbs. The sinking boat swayed out into the current; as her feet left it, Allit heard a horrible, crunching sound. Amid lashing foam, the boat, crushed like an eggshell, was drawn beneath the waters. Still the gate arose. Lalitha hung down straight from it. Her wet robe stirred heavily in the wind. She clung with the last power that desperation gives. Some one spoke to her. It was not Allit. She felt an arm about her, — not her lover's.

"It is my father's spirit," thought the girl. She let go, and knew no more.

Allit precipitated himself through the guard-house, and down the steps through the heart of the wall, to the gate below. All the doors that he had vainly tried before, were unfastened. He rushed madly, sword in hand, and emerged upon the steps within the water-gate. A man stood there, bending over the unconscious girl.

" Hold ! " cried the lover. " Stand back, on thy life ! "

The man raised himself. He had a strange expression, — half pain, half ecstasy.

" Take the maiden," said Daniel gently, " and bear her to a safer place than this ; for she is thine."

CHAPTER XXI.

DAWN fell gently upon the royal pleasure-
grounds. The air had cooled. The khamsin
was over. The day unfolded like an oleander,
in petals of white and pearl. The perfume of
a million flowers intoxicated the morning. The
freshly watered foliage glittered merrily. The
brilliant birds of Babylonia dipped, and rose,
and darted busily; they looked like the blossoms
of air plants. They sang madly. One would
have said that Nature gave herself trouble to
distinguish a spot where purity, mercy, gentleness, all holy deeds and peaceful thoughts abode;
where happiness had her sanctification; where
disease and misery, hatred and hell, could no
more enter than the scouts of a conquered enemy
beyond the desert.

In the " pasture " of Nebuchadrezzar's gardens, a desolate king groveled before the sunrise. The maniac had slept but little; he was
at best a poor sleeper. Perhaps a wiser than the
medical art of the court would have attributed
certain symptoms at the outset of the king's
disease to his prolonged and serious insomnia.

He lifted his gaunt eyes from the ground, and regarded the gay morning with a kind of horror. Then he dropped to his favorite position, and crawled pitiably about. . . . His unshaven face, his unkempt hands, his neglected robe; above all, the shifting expression of his mouth, half savage, half human, now settling to ferocity, now appealing timidly for the care and sympathy which the science of the times denied to the alienated intellect — these are things to dream of, not to tell. When was a sovereign so abased? When did so imperious a pride undergo such exquisite humiliation? Madly contradictory moods fell upon the royal maniac. His keepers learned to prepare for their coming. At times, he fondled the timid creatures who had been suffered to share his green prison: the fawns crept to him; the lamb nibbled beside him. Then came dark hours; then, what wild nature, what savage bestial blood, wrestled within him? The gentle animals recognized the symptoms of these waves of cruelty before human intelligence perceived them. When they fled, quivering, and remained hidden in the shrubbery, the guards redoubled their precautions, taking good care to keep themselves well out of the way. It was popularly believed that a scratch or a bite from the unhappy monarch would produce a fate similar to his own. On this morning of which we speak, a keeper called another, with quick and agitated cry : —

"Look! By Nergal, look yonder! Nay, but what I see is too terrible for gods or men. I look no more. Take *thou* the watch, for I am sickened of the business."

The first guard turned his back to the madman, and hid his face. The second took his place, with light curiosity. A cry of horror escaped him.

"*Where is the lamb?*" he whispered.

The royal maniac growled. The growl had a deep, strange sound, like an unsuccessful roar. Warm blood upon the grass — dripping blood where the loathing eye refused to look — answered the keeper's question.

In the hanging gardens, no one troubled himself about what went on in the king's guarded grounds. That was the physician's business, and the magician's. Why should a wife be uncomfortable? The queen troubled herself about nothing that morning. She was abroad early, in spite of last night's carousal. She was exceptionally gay. In hot summer, she adopted the custom of the Babylonians, who arose before the sun if they wished to have any day at all in weather when the thermometer, if they had known one, might have registered one hundred and twenty in the shade. It may have been at the first of the morning watch, or not long after, when the queen chose to saunter through the mountain garden to refresh herself for the day; when cares of state must come even to Amytis, and the light nature wear for a few hours the weight of human duty.

The gardens were well watered, and dripped luxuriantly. The human force-pumps had worked all night. Since the khamsin fell upon the city, the carrying of water had not been suffered to cease. Relays of captives took the places of those who dropped. Now, all signs of toil or suffering were scrupulously banished from the gay scene. The last gardener had departed. The last slave had done his last toil for some hours to come; until the approach of noon should call an invisible force of skilled hands to drop the awnings that shielded the more delicate and valuable flowers from the midday fire.

At this time of the morning, Amytis amused herself alone, or with a few favored slaves. She dipped through artificial dew and pollen, bloom and fountain, like one of the butterflies that circled above her small head, or one of the bright, cold lizards that crept about her feet. She bathed, she ran, she sang, and curled to sleep, and stirred and bathed again. Mariamnu only attended her. The queen thought of last night's

events apathetically. Perhaps she did not remember — for the Median wine had wrought
well upon her — exactly in what form she gave
the order. The girl was gone this time; that
was enough. Ashpenaz swore it to her by the
ring last night; by his own shaking voice he
had renewed the oath this morning. The queen
had dismissed him abruptly, asking no questions; he looked so disagreeably uncomfortable
over the business. At all events, the girl was
out of the way; Amytis laughed the louder, the
day was the fairer, for it. And now? Ah,
well, and now, — what pretty pleasure next?

"I would behold my lord Balatsu-usur," said
Amytis, after a few moments of what she called
thought. Mariamnu sent the summons silently.
The captive trembled in every nerve of her thin
body. She knew too well that her own head
sat upon her shoulders to-day more lightly than
the calyx of any flower in the mountain garden
on its stalk. She robed her mistress for the
visit of the Jew with a temporary sense of protection.

Daniel answered the command leisurely. His
countenance had a remote expression. One
would have said that he did not see the queen.
He did not speak, but awaited her order in a
mute scorn.

"I have sent for thee," began Amytis, coquettishly, "to say — to discuss — to see — My lord Balatsu-usur, thou art not in a tender mood toward me! I am too frivolous a woman. Yet, indeed, I have it in my heart to do some service to thee."

Daniel regarded her fixedly. He made no reply whatever.

"Come to me!" cried the queen. He obeyed her. She drew his ear to her lips, and whispered a few words. Her round arm stole about his neck. . . . The Jew released himself with a motion more like that of an offended spirit than a tempted man. He seemed to melt away from her, as if her touch had no means of expressing itself to his sensation. To this high rejoinder he added the rebuke of continued, scathing silence.

"Thou dost not understand me!" cried the Median. Burning blushes scorched her face. She turned her back upon him petulantly.

But Daniel had understood her perfectly. What the queen had offered him was nothing less than the utmost — the full of political authority, the crest of human glory, the vacant place of Nebuchadrezzar, his awful power, — practically his empty throne. This offer was accompanied with one soft stipulation.

Then, without hesitation and without mercy, the Jew spoke these few words : —

" Rather would I be cast unarmed into the cage of the lions upon the plains of Doura. Rather would I tread the furnace of fire where the convict scorcheth." . . . Amytis uttered a little cry of rage and shame. The Jew's cold voice went on above her ringing ears: " Rather these a thousand fold, Amytis, than touch *thee.*"

When the queen raised her abased head, Balatsu-usur had gone. Mariamnu stood cowering at a distance, by the scarlet Judean lilies; she did not dare approach, or raise her eyes.

Neither of the women had entirely recovered herself when dashing steps crushed the shrubbery, and the figure of an unannounced visitor burst upon the privacy of the garden of ascents. The man was tall and mighty of stature. His hanging sword caught the red lilies and tore them, as he rushed into the presence of the queen. When Amytis saw who it was, her heart failed within her. But she gathered herself right royally, like the leopardess she was, and haughtily waved the intruder away. He paid no more attention to her gesture than he did to the movement of a brown moth that circled over him and brushed his helmet. His manner, even more than his look, was terrible to Amytis. She melted and fawned, the tears started, her whole being seemed to creep to him ; she remembered how fond she had once been of him, how she had wished for his fondness. It seemed to her as if she should die, if he spoke — as he would, if he spoke at all. She knew in an instant that he understood everything. She breathed his name tenderly : —

. " *Allit !* "

His large lips moved as if he would answer her, but no sound came through them ; they were dry and clumsy with rage. Amytis observed that the soldier made no obeisance to his queen. She understood that she had lost her captain. Allit approached her with simple human fury. Throne and crown, power and peril, disappeared from his consciousness. His hatred clawed for vengeance within him. The man's great figure broadened and heightened with his sense of mere muscular power. He could have throttled her — but, after all, she was a woman.

"Allit," she repeated softly, "what aileth thee, Allit ? "

"I scorn thee !" hissed Allit.

"Thou art mad," whispered Amytis. "Thou hast an illness ; thy brain is wild. Seat thyself among my flowers and cool thy blood. See, we are alone. Only my slave is present. . . . Stand farther, Mariamnu. Observe not my lord the captain, for he is seized with a sudden evil spirit. Come hither, my captain. The queen forgiveth thy wild language. Amytis considereth thee too kindly to make memory of thine offense. Come to me, Allit, come!"

Amytis half hid herself in blossoming shrubs, and timidly held out her brown, bare arms. Allit did not see that they trembled. He did not divine that she was really afraid of him. He stared at the queen stupidly. She prattled like a dull child; she tossed aimless words at his awful rage, as if she threw withered flowers at a shield of bronze. He could not understand how she could be so imbecile. The narrow brain of Amytis, dazed by folly and fright, seemed unable to distinguish anything more than the waymarks of her outworn passion. She took the feeble course of an intellectually inferior, unprincipled woman. A cleverer or a better would not have added this last fuel to his loathing. Her manner nauseated Allit out of his poor feint of self-possession. He burst into a storm of terrible words. . . . Amytis raised herself from behind the foliage, and stood to receive them. She had grown very pale beneath her warm, dark coloring. She drew her supple form to its best proportions. Framed by a yellow acacia, full in the broad sunburst, she had a tawny splendor like some bright animal's. Even at that moment, Allit could not help thinking that she was a beautiful creature. If he had been himself a more thoughtful man, he might have wondered if she had more than animal conscience. The two were alone upon the topmost tier of the mountain garden. Only the Hebrew captive was witness of their meeting. Mariamnu had turned her blanched face away from the scene, which she found no less than terrible, yet before which she was as helpless as the lizard in the lilies at her feet. Amytis began to walk backward through the acacia bushes. The yellow blossoms closed about her. Allit burst into them. Then the queen found her voice.

" I have thy head for this," she said collectedly. " I have endured thine insolence too long. The queen of Babylonia is a woman — like a woman she hath fallen into folly. Like a woman she hath forborne. Learn thou, though late, that she is also a queen. The death agony may teach it thee, if thou art teachable. Look thy last upon thy last sunrise, Allit Arioch. See ! Turn thy curling head. Come hither. For the sake of what was once between us, look thy last upon earth beside Amytis — my Allit."

To save her crown, the queen could not have withheld those last soft words. Allit answered them with one hard enough to strangle the dying delusion out of any folly in Babylon.

" *Murderess !* " he said, and said it over ; repeated it distinctly ; dwelt upon it ; dashed it at her ; drew his breath in between his teeth, and said it again. The acacia had closed behind them. The thick shrubbery of an imported Persian bush with a scarlet flower grew between them and the wall, whose low edge skirted that side of the high gardens that rose perpendicularly from the reservoir. Amytis retreated before Allit with slow, sinuous steps. He followed her, raging. He could have stamped the life out of her — but she was a woman. The soldier withheld his hand. Yet with his tongue he beat upon her. Her threat seemed to have no more effect upon him than the little thorns of the Persian quince that pricked him as they swung against his cheek. He followed her with a frightful slowness. She caught his broken sentences : —

" My wife — she is to be my wife — I wed with her — and thou — and *thou* " — Amytis uttered a low exclamation. He clenched his two iron hands within each other like padlocks that he might not touch her. If he had given himself a moment's freedom, he would have killed her before she could have cried out upon him. What he said he never knew. Awful words fell from his hot lips. What queen? — no woman — could forgive. Denunciation blazed

upon denunciation. Scorn hurled after scorn.
Then came insults — the worst and last.

Amytis had retreated steadily before him, in
who knows what? terror of the outraged man.
As steadily, Allit followed. The Persian bush,
sending forth soothing odors, crackled and was
crushed beneath his heavy feet. The thorns
tore her soft flesh. Neither saw — both were
too blind with the flash of the scene — that the
queen had reached the limit of the wall's edge.
Still retreating, she swayed before him.

" And you missed it, after all ! " he said between his teeth. " Do your worst, but in spite
of you, this night I wed her."

Amytis started, and threw out one arm to
steady herself. Her beautiful body stood high,
for one hot instant, against the quivering sky
— then curved — her robe fell — and she top-
pled.

The terrible cry which tore the air recalled
the soldier to his senses. He unlocked his
hands and sprang to the precipice, holding them
out to snatch, to save. He looked over the low
parapet, and shrank back ; he covered his eyes
and crouched against the Persian shrub.

.   .   .   .

Mariamnu stood shrieking.

" Have silence," commanded Allit hoarsely.
" Thou art the only witness. Thy life and

mine are the forfeit of this morning's work. There is a moment left. Make the most of it," urged Allit dully. " Fly while thou canst, if thou canst. It only remaineth for me to do the same. I did not do the deed," proceeded the captain argumentatively; he looked about him with bloodshot, bewildered eyes. " She fell. I touched her not. She fell. Amytis fell. Look thou over the wall — I dare not — for she fell."

He tore through the crimson quince, pushed through the yellow acacia, crushed the Judean lilies, dashed down the path and down the steps. At sight of the first guard, he recovered himself. He passed them all with the ease of the queen's favorite. The soldiers saluted their superior officer. He reached the lowest platform of the hanging gardens, and walked on leisurely. As he went by the king's pasture, Allit paused a moment. The keepers also saluted profoundly.

" How fares the king ? " asked the captain in what he thought to be quite a natural voice.

" As the beasts of the jungle fare," was the significant reply. Allit turned his white face toward the sunny field, lifted his helmet in silent obeisance to his sovereign, and passed on.

CHAPTER XXII.

A LITTLE after the setting of the sun, a caravan of merchants, about to make the great journey across the desert, left Babylon for Tadmor, and thence by way of Damascus to Tyre and Sidon or Judea. This incident, of very common occurrence, attracted less than usual attention on account of the tremendous public excitement aroused by the fate of Amytis; and a group of travelers who left the mansion of Egibi found themselves of less than no consequence in the general uproar. Foreign visitors at the residence of the distinguished banker were an every-day affair: traders from all parts of the commercial world had errands there, — to execute wills and deeds before a hazardous trip, to exchange their stuffs for well-coined silver shekels, to make deposits of moneys at the bank, to receive letters of introduction and of credit needful for their journey. Why observe the commonplace, well-to-do merchant who, with his family, — a lad, presumably his son, and two women of his household, — took leave of Egibi, and with the usual composure of his class, motioned his servants to lead the camels nearer?

The tumult in the city was in no wise lessened by the fact that nobody in it had ever loved Amytis. She was their queen. The throne was once again empty. What was to be done with a mad king and a dead queen? The city of the Gate of God was on fire with dismay. Between Evil-Merodach, the boy prince, and the throne, nothing visible in the way of a sovereign or even of a regent now intervened; and this heir of the pious name had up to this time given no particular proofs of any kind of aptness for the crown, beyond a very bad temper and his father's nose.

At all events, Amytis was dead, — murdered, it seemed past a doubt. By whom and to what end who should say? Ashpenaz, for that brief wild day *ex officio* ruler of Babylonia, made the most of his short-lived glory to stir the swirl of events to their dregs. As chief of the royal eunuchs, as major-domo of the palaces, as personal guardian of the queen, it was the duty of Ashpenaz to circulate a theory of the horrible accident. His own life would none too slowly pay the price of his neglect or of his dullness if a satisfactory murderer did not turn up. His personal objections to the captain of the guards were several and serious, the testimony was sufficient, and the rest followed glibly. Before the crimson banner on the Ziggurat of Bel told the hour of noon, criers were patrolling the city throughout its vast extent, proclaiming Allit Arioch, captain of the guards of our lamented King Nebuchadrezzar, the murderer of the Median queen. The enormous price of two talents of gold was set upon the curling head that half the beauties of Babylon would have counted themselves happy to caress. Thus were laggard detectives stimulated into enthusiasm. Soldiers at the gates were doubled. The ferries between the east city and the west city were watched. A military signal of alarm ordered the hundred huge brazen gates that pierced Imgur-Bel to drop in their bronze grooves; they opened sullenly only for accredited passengers, and snapped again. Every trap was set for the fugitive. The reluctant witness of the guards at the mountain garden was enough to have condemned any man in Babylon without trial or reprieve. Rank was no protection against the doom of the regicide; that doom was too hideous for the pen to dwell upon. Allit had been seen to enter the gardens, unbidden and unannounced; after a brief interview he had been known to depart unchallenged; and between his coming and his going the queen had met her fate. The watchmen on the Yapur Shapu told a ghastly tale. It was said that she struck once in falling, and bounded from the perpendicular wall. It was rumored that she was mangled before she hit the great reservoir, whose sluggish current mercifully received and clothed the pitiable body of the daughter of Astyages. Shrinking slaves dragged the canal for a few recoiling hours; and then they found her. Before the throne which she had disgraced, and the averted gaze of the people whom her caprices had oppressed, the Median now lay for an hour in such state as death and compassion allowed her. One of the most appalling rumors of the day was to the effect that the death of the queen had been observed by the poor maniac in the walled pasture. It was said long afterwards that the shock had profound and remarkable effects upon the king. There were not wanting opinions that this mental concussion was not wholly injurious to the sufferer; and one very aged magician claimed that in consequence of a conjunction of certain stars the slow restoration of the royal patient to normal health had on that dreadful day begun its almost imperceptible course.

But the queen was dead. "He who is alive at even is dead the next day." Thus runs the Babylonian proverb. The evil doer was traveling to a distant land which cannot be seen, while her former favorite was hunted down like common game. Every probable hiding-place in Babylon was searched for the captain of the guards. The governor of the province even offered his own palace to the official inspection; but the officer of ten protested that it was impossible to extend such an indignity to the highest civil authority of the city. Was not Balatsu-usur now the sole hope of the troubled nation; its moat, its ramparts, and its shield in this terrible crisis? Yea, verily. The officer and his men saluted, and passed on.

It was some hours after their visit to Balatsu-usur's palace before he found time to accompany a guest of his, a portly merchant, to the banking firm of Egibi and Sons. This was done slowly, in broad noonlight, and with perfect assurance. Who concerned himself with the guest of the governor? Or who, indeed, with the palace of Egibi? The last place in Babylon which the keenest detective wit in the city would have thought of searching for the condemned captain was the home of the treasurer of state.

Into that gorgeous house — the most sumptuous private home, probably, then in the known world — her guardian had, in fact, removed Lalitha immediately after her rescue from the river the evening before. Allit had accompanied them, in a tempest of love and rage, which would have borne down the reluctance of a far less good-natured household than that of Egibi. In short, Lalitha was thrown, on the impulse of one wild, wise moment, upon the mercy and hospitality of her own uncle; and Egibi, always a generous though sometimes a politic man, did his simple duty by the daughter of his dead brother. This was natural enough; but when the tragedy of the next day threw two more refugees upon the favor of Egibi's household gods, and when Allit, skulking under sentence of ignoble death, demanded an immediate marriage with the banker's niece, in the name of love and flight and mortal peril, the case became complicated. As for Mariamnu, it was simple enough to shelter a slave. But a condemned officer of the court — a wedding — disguises — a flight, — these things were not within Egibi's distinguished experience. The distracted appearance of Susa, wretchedly hunting for his brother at the banker's door, added to the unprecedented perplexity of that influential man.

"By Merodach, verily, here's another," said Egibi to his daughter. "Are we to sneak all Babylon under our roof in behalf of this curly-pated courtier? Judge thou; for I am awearied with the business."

Then Ina cast down her sad, fine eyes, and remained lost in thought for the space of many minutes, and no person addressed her. When she raised them, Allit Arioch knelt before her, silent too. And he looked upon Ina. And she began to tremble. For she felt in her soul that his eyes commanded her; that whatsoever he did will she should perform, — yea, though it were to speak the word that did give him for all time to the arms of a happier woman than herself; for Allit was lord of her heart, and her nature did serve him.

"Go thou," she said, in an almost inaudible and most touching voice. "Go thou. Take my cousin Lalitha to her own country, and wed her as thy heart desireth. My father and I do not deny the shelter due our kin, nor I the courtesy due from a lady to an old friend."

Thus and there, that day, in concealment and haste and alarm, was Lalitha wedded to Allit, who took her from the hand of her guardian, Balatsu-usur, and from the protection of her uncle's house, in the presence of her cousin Ina and his brother Susa ; the slaves Mariamnu and Kisrinni witnessing. The ceremony was completed without festivity, but with all possible solemnity.

The Babylonians honored marriage, in spite of, perhaps because of, their light morals; and although Allit must needs wed the maiden, so far as the circumstances permitted, according to the Jewish customs, yet the Babylonian heart of him rejoiced that the great seal of the city, set by the governor, signed his marriage vow, before he turned his life forever from his home and from his country.

Lalitha, very gentle, very sweet, so spent with the excitement of the past few days that she looked as if a little wind would waft her off her feet, gathered her color and her courage for her marriage hour, and lifted to Allit the pure, helpless, and adoring eyes that make a man of mighty muscle and of eager deeds a woman's very slave. In the hurried little wedding robe, over which Ina had generously flung the jewels of the house of Egibi, Lalitha did not glitter, but she shone softly. Her long, loose hair half hid her face. She turned toward Allit delicately, like a flower stirring on its stem. Tears sprang to the soldier's eyes. How should he handle that tender life? He thought of the hard journey, the desert, exile, the founding of a strange home in a strange land, of his disgrace and flight and social ruin, and of hardships which her gentle experience could not by any possibility present to her imagination.

"Thou wilt regret!" whispered the chastened courtier humbly. "Thou wilt think coldly of me for the fate thou sharest with a ruined man."

"Where thou goest I will go, and there will

I be buried," said Lalitha. Her voice broke. She could not think of anything more to say. She was not a talker. And she thought it must be so evident to anybody that she was the happiest, that she was the most blessed woman in the world. Then Allit Arioch fell at her feet, upon his knees, and gave to the Hebrew marriage an unexpectedly Babylonian turn. For the power of his education and of his race and of his great love was strong upon him ; and he offered to his Jewish wife the prayer of penitence which he had been used to utter in the Ziggurat to the gray god Bel, or oftener to Ishtar, the Queen of Babylonian chivalry : —

"O my goddess . . .

O my goddess, that knowest that I knew not,
My transgression is great, many are my sins.
The sin that I committed I knew not.
The forbidden thing did I eat. . . .
God, in the strength of his heart, has overpowered me.
To my goddess, who knew, though I knew not, I make supplication.
My transgressions are before me, may thy judgment give me life.
May thy heart, like the heart of the mother of the setting day, to its place return.
The feet of my goddess I embrace.
Peace afterwards."

Allit had scarcely risen from his knees, when a whisper through the barred door of the banker's private room, where the marriage party had been hastily and secretly gathered, announced the arrival of the camels and of the servants of the foreign merchant who was expected to leave the house of Egibi at the sunset hour. Egibi himself responded to the summons. The merchant was a friend of his, and received the especial attention of his presence in the stir of departure. Allit, successfully disguised by the loss of his fine beard and the traveling costume of a middle-aged man, stepped boldly into the street, and tested the harnesses of his camels. As he stood there, a crier passed by, proclaiming, —

"*For the body of Allit Arioch, whether dead or living, two talents! Two talents! Two talents!*"

Egibi saluted the crier. Allit imitated his example with composure.

As the two men stood together beside the tall white camel, they exchanged a few hasty words.

"Thou wilt find the deposits all correct," said the banker. "The sum mounts well. The moneys and the bales attend thee."

"Hast thou accredited all my properties to thyself? I would not go from Babylon in thy debt. It hath not been my custom to be in debt."

"Concern thyself not. The matter is quite satisfactory," replied the banker prince, with a wave of his opulent hand. "I have accredited thine affairs and the maiden's duly. My niece hath a sufficient dowry. If I took the liberty of adding unto it by a tithe or so, who gain-sayeth me? Am I not brother to Mutusa-ili? May Jehovah rest his soul!"

"And thine!" replied Allit, with emotion. "And thine, also, Egibi."

Egibi turned his grave face toward far, in-visible Jerusalem; he made no reply.

"I have feared," suggested Allit, "that — under the circumstances — my little property would be confiscated to the crown, and thou, therefore" —

"Trust that to me," said the treasurer of state, with a shrewd glance.

"The caravan moveth," cried the driver of camels restlessly. "Thy friend will be late, my lord Egibi."

In the sudden haste and little confusion that fell upon the banker's household, nothing went exactly as it was expected to go. When the merchant who would hasten toward Damascus was well upon his camel with his son; his women following upon another; the goods, the servants, and the many matters of the journey attended to in such order as the hurry of the start per-mitted, two persons stood in Egibi's glittering rooms, and stared at each other in a kind of stupefaction. These were the daughter of the banker and the governor of Babylon.

" Did she not say farewell to you?" stammered Ina.

" Nay; I heard her not."

" Nor he to me! Nor he to me!"

Ina leaned against the long tapestry of heavy gold embroidery that rattled behind her. She hid her face. But Daniel comforted her.

" Farewells," he said, " are but stabs in the heart. There be wounds enough without them. . . . Nor would I blame the maiden, or the youth," he added gently. " For the haste, and the disguise, and the danger thereof, these are serious matters. Pray thou, the rather, that they escape, and God go with them."

But Kisrinni, prostrate on the floor, in a dark corner of the splendid room, prayed while these were talking about it. The old slave wept silently, as she repeated the name of Beltis sixty-five times. *She* had kissed her mistress good-by, before the wedding, to make sure of it. They thought she was too old to take the journey. She had no price set upon her head, like Mari-amnu. And probably the lady Ina would feed her well.

" But how can they pass the walls?" Ina recovered herself, and looked at Balatsu-usur anxiously. " The guard is doubled, my father says, at every gate. It is such a horrible thing — it has been so sudden — no time to explain

—and women know nothing. Nobody has told me how Allit will pass Nevitti-Bel, and beyond Imgur-Bel how shall he escape? For these are terrible walls, and terribly are they watched to-day!"

Balatsu-usur smiled.

"The passport beareth the official seal of the governor of Babylon," he said quietly.

Then Egibi came back into the room. He looked pale, and walked slowly. No one spoke to him. The Assyrianized Jew had committed his first disloyalty to the state which had entrusted him with its highest financial position, for the sake of a dead brother, whom, living, he had never taken the trouble to acknowledge. His daughter came to him after a moment's hesitation, and hid her face upon his knees. She wished that her mother were living. How could fathers understand? She heard the noise in the hot streets drearily. Desolate Babylon! In a moment, in the twinkle of an eye, what a desert!

But Balatsu-usur departed silently, and went alone unto his own place.

As he entered the palace, the voice of a distant crier came faintly on the sluggish air: —

"*For the head of Allit Arioch, two talents! Two talents! Two talents!*"

CHAPTER XXIII.

IT was well into the dark of the night. Weary Babylon slept heavily. Only the extra guards and the sleepy criers, still proclaiming a price for the head of the king's captain, patrolled the streets at less frequent intervals.

At the great gate of Imgur-Bel, an unattended horseman halted.

"Stand!" cried the guard anxiously. "The countersign! Thy passport! Who art thou, and on what errand wouldst thou, alone and undefended, pass Imgur-Bel, on a night like this?"

The horseman removed his turban, baring his head and face fully to the guardsman's torch. He extended his hand, upon which the seal of the Province glittered, cut in one priceless sapphirine.

"My lord the governor!" cried the guard, bowing to the ground. "I pray thy pardon. In mercy, pass thou on."

He saluted and protested. The governor saluted and praised. The gate opened and closed with important resonance. Balatsu-usur spurred his Arabian horse, and, once well without the city, sped through the dark, hot air as recklessly as a boy in the university of Bel at his riding-lessons.

He made tremendous time, to which he gave no check until the outlines of the caravan to Damascus met his fixed and sunken eye. Then the saint halted mightily, drew his horse upon the haunches with a soldier's muscle, and fell into a slow and thoughtful pace. What unmanageable human impulse moved this holy heart now, after all, at the end of so much struggle and supremacy of soul? But it came to seem to the Jew that his breath would die out of his body, if he might not look upon her face again. Just to see her for one moment, — only for a single moment; he thought, if he could see that curve of her chin, and the way her under lip trembled — perhaps she would even be glad to speak to him, and tell him that she was happier for saying farewell to him, after all.

Daniel rode on softly. The caravan, skirting the Euphrates, had just camped for a few hours on the luxuriant bank. The full starlight fell on it. The camels were lying down peacefully. Lights glimmered still from the tents. A nodding watchman recognized and admitted him; a watchdog barked at him dutifully. He left his horse, and entered the camp on foot.

Before a cluster of tents, bearing in Assyrian

characters the ideogram of the great firm of Egibi, the Jew paused. His movements were almost stealthy. To avoid attention seemed to be his absorbing purpose. He had pursued the bride of Allit upon the wings of the wind, — upon the wilder wings of a mad emotion; but now that he was within a spear's toss of her, it was as if he were afraid to make his presence known, or to behold so much as her shadow on the sand.

As he stood there, hesitant, humble, one might say embarrassed, and uncertain in his movements, a familiar sound, without any embarrassment whatever, startled the drowsy air. It was a boy's laugh.

Then Daniel lifted his head and looked, and the nearest tent-lights flashed upon him merrily. At the door of her tent, Mariamnu, the captive, sat half within and half without the curtain. Before her, stretched lazily upon the ground, Susa lay chattering like a hoopoe. He regarded Mariamnu with pretty, boyish admiration.

"For my part," said Susa loudly, with his usual dogmatism, " I have no confidence in the government. What is a throne without so much as a regent? I have seen too much of it! I know how Babylon ought to be ruled. Turn your king to grass and toss your queen into a reservoir, and where are you? In my opinion it will be some days before they will find that fellow Arioch. He's well hidden in that cat's-cradle of a city, — trust him for it. *I* should search the big Ziggurat. But — ah — I was not consulted." Susa had the air of having made a fine political point: he looked about the camp to see if any one had overheard his views; he thought himself exceedingly adroit.

Mariamnu assented in a sleepy, happy tone. The captive gazed about her confusedly. Her freedom perplexed her as much as the stars in heaven, and seemed still as far away. Susa rattled on contentedly. He took a lower tone, that he might not be overheard by his neighbors : —

" The only thing I regret about it is this. There was my translation from the Akkadian. Mutusa-ili thought it extraordinary. It is packed away in the library of the university for all time and times and a day. Now my grandchildren will never see it. How shall I prove to them that I was talented ? That's a great pity ! "

He threw back his head, and laughed like a fountain. Then he stretched his stout young arms, clasped his hands behind his neck, and yawned.

" Sing, Mariamnu. It is very stupid of those two, — leaving us to ourselves, this way. I sup-pose we 've got to expect that, till this tiresome journey is over. We shall have to make the most of each other. I 'm glad you 're such a *pretty* girl. Sing, Mariamnu, sing!"

Mariamnu, with the instinct of captivity, obeyed the young Babylonian. She took her little lyre; it was cut from a tortoise-shell; it had seven strings; she leaned her head against the tent-pole, and turned her eyes toward the stars.

"Look there," whispered Susa. "Look at *them.*"

He pointed down between the tents, toward the outer circle of the encampment. Mariamnu looked and smiled, and sang : —

> " Fold the tent, fold the tent.
>   Start away!
>   Love is but a traveler,
>   Camped for a day.
>   Oh, though he kiss and whisper,
>   Though he be fair and fond,
>   Love is but a traveler, —
>   The desert lies beyond.

> " Strike the tent, strike the tent
>   Strong and fast.
>   Love, like any traveler,
>   Cometh home at last.
>   Oh, sing it to the sunlight!
>   Oh, tell it to the wind!
>   Love hath been a traveler, —
>   But the desert lies behind."

Daniel's haggard gaze had followed the lad's finger. Were they figures? Were they shadows? Soft, blurred outlines moved from out the tent of the merchant, friend of Egibi, and bound by way of Damascus for Judea. The Jew followed them silently.

The two stole down between the tents, and turned their faces toward the wide night. They made as if they would be a little apart from humanity, from which, indeed, they might not free themselves. He, the man, stood erect; he had the air of a god at the moment of his apotheosis. She, the woman, shrank and seemed to tremble; she looked like an enraptured sacrifice. It was too dark to see their faces; but their eloquent forms, modeled against the starlight, spoke like the festal figures on a frieze.

Daniel delayed his foot and cast down his eyes. He had meant to speak with her, just one word; to see her face for one precious moment. His heavy lids lifted uncertainly. Then, in the dark, the man and woman turned and clung . . .

The Jew thrust his hands against his face. His head fell. From the tent behind him, the low voice of Mariamnu sang delicately: —

> " Oh, happy, happy! Sacred thy delight.
> To life belongs the day, to love the night.
>
> Oh, blessed, blessed! for the gods give breath.
> But love's are day and night, and life and death."

The two figures unclasped, and seemed to listen to the song; then clung again. When Balatsu-usur raised his eyes, he saw that they had moved, and set their invisible faces toward their own tent. Their footsteps made no sound in the soft soil.

Without a word, without a sign, and without another glance, the Jew turned. He left the camp at once.

When the governor of Babylon reached the city, the guard at Imgur-Bel noticed that the eminent horseman did not take the street leading to his own palace. Daniel, on the contrary, rode straight to the temple of Bel. He rode slowly. He was absorbed in patient thought. Now this Ziggurat was the highest elevation in Babylon. Daniel dismounted at the Ziggurat.

His appearance at that place and at that hour surprised the idolatrous priests, to whose shrine the governor of the province was not accustomed to give countenance by even the merest visit of curiosity. But they saluted him with enforced respect, and admitted him without question.

Daniel slowly climbed the interminable slope. He walked wearily. He seemed tired out. The night was far spent. The dim temple lights were not enough to reveal the colors of the Ziggurat. The Jew counted them from memory, in a dull way, as he ascended.

"I have passed the black and the white. . . . This is the orange. . . . Was that the blue? How far to the red? for it holdeth the color of the heart's blood. . . . Fair is she as this silver. . . . When the sun ariseth, will she look back, if so she may once more behold the glitter of the day upon the tower of gold?"

He climbed to the topmost foothold of the temple. At his peremptory request, the astrologer on duty there descended. Daniel clung with his long fingers to the marble railing; he was so giddy with exhaustion that he might easily have fallen from the height. He stood with his face toward Damascus, toward Judea.

Dawn came. The pale, violet light touched his solitary figure solemnly. Far down the plain the outline of the cavalcade could be seen. It must have been stirring for some time. It fell into shape like a huge serpent, crawled on, and began to grow small. Then it faded gently. He passed his hand over his eyes, rubbed them, and strained them piteously. But the white caravan had vanished in the sand. Beyond was the desert. As the sun rose, Daniel extended his hands, palms outward, and fell upon his knees.